UNSUNG
THE HENRY BROTHERS

AMY KNUPP

CHAPTER 1

EVERLY

It was a perfect day for a wedding.

The June sky had been a bright blue all afternoon and was promising a spectacular color show this evening as the sun dipped lower, just as we'd hoped for. The temperature was a mild-for-Nashville eighty-one degrees.

The rooftop of the historical Wentworth Hotel had been transformed into a stunning oasis of greenery and flowers for its first-ever wedding. My dad was like that. He would move mountains for me, his only daughter, whether I wanted mountains moved or not. For the record, the rooftop idea had not been mine but was the love child of my publicist and my manager. I hadn't argued, so my dad had taken it from there. His motivation was pure and steeped in love, so I couldn't hold it against him.

The wedding coordinator had showed me phone pics of the finished rooftop setup twenty minutes ago. Three hundred guest chairs sat in perfect rows on either side of the narrow white carpet. The wedding arch was laden with salmon-pink hydrangeas, white dahlias, and the palest pink peonies, plus an ocean of shades of green. Countless potted topiary trees had been dressed to the nines with white hydrangeas and lined both sides of the terrace to give the illusion of privacy.

Five minutes ago, my best friend and matron of honor, Drea Verne, had whisked me out of the bridal preparation room without even asking, away from the other bridesmaids, who happened to be two of my cousins and my fiancé Trey's two sisters. Somehow Drea had known I wasn't okay. The walls had been closing in on me, the chatter of the women ringing in my ears undecipherable, and I'd felt like I couldn't get a full breath.

Like a couple of thieves in the not-quite-night, we'd rushed up three flights of back stairs to Drea and her husband's empty hotel room. We'd made it without being seen by anyone, in part because her room was right across from the stairwell.

When she shut the door behind us, enclosing us in a welcome silence, I sagged my back against it, willing myself not to slide down to the floor in my designer wedding dress.

"Talk to me, Everly." Drea busied herself at the mini bar, glancing at me every few seconds, waiting for me to speak. "You're pale and you looked like you were going to pass out back there."

"I…" I cleared my throat because my voice didn't sound like me. "I thought I was going to pass out back there."

"Come here." She took my hand and led me to the chair by the window that looked out over the front side of the hotel.

I was too antsy to sit, so I gazed outside, down Hale Street, which had cars parallel parked bumper to bumper and people everywhere. I stepped closer to the fourth-floor window, and my attention was pulled to what was happening right in front of the hotel, directly below me.

A crowd had gathered on the grassy areas on both sides of

the semicircle drive up to the main doors, spilling into the street and filling the little park across the way, as if gathered for a concert.

"Oh, my God," I muttered, and Drea came up by my side to look out too. "Is that... Are they..."

"Trying to get a glimpse of the country power couple, Everly Ash and Trey Gilbert? You bet your ass. Y'all are a hot ticket." Her voice went from false cheer to concern. "You should probably back away from the window before someone spots the bride up here and all hell breaks loose."

With a gasp—because I knew all too well she was right—I stepped away from the glass and fell into the chair she'd originally offered, this room now starting to close in on me too, making me feel like I was stuck in an underground tunnel that was low on oxygen. A bone-deep chill went up my bare arms, and I covered them with my hands, running my palms up and down, as if I only needed a little circulation.

Drea pulled an ottoman over and sat in front of me, holding out a hotel glass with an inch or so of amber liquid. After getting a whiff of it, I raised my plucked-to-perfection brows at her. "Whiskey?"

With a nod, she said, "It's big-guns time. You need Jack."

Not a single argument came to my mind, so I tipped my head back and shot the liquor. The burn in my throat was startling at first, but I closed my eyes, focused on the sensation for a few seconds, and it became pleasant. Reassuring somehow.

When I opened my eyes, Drea peered into them, hers full of empathy and concern. "What's going on, Ev? Are you getting cold feet?"

I was cold everywhere except my throat, as a matter of fact, but I shook my head, knowing that wasn't what my friend meant. "Just... it's a lot. Wedding-day nerves are a real thing, turns out." I tried to laugh it off, but the laugh was more of a croak.

I could feel Drea staring at me as I silently coached myself through inhales and exhales, needing something to level out the shakiness I felt down to my bones.

"You know, I've been paying attention since I got in Wednesday night. You and Trey…"

Alarmed, I darted my glance to her face. Our eyes met, and hers said so much more than her words. My breath hitched. I pressed my lips together, not knowing what to say. Forcing her to finish her thought.

"Do you love him?" she asked, cutting to the chase as Drea always did. Most times, I admired her directness, but today it only made my skin feel a little too tight.

"Of course," I said, probably too quickly. I did love Trey. He was a kind guy, a likable man, a charmer with very few enemies, if any. "Everyone loves Trey."

Drea let out a breath, not of relief but more like exasperation. "Everyone's not marrying him, sweetie."

I couldn't hide from my BFF since seventh grade, but I could reassure her. "I'm not sure if I'm in love with him yet, but how would I know? When have I ever been in love? Maybe I am—"

"You would know, Ev."

"Would I though?"

With an exhale that was half amusement and half contentment, leaving no question whether she was madly in love with her husband, she smiled and said, "You would."

I wasn't sure I believed her. I cared deeply about Trey. If something bad ever happened to him, I'd be heartbroken. If he cheated on me, I'd be upset. If we one day had kids, I knew we would become a team in raising them with similar beliefs and values.

We were a good team. We had been since our first date. Actually, from the first time we'd met, at an industry party about a year ago.

I'd known of Trey Gilbert since I was a teenager—he'd

been a household name in country music for the past ten-plus years—but I hadn't met him prior to that party. I had to admit to being a little star-struck when he'd sought me out, poured on the charm, and pulled me aside. He was seven years older than my twenty-nine, and we'd clicked on a professional level, relating to each other as hardworking singers in country music. We'd talked music for over an hour.

Apparently, an hour was all the press and paparazzi needed. They'd taken it from there, and before I went to sleep that night, rumors were flying. While there'd been nothing but business talk between us at that party, entertainment sites had had us halfway to eloping. Fans had grasped on to the speculation, both his followers and mine. My team, of which my world-famous producer dad was a key part, had been smiley and sparkly-eyed over the publicity boon.

It turned out my publicist was close friends with Trey's, and the two had cooked up an idea to continue the buzz. They'd suggested Trey and I go out on a proper date. It hadn't taken much to convince me—Trey was handsome and easy enough to like—and our first official date had been designed to include plenty of "random" opps for the press to perpetuate the rumors.

After the past few months, I now had an up-close-and-personal understanding of the phrase snowball effect. Trey and I got along well. We'd been in it together from that first date, being open about riding the wave to help our careers along. We'd recorded a duet together that shot up the charts. It'd been a partnership both professionally and personally, and it had slipped into romance naturally. I'd liked him from the beginning. My team adored Trey, and they loved Trey and me together even more.

We'd been tagged as "the power couple of country music" and "country music's best love story" and "Nashville's hottest couple." In a short time, our lives had been woven together so tightly my head was spinning. Now, suddenly, it was our wedding day.

"If you're having any doubts, Everly, it's not too late to change your mind."

An incredulous laugh escaped me. "Are you kidding me? What are you thinking? I just... call off the 'wedding of the year'?" I laughed again, and this one sounded closer to hysterical.

The idea was hysterical and impossible. So why was there a little rebel part of my brain that clung to it and imagined escaping? And why, oh dear sweet Jesus, why were there ribbons of hope and relief wisping through my mind when I thought about it?

"It'd be better to do it now than after you tie the knot. I know y'all have everything financial sorted out with the prenup, but a clean break in every other way will be a lot harder once you say I do."

My heart raced at her words. There was no denying they were true, but this wasn't just any wedding. This was so in the public eye I couldn't even help decorate for my own big day for fear of being mobbed by fans. And the money my dad had spent... the people I'd be letting down... Flaking wasn't an option. Not to mention, I hadn't been raised to be a flake.

"I'll be okay," I said, hoping I could fight down this sudden nausea before it was time to rejoin the rest of my bridesmaids. Which was probably really soon. They were undoubtedly already curious about where the heck I'd disappeared to.

I'd like to say Drea smiled, patted my hand supportively, and reassured me that I would indeed be okay, but instead, she tilted her head, furrowed her brow with worry, and bit her lip.

"I know you have an extreme amount of external pressure, but this isn't just art for your album cover or what dress to wear to an awards show. This is your *life*, Everly. Your future.

Marriage is a long fucking time, and even when you're head-over-heels in love, it can get tough."

My brain shut down on everything she was saying, because hello, show time was thundering upon us and I needed to be okay. I forced a smile. "I'm good. This is normal pre-wedding jitters. I just need one more little bit of Jack and about five minutes."

"Why I'm here," she said, grabbing my empty glass, bolting off the ottoman, and gliding back to the mini bar. In seconds, she handed me the glass with another inch of smoky, smooth spirits.

I took it and downed it just as there was a noise on the other side of the door. I'm pretty sure the soothing burn making its way from my throat to my stomach was the only thing that kept me from looking for a hiding spot.

"I'll see who it is. Probably housekeeping. I'll get rid of them," Drea said like the sparkling, awesome best friend she was. "Oh," she said when she peeked out the peephole. "One of the good guys."

She opened the door to her husband, Tim, holding up his key card and looking startled to have the door opened for him.

I let out my breath and tried to smile at him, the alcohol softening the edges of my anxiety. I loved everything about Tim Verne. He was, without a doubt, perfect for my dear friend—protective, unselfish, and indisputably in love with her. He made her laugh and would do anything for her.

When he saw me, he looked even more confused. "Hey?" he said, yes, as a question. "What are you doing here?"

I held up the empty glass. "Pre-wedding liquid fortification." My smile was less assured now, on the wavering side.

Drea kindly didn't mention that I'd been freaking the hell out, but the look she shot my way was filled with concern, letting me know I hadn't managed to convince her I would be okay. That I was doing the right thing.

"What are you doing up here?" she asked her husband after planting a kiss on his jawline.

"Headache. I came up to get some ibuprofen."

As Drea went to her bag on the desk and found what he needed, I slipped back into my thoughts, giving myself the final pep talk to stand up, walk out of the sanctuary of this room, head back down to the bridal prep room, summon up a confident smile, and marry Trey Gilbert.

Marry.

Trey Gilbert.

This is your life, Everly... Marriage is a long fucking time...

The warmth of the whiskey disappeared as cold fear froze the blood in my veins and flooded my chest with a heavy, paralyzing blackness that made it hard to breathe. I sucked in a breath, thankful Drea had gone into the bathroom for water and Tim was talking to her at the doorway, not facing me.

I had twenty seconds to get it together.

I carefully held my head in my hands, making sure not to smear any makeup, and closed my eyes to focus.

I could do this. I *would* do this. I couldn't hurt Trey, could not stand the thought of humiliating him so publicly. And my parents... They were so stoked about this wedding, so proud of their daughter, the rising country star who'd landed the biggest catch in recent history. And the money they'd spent... I'd been struggling with that on a good day. The total for this wedding was well into six figures. I had plenty of money of my own, and Trey and I had footed the bill for some things, but my dad was old-fashioned that way, plus stubborn, and had insisted on giving me an unforgettable wedding.

I couldn't let any of them down. I *wouldn't*.

Sucking in a deep, maybe slightly steadier breath, I looked up to see Drea and Tim at the door, in each other's arms, speaking quietly enough I couldn't make out the words. But I could decipher the tone. It was... *so full of love*. And smiles.

And mutual caring and—I don't use this word lightly —*adoration.*

Tim caressed Drea's cheek, peered into her eyes, and kissed her.

God, that kiss.

That kiss was filled with so much obvious love, and I knew in that instant that I had never been kissed like that. That kiss was not what Trey and I had ever shared, and in that instant, I faced the truth.

Trey might be the kindest, most likable man in the world, but he and I would never share the kind of love Drea shared with Tim.

Bile rose in my throat and I leaned forward, hoping to not pass out. I heard quiet goodbyes and *love you* and *see you after*, but it was distorted, as if I'd fallen into a hole I couldn't climb out of. I gasped, imagining there wasn't enough air, and when Drea had closed the door and turned back to me, a contented, blissful sort of smile on her face, I licked my lips and fought to swallow down the bile.

Her smile vanished in an instant, and she rushed toward me. "Ev?"

I stood, filling my lungs with another breath, and met her eyes. Shook my head. "I can't do it. I can't marry Trey."

CHAPTER 2

Spontaneity had never been my strong point.

I was a planner, probably to a fault, so my radar had already been triggered by the text exchange with the last-minute renter. But I also liked to think I was open-minded, and I was willing to rent my newly remodeled garage apartment without judgment as long as the renter followed the rules and didn't infringe on my life more than necessary.

As I pulled my Subaru into my driveway, I realized I'd never gotten the woman's name. Matter of fact, I wasn't sure what made me think it was a woman.

I pulled up as far as the front walkway and killed the engine. I hadn't parked in the garage for weeks as that was my remodeling headquarters and had enough construction supplies to build a whole new city. Grabbing my phone from the console, I tapped to the brief conversation and reread the exchange. Phrases like *so much appreciated* and *that would be awesome* were what made me guess at the person's gender, but really, it could be anyone.

This was my first renter ever, but that was no excuse. I needed to up my landlord game significantly. And I would, particularly if I received inquiries at some time other than ten thirty p.m. while I was at my brother's wedding reception.

Still sitting there in the dark in my driveway, I flipped to my email and saw a notification that the month's rent for the apartment had been paid in full. Nearly three G's sitting pretty in the account I'd opened just for my new rental business. I frowned. It was from an LLC, not an individual. That told me nothing.

Instead of googling, I got out of the car and hurried to my house. Thanks to being blocked in at the reception, I was down to twenty-five minutes until the renter was scheduled to arrive. Though I'd made the bed and put bath products and towels out two weeks ago when I'd posted the listing, I needed to do a final run-through to make sure everything was ready. That and add the welcome basket my sister, Hayden, had suggested, with coffee, tea, chocolates, fruit, and break-fast bars—which weren't nearly as good as fresh donuts from Sugar, but that's what you got when you were last-minute.

I unlocked my door and was met by Chaos, my big yellow tomcat, as usual.

"Hey, Chaos. Where's Mayhem?"

The lazier of the two, the solid black male sauntered into the living room, more than likely curious about what was going on that would not only keep me up late but have me out of the house after dark.

"I fed you earlier, Mayhem. Kitchen's closed." I leaned down enough to give each of them a quick ear scratching, then headed to the kitchen counter to grab the welcome basket. Chaos gave me a sassy meow as I went to the back door.

I flipped on the back light so I could see my way across the yard, but nothing happened. I'd have to replace the bulb later.

The yard was dark, as the moon was a sliver tonight. You could barely make out the shore that edged my property or the rack where the kayaks, paddleboards, and canoe were stored or the dock with the boat. In the late-night quiet, though, I could *hear* the lake, the gentle lap of the water on the pylons, the chirp of the frogs, a boat motor in the distance. Peaceful sounds. Comfort sounds.

I let them wrap around me as I walked toward the detached garage and the steps to the apartment—and nearly jumped out of my skin when I realized someone was sitting on the steps less than twenty feet away from me. I stopped momentarily, allowing my eyes to focus.

It was a woman, a young one, wearing short shorts, a white tank top, and a dark ball cap. I couldn't really see her face in the shadow from the bill, and even as she stood, she kept her face somewhat averted. She was short, slender, just a little slip of a human. It didn't seem wise for her to be here on the steps of a random rental property at eleven thirty at night by herself.

"Hi," I said as I approached, wishing I'd gotten her name earlier. "I'm Seth Henry, the owner."

"Hi. Thank you for meeting me so late." She let out an exhale. "I appreciate it."

"Not a problem. Do you have a name?" I asked lightly.

She didn't smile but kind of glanced toward the lake as she said, "Andrea. Did you receive the payment?"

I got the distinct vibe that was shorthand for *I paid my money, so no more questions.*

I could honor that—for now.

"I did. And the digital rental agreement. We're all set."

There was nothing obviously suspicious about her. She had one suitcase that seemed tiny for a month-long stay plus a plastic shopping bag I could only partially see because it was behind her, but other than her hesitancy to make eye contact, I couldn't spot any overt reason to worry for the safety of my property. However, even though I was up later than usual and worn out from being around so many people this evening, I wasn't ready to just hand over the entry code and say good night.

"Come on up. I was about to triple-check that everything's set, but you're here early."

She hesitated, nodded, and stepped to the side to let me go first up the stairs. I reached to help her with her suitcase, but she grabbed both it and her bag before I could.

"I've got them," she said, her tone lighter than it had been so far, friendlier.

I shrugged and headed upstairs.

"So Andrea," I said over my shoulder, "what are your plans while you're in Dragonfly?"

"I... don't know yet. This is sort of a spur-of-the-moment vacation. Sometimes you just need to get away for a bit, you know?" She added an attempt at a light laugh, but it didn't sound natural.

"Do you travel a lot?"

"I do."

Maybe it was my imagination, but it felt like she was weighing everything before she said it. On the one hand, I was a proponent of not blurting things out without thought. I tended to think before speaking, probably to a fault. But if it was done to hide something...

I could swear Andrea with no last name was hiding something.

Did she have a secret lover who was planning to meet her here? Not my problem or concern.

Had she had a fight with a family member and needed some time to herself? Fair enough. I liked being alone myself.

Had she escaped from a drug dealer ex-boyfriend who wanted to hurt her? That was a problem, on multiple levels.

Somehow I didn't think she was going to open up and share with me. Not tonight.

At the top of the external stairway, I stopped, punched in the entry code, and opened the door. Breathing in through my nose, I noted it still smelled fresh, with a hint of citrus, even though it'd been over a week since I'd had Viola Berry in to clean it.

"Welcome," I said, flipping on a light and doing a quick scan of the living and dining area and the kitchenette across from the door. Everything looked in order.

As I stepped farther in, a gasp came from behind me.

"This is adorable. You never know if the photos are recent in these places…"

"Taken two weeks ago," I told her. "You're my first renter. I just remodeled the whole place."

"Wow."

Setting the suitcase aside but still holding on tightly to her overstuffed plastic bag, she took in the kitchen—simple white cabinets, a stainless three-quarter-sized fridge and full-sized oven and microwave, a compact sink, and light butcher-block counters—and the dining area, which consisted of a high-top table with four chairs, two of which faced the French doors that led to a small balcony and a view of the lake. Turning to the right a few degrees, she checked out the living room, just big enough to hold a sage-green queen-sized sleeper sofa with an end table, a coffee table, and a TV mounted on the wall.

"I love this. You have great taste. It looks more like a home than a rental."

"That's the idea," I said. "I can't take the credit though. My sister is a designer and I set her loose."

"She's fantastic." She continued to look at all the details, and thanks to Hayden, there were a lot. "The art and the signs on the wall, the neutral palette with nature-colored accents…"

"You kind of sound like her." A grin worked its way across my lips. I couldn't deny that her approval of my baby sister had me warming up to her. I had a soft spot for

Hayden, and I was inordinately proud of the businesses she was building with all her talent and hard work. "Are you a designer too?"

She shook her head but didn't say more, instead walking over to the bathroom and bedroom doors, which were near each other on the opposite wall. Finally, she turned back my way and said, "It's perfect," but I noticed she still hid beneath the hat.

Dammit, I wanted to see what she looked like. It was beyond the worry that she was trying to hide something now. I was dying of curiosity. Her legs were slender and toned and appealing, and her voice had a sugar-sweet tone to it that did something to me inside, even though that made no sense. Her chest was average size, her tank leaving little to the imagination, and I suddenly couldn't imagine why a guy could ever need more than beautiful, average-sized breasts.

And what the actual hell was going on with me?

Andrea, whoever she was, waltzed across the small space to the French doors, put her face and one cupped hand up close to the glass, and tried to see out. "I could sense that the lake is out there somewhere but I couldn't see it from the stairs."

"It's out there. No more than forty feet from your balcony, although your view is partially impeded. Lots of towering trees keep the balcony shaded and semi-hidden from people on the water."

"Even better," she said quietly.

I stepped to the table and set down the welcome basket, but she must not have heard me, because when she whirled back around, she bumped into me, dropped her bag, and rushed to bend over and retrieve it but knocked her hat off, then whacked her temple on the back of the chair. Not so hard that I was worried about head injuries but hard enough that she let out a restrained *damn!* and pressed her fingers to the point of impact as she straightened.

"Are you okay?" I barely got the words out before she straightened all the way, took her hand away from her temple, and made eye contact with me.

We both froze, her with a deer-in-the-headlights look, me with my jaw figuratively gaping to my chest because, my god, she was beautiful.

Her eyes were a stunning green, her lashes long and thick. She had apple cheekbones and kissable lips and dark hair that was intricately done up like nothing I'd ever seen before. Her skin looked baby soft and smooth, like a TV ad for makeup. The only sign she'd had a long day was some smudging of eye makeup under her eyes, but it didn't take away from her natural beauty. Not one bit.

I took all of this in within about three seconds flat, and then my gaze veered back to hers, which was still glued on me in… fear? Dread? I wasn't sure what I read in her eyes, but it wasn't remotely similar to the intense attraction that was pulsing through me.

Which was the reality check I needed.

I went from one shock to another when I turned my attention to the bag she'd been going after, intent on picking it up for her. I was halfway bent down when my brain made sense of what my eyes were seeing. I picked up the bag by one handle, and that only made it gape farther open, revealing even more of the white, shimmery, silky fabric and bits of lace and sequins.

"Is this a wedding dress?" I asked as I straightened.

The mysterious woman's gaze darted to the bag, then back to my face.

A couple of seconds ticked by, and then she said, "Yes."

"Shouldn't it be in a better bag? Like, a wedding dress bag or something?" I had no idea what I was talking about, as I had zero experience with wedding dresses, but I was reasonably certain most people didn't stuff a thousand-dollar gown into a plastic bag from a big-box store.

She snatched the bag from me and pulled the two handles together, as if hiding it now would do any good.

Though she remained standing, her shoulders sagged as if in surrender. She dropped the bag with the dress on the table, rubbed her fingers over the spot on her head where she'd hit the chair, then paced away from me.

"It should be in a better bag. It *was* in a better bag."

When she went silent, my brain filled with possibilities as to what had necessitated the change. She'd stolen it? There'd been a fire? Someone had been chasing her?

"When I decided not to go through with my wedding today, I snuck away like a common criminal to the getaway car. I ended up changing out of the conspicuous dress in the backseat of my best friend's rental, and the only place to put it was in a Walmart bag."

This time, I was pretty sure my jaw actually did hang open as I processed her words. Slowly, the pieces fell into place.

The hairdo… It was done into loose braids and twists and curls that started at her hairline and wisped to the back of her head, where it all came together in an ocean of waves and swirls of coffee-colored locks that looked barely controlled and yet didn't seem to fall out of place. It was a masterpiece that must've taken hours and only made sense for a woman's wedding day.

And her makeup… It was a little on the heavy side but not at all distasteful, her eyes a work of art on their own with dark liner on her upper and lower lids and a dramatic gradient of shadow on each lid that went from a tannish mauve to a shimmery cream color that I imagined would stand out well with a white dress.

The question that fell off my tongue was asinine, considering all the things I should've asked. Things like, *Why did you decide not to go through with your wedding?* or *How's the poor schmuck you left?* or *Are you okay?* Things she likely wouldn't answer anyway.

Instead, what came out was, "The getaway car dropped you off here?"

It'd been a half thought floating in my mind, I guess, that there was no extra car in the driveway.

"Nearby," was her answer, and maybe if I hadn't been absorbed in all those other questions, I would've noticed how odd that answer was in itself.

Before I could fire off anything else, she said, "So it's been kind of a long day, and if we're done with all the things, I need to crash."

"Of course." I reluctantly flipped back into my property-owner role, reminding myself her problems were not mine. "This is for you." I gestured to the welcome basket, then pulled an info card out. "The door code is on this. There's a brewing machine that can do both coffee and tea." I pointed to the item on the sliver of countertop. "You'll probably want to get some groceries at Country Market, and let me know if you need a grill. Text me anytime for restaurant recommendations or directions."

Andrea nodded. She'd put her ball cap back on—a Seattle Seahawks cap, I belatedly noticed—but she managed to meet my gaze. Now that I looked at her, knowing a little of what her day had consisted of, I could see exhaustion and weariness.

"Thank you," she said in that sweet voice that had just a touch of a Tennessee drawl.

When I turned to go to the door, she said, "Seth, the fewer people who know I'm here, the better, so if you could keep it to yourself…"

"Of course." It was a strange request. If she was traveling, no one here would know her from Eve, but I was compelled to put her mind at ease in whatever small way I could. "Your secret is safe with me."

She looked momentarily startled by my words instead of comforted, and I decided this woman had complexities and oddities that I would likely never understand, even if she stayed here for the entire month.

And that was okay.

Because her problems were her own and I was merely the property owner.

"Let me know if you need anything," I said as I opened the door. "Good night."

As I went down the stairs toward the house, it hit me that I had even more questions now than I'd had before I met her.

CHAPTER 3

stood, frozen, in the garage apartment, listening to Seth Henry's footsteps descend the stairs, my heart still pounding too fast from the moment I'd let him see my face head-on.

Once the footsteps stopped, I exhaled and let everything drain from me, maybe for the first time in hours. I gripped the chair back as if that could keep me grounded and just breathed. For five seconds. Then I went to the door Seth had walked out of and locked it.

Next, I went to the French doors and assured myself they, too, were dead bolted. As curious as I was about my balcony and partially blocked lake view, tonight I was just about privacy. Being alone. To breathe.

And eat.

Now that I was safe from the media, my stomach made its empty state known. I hadn't eaten since brunch with my attendants, and that hadn't been more than a few bites. Wedding-day jitters, I'd told myself. I hadn't fully let the idea of bolting enter my mind until Drea had taken me to her room, away from all the commotion.

I shut down all thoughts of earlier today and went to the welcome basket. There were packets of microwave popcorn. Bless that man or his sister or whoever had put this together.

While the popcorn popped, I stood against the counter and chomped down an apple. If the paparazzi could see me now, they'd be appalled. My Sweetheart of Country Music moniker would be out the door like yesterday's trash, because I had juice dripping down my chin, and I was so hungry I barely swallowed one bite before going after another.

By the time the microwave beeped, the apple was history. I looked in the cabinets for a bowl and smiled when I spotted a large white bowl that said POPCORN on it in raised white letters, with four matching smaller bowls. Yeah, I grabbed the big one because I was eating every last kernel myself.

Once the bag was dumped into the bowl and I had shoved the first handful into my mouth, I glanced around the place again and realized the blinds were open. With a panicked start, I left the popcorn on the table and went from window to window, closing the blinds and shutting out the small-town world.

I'd never been to Dragonfly Lake before, but Drea's husband, Tim, had been here a lot as a kid and assured me it was a great little town, with loads of character and friendly people. Neither of those mattered to me, but hiding in plain sight, as Drea had suggested, did. Now that I was here, I wasn't at all sure it was the right plan. Wouldn't I be completely conspicuous in a place where there weren't as many people to hide among?

Drea. Shoot. I'd promised to update her when I could, and there wasn't a doubt in my mind that she was frantically checking for a message from me.

I grabbed the bowl and my suitcase and went into the bedroom. My second burner phone, which Tim had picked up for me while Drea and I hid in the rental car, was in the outside pocket, and I went for it now.

I powered it up and punched in Drea's number, one of the few I knew by heart.

"You are killing me," she said instead of hello.

"I'm fine. Well, starving but fine."

"We should've stocked you up on food."

"Burner phones seemed more practical at the time."

Before today, I'd never used a burner phone, never had reason to, and now I was on my second. The first I'd used to call Trey. I'd nearly thrown up as I dialed his number, because I hated what I'd done to him. Hated it. When I'd gotten his voicemail, I'd done the only thing I could think to do—told him I was sorry, that I hated to do this to him, that I'd never planned it, but I couldn't go through with the wedding. It wasn't fair to him and it wasn't fair to me. I'd promised we could talk soon if he wanted to.

Frankly, I wouldn't be surprised if he never wanted to talk to me again.

I'd never, ever wanted to hurt him. Deciding not to marry him was bad enough, but the way I'd done it... I wasn't proud of that, but the truth was, if I had to do it over again, I would've done it pretty much the same way. Well, ideally, I would've found my bravery and my common sense weeks ago and called off the wedding then. Short of that, though, I knew there was no other way this could have happened. Had I told anyone besides Drea about my doubts, I'm pretty sure they would've talked me into going through with the wedding, convinced me it would be okay.

"Tell me everything," Drea said into the phone now. "How's the apartment? How are the owners? Do you trust them? Do you think you'll stay there for a few days?"

Chewing another bite of popcorn, I put the phone on speaker and set it on the bed next to me so my chewing wouldn't be so obnoxious.

"The apartment is perfect." I described it to her and told her about the balcony I had yet to see.

"It sounds like exactly what you need. Some peace."

Nodding, I said, "And space. Mental space. What's going on online?"

"You don't want to know," Drea said, her tone hardening.

I knew she was right. I could imagine all too well what the media was saying about the selfish "sweetheart" who'd crushed fan favorite Trey Gilbert's heart.

I squeezed my eyes shut against that. All of it, but particularly the Trey part.

"Has Trey said anything yet?" I asked, eyes still shut.

"Not a word. No one's seen him for hours. I'm sure he and his best man had to do a disappearing act like we did. All the media has is conjecture, and trust me, they're doing that to the hilt."

Of course they were. It was an unavoidable part of my life. The press made everything worse. I had to force all of that to be secondary right now, because this was my real life. Mine and Trey's. The media tended to forget we were actual humans behind all the stories and rumors and news. "I hope he's okay."

"Physically, I imagine he's fine," Drea said, and neither one of us needed to say out loud that, emotionally, mentally, he probably wasn't okay.

"He's never going to forgive me."

"I don't know him well enough to say either way, but even if he doesn't, it's better than being married for eternity to a man you don't have a passionate, undying love for."

"I don't see me ever finding a man I have a passionate, undying love for."

Yeah, I was slipping into morose territory, but after the drama of making the decision and then the practical details necessary to escape without being recognized, I hadn't yet had a chance to absorb the ramifications of walking away from Trey.

"We'll talk that through another day," Drea said. "First you've gotta get through tonight. Then tomorrow. One day at a time. One thing at a time. How can I help?"

"You already did." A big knot of emotions clogged up my throat, and I tried to breathe past them. This girl… What would I do without this girl who knew me better than I knew myself? Don't get me wrong—I had a loving dad and mom and had grown up blessed. But I wasn't always sure about what drove my parents, and sometimes I suspected there were angles besides love. Drea? She was, without a doubt, a fan of whatever was best for me, the same as I was for her. "I don't know what I'd do without you."

"Probably marry the wrong guy, but I got you," she said, and I could hear her affectionate smile. "You're going to be okay, Ev."

I swallowed hard again and nodded even though she couldn't hear it.

"One question," she said. "Be honest with me. I know you feel terrible about breaking it off today, but do you have any regrets in your heart that you're not going to be Trey Gilbert's wife?"

I drew in a deep breath and then blew it out, long and loud, thinking. Allowing myself to *feel* so I could answer her question.

I registered exhaustion. Embarrassment that it'd taken me so long to figure out my heart. Regret that I'd likely humiliated and hurt Trey. Worry over what my parents would say once I finally got the nerve to do more than I had earlier, which was to text them that I was okay and needed time alone. There was probably a long list of other emotions twisted up in there too. But what I didn't feel was any sense that breaking up was the wrong thing to do.

"I don't," I finally said quietly. "I have some big questions for myself, like what was I thinking? How could I just drift into the situation I did? Why didn't I speak up earlier? But no, I don't think I'm the right person to be Trey's wife."

"Okay." Drea's voice was matter-of-fact. "That's what I thought, but I had to make sure. So hear me. You did the right thing—"

"I did it in a terrible, unforgivable way."

"You didn't have a lot of options, sweetie. We did the best we could. Now we need to move forward and figure out what's next."

"Right now?" I said, then collapsed back onto the pillows, unsure I could do one more thing. Maybe not even brush my teeth.

"All we need to figure out tonight is whether you're in a place where you can stay a few days. Do you think the owners will recognize you?"

I rolled to my side, the popcorn bowl empty except for a few unpopped kernels. "The guy I met tonight is a no. I accidentally looked at him directly and froze. Nothing. It was a terrifying few seconds though."

"Let's hope he doesn't pay attention to entertainment news."

"He doesn't seem like the type."

"What makes you say that?"

I stopped and thought about it and couldn't quite put my finger on it. "Just a vibe. He seems quiet and serious and more like the world news type than entertainment."

"Ah. Older generation."

"No," I said, amused. "In his thirties. Good-looking. Maybe single. Who knows?" I was egging her on purposely now.

"Oh?" The one syllable was full of imagined possibility. She was so easy.

With a laugh, my first in hours or maybe days, I said,

"Shut up. You're nauseatingly blissfully married and I'm off the market for ten years, minimum."

"Maybe for a relationship, but there's always a fling."

I rolled my eyes. "Not remotely possible in my world. Last thing I'm up for. And after the media gets done with me, no one will be interested anyway." I shrugged tiredly.

"Yeah, you need some you time. Recovery. Reflection. A month in Dragonfly Lake will be the best thing. You haven't slowed down in forever."

That was no lie. But... "I don't know. I'm afraid I'll stick out."

"There are ways to get around that. What we need is a discreet delivery service, a little online shopping maybe for when you want to go out, but once you get food, what more do you need? You have a balcony on the lake. Peace. Privacy."

"Maybe. I have no idea how to find a trustworthy super-secret delivery service—"

"We don't have to know that tonight. Tonight, you need to sleep. Sleep the day away tomorrow. Text me when you wake up and I'll have more ideas. Promise."

A warmth took root in my chest and my eyes teared up in gratitude. I hadn't been this alone in years. I still lived in my parents' home, and yes, I knew, at twenty-nine years of age, I needed to get out. But I had my own wing. The one time I'd gotten serious about finding my own place, they'd convinced me to stay. Now, suddenly, I finally had the space I longed for and it was daunting. Having Drea so willing to help, even from a distance—she and Tim had to fly back to Seattle tomorrow—made it less daunting.

"Thank you for being my ride-or-die girl," I said.

She let out a light laugh. "Who knew it would be literal today? At least the ride part. I know this is hard, but you're in a safe place, away from the press. You can call me anytime."

"I know."

"Okay. Tim says he needs his wife now and you need your rest." Her laugh was closer to a giggle, which made me laugh too and try not to think about their closeness and affection that I wondered if I would ever have. "Turn off the burner and pass out, dear girl. We'll figure out the next thing tomorrow."

"Love you, Drea. Tell Tim thanks for driving the getaway car."

We hung up, and I shut the phone off. I had every intention of trying to puzzle out my next move, but the day had been too much for me, and I fell asleep on top of the blankets, still in my clothes, without brushing my teeth.

CHAPTER 4

As I retraced my steps across the yard toward my house, my gut twisted with uneasiness.

For starters, it turned out that having a renter felt intrusive. I valued my privacy, most people would say to an extreme. Having someone living in my backyard was a little suffocating. But letting the garage apartment sit there unused, especially after all the money I'd put into the remodel, was bad business, and bad business went against everything in me. For the money I would make, I'd get used to a close-up neighbor.

The bigger issue was this particular renter.

Andrea Whoever was uneasy herself. Beyond uneasy. I'd have to be inhumane not to be concerned about her, whether it was my business or not. She seemed harmless, but she was scared of something. The bitch of it was, something about her elicited a protective urge inside of me. It was a foreign feeling, unlike anything I'd felt before. Yes, I could be protective of those in my inner circle, particularly my sister, but I wasn't a save-the-world type who wanted to get involved in others' situations under any circumstance. That wary, vulnerable look in my renter's eyes though... Add that to her unparalleled beauty...

I went up the three steps to the deck, let myself into the kitchen, and slammed the door on that line of thinking.

I wasn't about to get tangled up with a renter, any renter, whether they were here for a month or a year. Truth be told, I wasn't in a rush to get tangled up with anyone. I was fine on my own, and a pair of arresting green eyes wasn't going to change that. I knew better than to fall for a pretty face.

Unable to stop myself, I kept the lights off, walked over to the windows in the eat-in area, and peered out toward the garage, Chaos winding his way around my ankles. The apartment was still lit, blinds open. I watched for a glimpse of my dark-haired renter, then swore at myself for being creepy. Although I didn't usually bother to close all the blinds in this room—the nook was enclosed by tall windows to capitalize on the view of the lake—I snapped them shut now, telling myself I'd do the same regardless of who the renter was.

After turning out the lamp in the living room, I continued to my bedroom, shedding my clothes and tossing them into the laundry basket. I brushed my teeth, then I pulled the covers back and sank into my bed with more than a little relief. One of the cats—Chaos, I knew, even though I couldn't see him—jumped up to the foot of the mattress and settled in, as he often did.

Though I normally read before bed, it was about two hours later than usual, and I was beat after socializing with half the town at Holden and Chloe's wedding reception. Turnout had been great, as expected, since my younger brother was friends with everyone. I'd enjoyed the party, wished my brother and new sister-in-law the best, but I was more than ready for the peace of home even before I'd received the late-night text about the apartment.

I grabbed my phone, flipped the lamp on the nightstand

out, and settled in to skim the headlines until I felt sleepy. I glanced over the world news, sports, business, local…

My lids were getting heavy, and I was about to set the phone down when a thumbnail-sized photo caught my eye. A photo I could swear was my mysterious renter.

Sweetheart of Country Music bolts, the headline read, and you bet your ass I clicked on it, my pulse pounding.

The source was one of the Nashville networks, and the article was short and to the point: Everly Ash had apparently left Trey Gilbert, a household name in country music that even I'd heard of, at the altar earlier this evening at the Wentworth Hotel in Nashville. Everly—not Andrea—had recently gained the Sweetheart nickname as she and Gilbert got involved in a "whirlwind" year-long romance that the public devoured and adored, and her popularity and career had soared.

The article didn't give much more information, saying they'd report when more facts were known.

I did a search for her name, and a bunch of entertainment sites popped up with articles timestamped in the past two hours. I couldn't help myself—I clicked through several of them, voraciously reading the first several I came across.

The facts were few and far between but the conjecture was all over the place, most of it unkind toward Everly. The general consensus was that she'd devastated the singer, the more established of the two, though Gilbert hadn't been seen or hadn't commented publicly.

Hell. I'd like to say I shoved it all aside, put my phone down, and went to sleep, but my curiosity was piqued.

I slid out of bed, pulled on some shorts, and headed upstairs to my office, leaving Chaos snoring. Without turning on the light, I powered up my laptop and continued my deep dive into Everly Ash.

Two hours later, I knew enough to write a Wikipedia entry on the woman in my garage apartment. Some of it was probably even fact, though I knew all too well that plenty of what I'd found online was garbage. I knew better than to read all the fodder, but I hadn't been able to help myself.

From what I'd gleaned, she was the only daughter of world-famous, in-demand producer Eddy Ash and his wife, Jane. Everly was twenty-nine years old and had recorded her first solo country album at twenty-one, with her dad producing. She apparently wasn't an instant success but had been building a steady following as her catalogue grew. She'd met Trey Gilbert just over a year ago at a party, and it appeared that's when her fame exploded. Soon after, they'd recorded a duet that hit number one on the country charts. The media had dubbed Everly the Sweetheart of Country Music, and both her and Trey Gilbert's celebrity had grown exponentially. It appeared they hadn't shied away from the press during their courtship, as there were hundreds of photos of them, from formal awards ceremonies to candids around Nashville to trips together around the country.

I confess I got lost in the photos.

As the whole world knew, Everly Ash was gorgeous from every angle, whether she was dressed to the nines or wearing cutoff shorts and a tee.

There was no official word on why she'd ditched her superstar would-be groom earlier tonight, but the more guesses and rumors I read, the angrier I got.

Maybe she'd never intended to go through with it, using the wedding hype as a publicity stunt.

Maybe her powerful dad had wanted her to marry "up" career-wise and she'd finally decided to rebel.

Maybe she'd run off with a secret lover.

Or so the trashy websites that fed off mistruths and bullshit said.

Fed up, I shut my laptop harder than I should have, pushed my chair back, and stood.

I left my office, went into the spare bedroom on the garage

side of the house, and looked out toward Everly's apartment. Her blinds were closed now, and the place had gone dark. I hoped she was sound asleep, recovering from what must have been a nightmare day.

I headed back downstairs, my mind spinning. I wasn't proud to admit that I, too, was curious as hell about what had made her call off her wedding, but I was just as preoccupied by what the press was trying to do to her reputation.

One might think that, in her position, as someone who'd been in the public eye for years, she'd have a thick skin and be used to the media's sensationalism and attempts to ruin people's lives. However, though I'd only just met her, I suspected she wasn't indifferent to the terrible lies zipping around the internet.

The look in her eyes made more sense now. The look when her hat had fallen off and I'd seen her face directly made sense. She was terrified I'd recognize her. From what I'd read, ninety percent of Nashville—hell, the country—would've recognized her. But I'd never been big on pop culture or following celebrities or staying up on the latest hits. Though I was familiar with Trey Gilbert and probably knew a couple of his songs, I wouldn't have known him from Adam if I met him on the street.

That inexplicable desire to protect the woman in my garage apartment surged, and it wasn't because she was drop-dead gorgeous. In fact, that was a compelling reason to keep my distance. In general, I had no intention of nosing my way into any renter's business, and probably staying away from Everly Ash would be wise. Her situation with the predatory press was all too familiar to me, though, and I would butt in just enough to see if there was any way I could help her.

CHAPTER 5

EVERLY

There was something about this place.

This apartment. This lake. This air.

I hadn't slept so peacefully in... I didn't know when the last time I'd slept like that was. It was as if there were tiny little peace-bearing fairies floating in the wind.

I'd woken a couple of times throughout the night, but the mattress was so comfortable and the air temperature so ideal and the bedding so soft that I'd merely turned over and gone back to sleep instead of diving into worry and stress as I would've expected.

It was just after seven when I'd stirred, seen daylight, and come awake for the day, but again, not in the panic I would've thought, considering yesterday.

First thing, I'd showered, as I'd had yet to wash off the loads of hair product my stylist had used to keep my intricate wedding-day paparazzi-ready style in place and the heavier-than-normal makeup. I'd used the honeysuckle-scented sample-sized products that came with the place instead of my own. The aroma brought to mind summer and a carefreeness I hadn't felt for years.

After dressing in shorts and a tee, I veered from my usual latte and brewed a peach oolong tea from the basket. While the magic machine made my beverage, I worked up the courage to check out the balcony.

Though I had my regular cell phone as well as my burner phone in the bedroom, I hadn't powered either one up, so I had no idea whether the media had somehow tracked me down. My plan was to stay unplugged for as long as possible, but that left me blind to what might be waiting for me outside these walls.

My heart pounding, I eased one side of the double doors open and peeked out, wary and vigilant. What I saw was green foliage framing a view of the lake. Willow branches draped and shaded a grassy lawn that went from below the balcony to the sandy shore. Sunbeams danced their way through the leaves in places, dappling the ground and making the water sparkle like diamonds.

The door opened outward, so I pushed it farther, enlarging my vista gradually, still keeping an eye out for people, but there was no one close enough to see me. I exhaled, grateful that my hideaway hadn't been discovered.

Keeping the blinds on the door closed provided a sort of privacy screen. I opened the second door as well, propping both of them at an angle, positioning one of the two outdoor chairs with red and white striped cushions between the door shields so I was protected from sight on both sides.

The balcony was barely big enough for the two chairs and a tiny side table and had a white-painted wood railing with vertical posts close enough that a kid couldn't fall through.

Before taking advantage of the balcony, I grabbed Tim's Seahawks cap and pulled my long hair up under it, just in case. It didn't qualify as a disguise, but it might prevent someone from recognizing me from afar.

After sweetening my tea, I parked myself right there in the doorway and just sat. I stared at the mesmerizing dance of the sun on the water. Watched the boats in the distance, none of them close enough to make me uneasy. Listened to the rustle of the leaves and the willow branches as they swayed in the early-morning breeze.

Last night, I'd been leery of staying here, but at this moment, I wasn't sure I ever wanted to leave.

I spent the next however long watching the serene show put on by nature—a duck here and there paddling by, a turtle popping its head above the water then disappearing until it surfaced somewhere else, fish jumping sporadically, the water sloshing against the dock from waves that came from a couple of fishing boats out in the middle of the lake. And the dragonflies… It was clear the lake came by its name honestly, because I'd spotted at least a dozen of the most beautiful blue-and-purple-winged insects fluttering around and doing whatever it was dragonflies did. Those were something I didn't see often in the city, in part because I didn't spend much time in nature. I needed to change that.

You need to change a lot of things, a little voice in my head said.

I definitely had a ton to figure out, but I refused to let reality intrude on this moment. I needed this gorgeous morning to come down from yesterday. Or maybe from the past year.

I was sipping my tea when a knock sounded so softly on the main door that I wasn't sure I'd actually heard it. My heart started pounding anyway, because there was no chance of that being anyone I wanted to see right now, mainly because there was no one I wanted to see.

Thinking maybe it'd been a woodpecker or some other non-human creature, I decided to ignore it. Until the sound came again, still quiet but definitely a knock.

A peek out the peephole showed me it was one tall, good-looking, pesky apartment owner. I didn't want to talk to him, but he definitely beat some photographer looking for a money shot. Unless he was looking for a money shot...

Another glance and I could see he was holding a paper bag instead of a phone or camera, so I braced myself and opened the door.

"Good morning, Everly."

It took two full seconds of me standing there, staring up at his warm eyes, for it to sink in that he'd used my real name. He wasn't supposed to *know* my real name.

I reacted by slamming the door. Yep, in his face.

"Shit," I said to myself as I realized what I'd done.

I couldn't afford to piss him off or offend him, particularly since he apparently knew my secret, so I whipped the door back open. "Sorry." I sucked in a breath, my shoulders rising, then blew it out. "I shouldn't have done that. Gut reaction."

"Your secret is safe with me," he said, and he seemed to mean it. However, the stakes were too high for me to just buy what he was selling without question. "May I come in? The longer I stand out here, the more suspicion it might arouse."

"Can someone see you?" I asked with a start.

He casually glanced both ways, shaking his head. "Not yet, but give it about twenty minutes or so..." When he looked back at me, a smile tugged at one corner of his lips. "I brought fresh donuts."

I still wasn't totally sure if it was smart, but I stepped back and let him in. I was starving and donuts were my weakness, one of the things that had been outlawed by my trainer, James, whose job it was to keep me fit for performances and the camera.

Seth came in, closed the door behind him, then asked, "Do you want me to lock it? I'm not going to stay long."

"Yes." I didn't care whether it was rational or not or if it revealed too much. My peace of five minutes ago had disappeared in a snap, or rather a knock. The sooner he left, the sooner I could breathe, but I wanted those donuts.

He walked over to the table, set down a bag that said SUGAR on the side, and checked out my half-hidden chair setup in the doorway of the balcony.

"Clever," he said, pointing to the way I had the doors propped open like shields.

"It would be bad if the press found me," I said defensively.

It looked like I was going to have to leave this formerly peaceful place after all, but where to go next was a conundrum I couldn't focus on at the moment.

"I understand that," he said, then he muttered, "more than you know."

At least I thought that's what he said, but he was looking away from me.

With my head tilted as I pondered that, I dug into the donut bag. There were four, and I could see one had white frosting and sprinkles, one had chocolate, also with sprinkles, one was a glazed, and the last one had pink frosting, no sprinkles. The sugary aroma that wafted from the bag nearly brought tears to my eyes.

I still didn't know if I could trust this guy or not, but he'd won points with this.

Pulling out the vanilla one, I said, "Thank you."

When he turned to me, he smiled, a full-on one, and I couldn't help noticing how delectable he was when he smiled, even though I had no room in my life or my head to notice. It was no big deal, kind of like recognizing my donut was a simple work of art in passing. The donut, though, I would be devouring. The man… I just needed him to leave.

"Is there something else you needed?" I asked.

He stood there in the doorway to the balcony, his shoulder perched against the frame, staring out at the lake, and I wolfed down the best donut I'd had in ages, thinking I might die if I didn't inhale the other three of them in the next ten seconds. By the time he pivoted to face me, leaning his back against the frame now, I was biting into the chocolate-frosted donut.

"After the kind of day you must've had yesterday, I thought I'd see if you're okay," he said.

"Why?"

"Uh"—he let out a short, confused laugh—"based on what you said yesterday, you broke up with your fiancé right before the wedding and went into hiding. That might be a lot to handle."

It *was* a lot to handle, and hearing him say it out loud had an unwanted wave of emotion rolling through, pulling my throat tight and making it impossible to say anything without crying. Fighting it off, I managed to make eye contact and nod once.

God help me, the empathy in his compassionate brown eyes nearly did me in.

Damn this man and his kindness. He made it nearly impossible to maintain the facade that I was doing okay.

I turned away, picked up the precious SUGAR bag, and with my hair draping halfway over my face, asked, "Which one would you like? Or both?" I rushed to add, realizing what a pig I was being.

He shook his head. "I ate one at the bakery. Those are for you. I would've had them for you last night, but... last minute and all. The bakery was closed."

"Well, thanks again. You didn't have to do that."

"How do you plan to get food while you're here?" he asked, stopping me short.

"I'm leaving today." I tried to keep my tone matter-of-fact instead of defensive, but it felt like he was prying awfully deep for an owner-renter relationship.

He frowned. "Are you heading back home?"

"No." It came out too quickly, too emphatically. Too honestly.

"What made you come to Dragonfly Lake in the first place?"

"I didn't have a lot of time to make a plan. I didn't want to fly, and we thought staying close might be like hiding in plain sight. The press will check airports and beaches and big cities but probably not here. Or at least that's what my friends convinced me of in the panic of the moment."

"You're having second thoughts though?"

Was I? I gazed out the doors at the water. Breathed in the humid lake smell. Listened to the soothing breeze in the trees. If I thought I could stay undiscovered, I'd be perfectly content not to venture from this apartment for the full month I'd prepaid for. But that was a big if.

"Do you think somewhere else would be a better hiding place?" he asked.

I set the bag down, my sugar gluttony on hold for now, and stepped to the doorway, sticking to the opposite side from him. His gaze was locked on me, but I kept mine on the view outside and tried to act like his scrutiny didn't rattle me.

"Do you?" I asked, still trying to gauge how much I could trust him. My gut said he didn't want anything from me, didn't have any kind of hidden agenda, but my head wasn't there yet.

"It depends on your resources, I guess. I imagine you have the money to pay for your privacy. The more people you involve, though, the more chances for someone to blow your cover, right?"

I nodded. "I don't have a lot of experience at trying to stay out of the spotlight. For years, the name of the game has been publicity, publicity, publicity. Now I just want the opposite."

"I'm not a famous country star, but I do cherish my privacy," he said. "I know you have no reason to trust me, but like I said, your secret is safe with me if you decide to stay here." He hesitated for several seconds, then added, "I own a restaurant just down the way. We don't normally do delivery, but I could bring you a meal now and then. And I'd be willing to pick up some groceries to last you however long you decide to stay."

I whipped my head to him to gauge his sincerity.

"Why would you do that for me?" I asked, narrowing my eyes, watching every nuance of his handsome face.

"No reason other than trying to help you. I don't want anything from you, Everly. It just seems like you need a little kindness right now."

And again, his compassion made my throat ball up with emotion. Gratitude. Maybe I would turn out to be naive and stupid for trusting him, but my gut told me otherwise. Drea and Tim were flying back to Washington State today. I trusted them with my life, obviously, but they could only help so much from far away, and the truth was, I could use a little help while I did some soul-searching and figured out how I'd let myself get into my situation in the first place.

For my whole life, there'd been people making my decisions for me. My parents, my publicist, my manager, even my fans at times, in an indirect way. I'd let them, sometimes for good reason and sometimes just because it was easier.

That right there was what had gotten me in my current awful position.

I'd done it to myself. Allowed my life to be steered by other people. Obviously that hadn't worked out so well.

Somehow, this moment with Seth Henry felt like a big one, an important one.

To trust him or not to trust him?

I was the only one who could decide, and though I wasn't entirely confident about trusting my gut, it was time to start taking control of my own life, making my own decisions, and fighting for what I truly wanted in my heart.

In general, that was a muddy subject and would take

some time for me to figure out, but right here, in this moment, I wanted to stay at Dragonfly Lake. I wanted to soak up the peace outside my balcony doors. I wanted to trust this man who'd offered to help make my stay here possible.

I faced him head-on and met his gaze directly. "I'd like to stay for a week and see how it goes. Thank you for offering to help me get food. I'll take you up on it and I'll pay you back somehow."

I extended my hand to shake on the deal, and when his large, warm palm closed around mine, I swear a response sparked inside of me, involuntarily.

Okay, so I wouldn't touch him again and I'd keep my distance. It shouldn't be a big deal to handle whatever physical reaction my body had to this man, because God knew I was messed up enough by everything else. There would be no further involvement between me and Seth Henry. I was grateful for his offer to help, and that would be the extent of it.

As of this moment, I was taking charge of my life, and it didn't include any kind of attraction to a way-too-good-for-me man in Dragonfly Lake.

CHAPTER 6

As the business manager of Henry's Restaurant, I was the one in the family who had the closest to a Monday-through-Friday nine-to-five job.

My older brother, Cash, was the chef, and he was an incurable workaholic who often worked seven days a week even though our sous chef, Zinnia York, was more than capable of running a dinner shift with a packed house.

My younger brother, Holden, used to manage the front of house, but now Riley O'Brien had taken his place, and Holden was the general manager of the Rusty Anchor Brewing Company, the brewery next to and affiliated with Henry's that he was less than a month from opening with his friend Kemp Essex.

Saturdays and Sundays were generally my days off, though it was a rare weekend when I didn't make an appearance at Henry's for one reason or another. I'd planned to go in today to check on Riley. She was proving to be adept in her new position, but this was only the third Sunday brunch since summer season at the lake had started, and brunch could be a real test.

However, my plans had changed. I knew Cash was there if Riley needed anything.

I'd stayed with Everly longer than I'd planned, helping her put together a grocery list. As it turned out, her family had a chef who consulted with her trainer on her diet, all in the name of keeping her fit and in top performance shape. From what Everly had said, she lived a regimented life where decisions as basic as what went into her body weren't really her own. Because of that, she didn't have a lot of experience cooking, though she seemed determined to figure it out.

I had her list and had promised I'd come back with everything on it. I'd jumped in to help her, but now, as I drove the few blocks to the Country Market, rational thoughts were filtering in, telling me I needed to back off.

I could tell myself I was just being a good neighbor, but that was bullshit. I was attracted to Everly Ash, probably like three-quarters of the heterosexual males in this country. It went beyond her enchanting looks. Although I hadn't been familiar with her before last night's online research session—I'd never claimed to be up on music trends or entertainment news—I got the impression that I'd been exposed to a vulnerable side of her that the public never saw.

She was wary and guarded, certainly. Filled with regret. Knocked down in confidence, yes. But beneath it all, I sensed a good heart and a determination to come out of her situation stronger than before. She was younger than me by almost nine years, and it showed. But I couldn't deny her vulnerability mixed with that hint of underlying strength was a turn-on for me.

I needed to shut that down immediately.

I was content with my life the way it was. Alone. I had my house on the lake, Henry's restaurant, my family, good friends. I'd screwed up relationships enough for a lifetime in my early twenties and had my fill of the drama and the godawful trauma that one gone wrong could incite. I didn't need any of the turmoil.

Even if I was dumb enough to want to go down the romance road again, Everly Ash was the absolute last person I should get involved with, what with the press nosing in every aspect of her life. Any man she became entwined with would be scrutinized, researched, his past dug into with no stones left unturned, his secrets laid bare. The very thought of that had bile rising in my throat.

I parked in the market lot, absorbed in my thoughts. With Everly's list of about twenty items on my phone, I made my way through the store efficiently, with my head down to avoid being stopped to chat. That's why I didn't see Nick Carlisle, one of my best friends, until he approached me in the alcohol section.

"What's up, Seth?" he asked. "Glad to see you weren't abducted by the mystery renter."

Nick had been there last night when I received Everly's texts inquiring about the rental. He and Holden and Chloe had had quite the good time speculating on why someone would be desperate to rent my place so late on a Saturday. There wasn't a doubt in my mind Nick would follow up on that now, and that's why I changed the subject.

Peering into his shopping basket, I frowned. "Sugar, flour, eggs, chocolate chips? Are you turning domestic and baking me cookies?"

"Baking Gran cookies, smart-ass. She came home from church wanting chocolate chip cookies, so here I am."

Nick had given up his apartment and moved into his grandma's house a few months back when there were signs of her forgetting her meds some days and she'd said she no longer wanted to "fool with" cooking for herself.

"Hope you don't burn them." Though we flipped each other shit, we'd been buds since grade school. I was willing to bet money that, if he did burn the first batch, he'd start over and try again for his grandma.

"I'd say I'd bring you a couple but I'm not that nice."

"No debating that," I said, grinning as I located the type of wine Everly had requested, more than a little surprised our humble market carried it.

"You're not a wine drinker," my bastard friend commented, standing over me like a nosy hawk.

"My brother owns a brewery. Maybe I just don't advertise that I drink wine from time to time."

"That or Holden was right that the mystery renter was, in fact, a lonely lady who needed some loving and you've decided to romance her."

"You know me better than that," I said with a scowl as I propped the bottle of sweet white wine in the corner of the overflowing basket.

"My point exactly. Seth Henry doesn't do entanglements and he doesn't drink wine. Especially not some frou-frou shit with a silhouette of a stick-thin chick on the label."

"I'm not romancing anyone."

I headed off toward the checkout lanes at the front of the store, Everly's list fulfilled. Nick said something about forgetting Gran's chocolate milk and went toward Dairy. I wasn't sorry for the respite. Now if I could just get through the line and out of the store before he reappeared.

No such luck, of course. As I finished putting all the items on the conveyor belt, Nick's ugly mug appeared over the rack that separated Darlene's checkout lane from Jerome's. My friend eyed the items I was about to pay for with a knowing grin.

"You ready to go, Nick?" Jerome asked, and I thought about slipping the guy a twenty-dollar tip for interrupting.

Nick stepped to the other side of his lane and left me the hell alone—for now.

"How you doin' today, Seth, honey?" Darlene Lionetti asked in her outdoor voice, the only volume she seemed to have. She'd worked here longer than I'd been a legal adult and knew the whole town.

"I'm okay, Darlene. You?"

"You must be hungry this week. You were just through my lane with a full cart two days ago!"

"Forgot some things," I said, fighting not to clench my jaw. Darlene was overly friendly all the time, usually a welcome face, but today I wouldn't mind a bit if she'd go silent until I was out of the store.

I kept an eye on Nick, hoping he hadn't heard what she said. He didn't need any encouragement. I needed some time to figure out what to tell him and my family about my "mystery renter." I'd promised Everly I wouldn't out her, and yet my family and close friends were nosy as hell.

"What'd you think of the big news?" Darlene continued, not seeming to notice I was more reticent than usual.

At the question, my heart took off in alarm. Did she mean Everly's news? How the fuck had her secret gotten out so fast?

The look on my face must've shown my shock and confusion, because Darlene raised her penciled-in brows and said, "An uncle again. I guess it must not be a big deal anymore." She winked exaggeratedly.

I frowned, wondering if Hayden and Zane were expecting again and she'd somehow, for some reason, neglected to tell the family first.

Nick laughed, definitely at my expense, from the end of Darlene's counter, apparently done checking out. "That's right. You probably don't know because you ducked out early last night. Holden and Chloe are with child."

A grin crept across my face as happiness for my brother

and sister-in-law battled for relief on Everly's behalf. I glanced at Darlene to confirm Nick wasn't bullshitting me.

"Early January due date, Uncle Seth. How 'bout them apples?" she confirmed.

"My brother apparently doesn't waste time. Good for them."

Darlene had finished ringing up Everly's items, and I slid my card in the machine. I couldn't be seen using her card, so we'd agreed she'd reimburse me digitally.

"Come on, Henry. Some of us have a business to run."

I turned to see Cade McNamara in line behind me, his cart full of a gigantic pack of toilet paper and two cases of bottled waters on the rack beneath. With a laugh, I said, "You running a business with that or providing janitorial services for the new resort?"

With a laugh, he said, "Nothing so fancy, thank God. Good news for Holden and Chloe, huh?"

Of course, at least two of the McNamara brothers had been at the party last night and no doubt had heard the news before I did.

The McNamaras had grown up two houses down from us on Honeysuckle Road, and the two families had intermingled daily, between their six kids and our four. Cade was the oldest son and the manager of the McNamara Marina, which was next door to Henry's Restaurant.

"Another Henry running around," I said. "If you McNamaras don't get busy, we'll have you outnumbered in another year."

"No thanks to you." He grinned. "You can always be the career uncle since you can't get a date."

Laughing, I flipped him off, then picked up Everly's bags of groceries. "Later, Cade. Bye, Darlene. Behave yourself."

"What fun would that be?" the sixty-something woman said with a cackle.

Most days I'd be fine with Nick waiting to walk outside with me, but today wasn't most days.

"You better get your ass home and in the kitchen to bake Gran's cookies," I said as we went through the automatic doors.

"Not till you tell me why you're buying groceries for your renter. What's going on, man?"

All signs of kidding were gone, so I needed to tell him *something*.

I sorted through options as we walked across the hot asphalt. His car was parked next to my Subaru, so as I put bags in the back of my SUV, he did the same. Waiting. Then he shut his door and came up next to me.

"This is me, Seth. You know I'm not a gossiper. I'm curious as hell and coming up with all kinds of possibilities, half of them not good."

"Save yourself the trouble. Everything's fine. My renter is going through a rough patch and wants privacy. That's it."

How the hell I'd thought I could offer any kind of privacy in this in-your-damn-business town, I didn't know.

Nick stared at me for several long seconds, and I stared back to emphasize the message that that's all he was getting. Would it be enough to last the whole week Everly was planning to stay? I didn't know. I could sure do my damnedest to keep to myself and avoid him and everyone as much as possible though. Not a perfect solution since my brothers and I owned one of the most popular eateries in this tourist town, but I didn't need human interaction the way Holden did to survive. I could run the business from my office just fine.

"This isn't like you at all," Nick said.

With a caustic laugh, I snapped, "Renting out my space isn't like me." I shrugged. "It's the decision I made and I stand by it, just like I stand by my promise to my renter to keep her situation to myself."

"Okay. You gotta do what you gotta do, but I sure hope

that doesn't bite you in the ass, man." With a nod, he went around his car, got in, and drove off with a brief salute.

It wouldn't bite me in the ass in any way he was probably imagining, like putting me in danger. It sure as hell was already biting me, though, because as I drove off, I had to tamp down on a kernel of anticipation at seeing Everly again.

CHAPTER 7

EVERLY

By Tuesday night, my head was a hot mess, oozing with doubts.

I was in my semi-protected spot in the doorway of the balcony, doors shielding me on the sides, staring out toward the lake in the darkness, listening to the gentle lap of the water against rocks and docks. I'd turned off all the lights in the apartment in hopes of not attracting insects, but I'd applied the bug repellent I'd found in the apartment anyway.

It was late, maybe after eleven? I'd lost track, and it didn't really matter. Doubts didn't care one bit what the hour was. They just rampaged on around the clock.

Was staying by myself in this lakeside apartment a mistake? I'd never been so isolated in my life, and while it seemed as necessary as oxygen at times, there were moments when I wanted to return to my home, where my parents could keep the wolves at bay, even if they were pissed.

Was holding my parents at a distance, with a simple one-line text each day to reassure them I was okay and needed more time, a stupid move? Yes, they were upset with me and didn't understand, mainly because I hadn't tried to explain in detail, but I knew, underneath it all, they wanted what was best for me. Surely they would eventually cool off, and then I could try to make them see my perspective.

Would ignoring my publicist bite me in the butt? Rebecca Morris was one of the best in the industry—my dad had ensured that—but she too was not anywhere in the vicinity of happy with me and left messages daily.

Would Trey ever talk to me again? I sucked in a shaky breath. It would serve me right if he didn't. I knew he had to be hurt, mad, embarrassed, so many things and none of them good. I'd left messages for him three times now, trying to balance between giving him space and letting him know I really wanted to talk to him. Yeah, I got it… It was likely too little too late in his eyes, but we couldn't just never talk again, could we?

There was thunking from the garage below me, as there had been on and off all evening. I knew it was Seth, and I confess, a couple of times I went to the window that faced his house and watched him walk from the garage to the back door, carrying heavy things like wood and tools and I wasn't sure what else, mainly because I was too busy admiring what I could see of his biceps, and I might've appreciated how his thighs filled out an old pair of jeans.

A girl could *look*, no matter how messed up and not capable of getting involved she was.

It wasn't that Seth was one of those guys who benched five hundred pounds like his life depended on it. He was tall, with a medium build that might not catch every woman's attention at first glance. Muscles, yes, but they weren't in-your-face and bulging. There was no reason for me to have noticed and a thousand reasons for me not to, but noticed I had.

I shrugged into the night, not concerned about it. With everything else on my mind, a passing interest in some random guy's muscles, a guy I would never see again after this week, didn't even make a blip on the radar as worry worthy.

The side door below me shut soundly, giving me the impression Seth was quitting whatever project he was working on for the night. I was more than a little amazed that he'd kept at it so late. He'd told me Sunday, when he'd delivered my groceries, that he worked until at least five all week at his restaurant and to text him if I ever wanted him to bring me dinner. I hadn't. I'd taken the groceries from him, thanked him profusely and genuinely, wired him a payment, and hadn't interacted with him since.

He was my landlord for a week. Not a friend. Not a dinner provider. Not a savior.

One thing I'd figured out in the past two days was that I needed to learn how to save myself. Make my own decisions. Run my own life.

It hadn't been so evident how much I'd let my parents run things until now, when I was fighting to have time to myself. Not having time to myself, not being accountable to myself, was a major contributor to my current situation. My fault completely, and my only excuse was that it had been comfortable and easy. I'd been coasting. My dad and mom had all the experience necessary to guide my career, and I seemed to have handed over the reins to my life along with it.

It was time for that to change.

As I sat lost in my thoughts, the sound of footsteps in the grass below broke into my awareness. I shrunk back into the thick chair cushion and held my breath, expecting a flash on a camera to flare into the darkness. There hadn't been a hint of media contact since I'd arrived, but I'd been conditioned to expect it at every turn.

The steps continued away from the garage, toward the water, at an even, unhurried pace, and I started breathing again, realizing it was probably Seth.

Though there was a partial moon, the large, towering trees blocked most of its light. My eyes were adjusted though, so I could make out the white of Seth's T-shirt as he got farther from me and closer to the shore.

I'd been alone with my thoughts for so long, trapped inside of this admittedly really great apartment, that the strangest combo of feelings washed over me at the sight of him. There was relief at seeing another human, one who knew my secret. Trepidation because I had an undeniable urge to reach out to him, say something. What? No idea. Why? I wasn't sure other than I was sick to death of my own company. And a frisson of excitement because, well, all I could guess was those biceps.

Ignoring that last feeling, I sat up straighter and studied the surrounding area for other people. In the past two days, I'd watched countless boats go by, seen a lot of commotion on the dock two houses over, which appeared to be right next to the busy marina, and noticed some other neighbors out and about, checking fishing lines on their docks or taking a dip in the water or riding off in their boats. At the moment, all was quiet. I didn't see anyone around.

"Psst," I said into the night, my eyes on the white tee.

It took two more tries before he turned around. Though it was doubtful he could see much, he must have noted the doors were open, and he made his way toward me. He, too, looked left and right to assure himself no one else was around, and that little action meant everything to me.

"What's up?" he said in a low voice.

Whether it was purposely or not, I also appreciated that he didn't say my name. There were other Everlys, but it wasn't that common.

I shrugged even though he likely couldn't see it, realizing I didn't know what to say.

"What are you up to?" I asked in a loud whisper.

He glanced toward the water. "Taking in the peace. You?"

Instead of continuing to communicate from fifteen feet up, I said, "Give me a minute," went inside, and closed the doors. I slipped into my flip-flops, then went out the main door, checked for people yet again, and descended the steps. We were in shadow anyway, and my tank was navy blue so probably hard to see.

Seth was standing where I'd left him but turned toward the lake. As I approached, he faced me. "Is something wrong?" he asked.

"No." I blew out a breath as I suddenly wondered what the heck I was doing. I didn't know this man. We didn't have any kind of friendly relationship, thanks, at least in part, to me dismissing him so quickly when he'd brought my groceries. "I… I guess I was just overexcited to see another human. Sorry to interrupt your peace. I think I'll go sit on the dock if that's okay."

Feeling like a dork, I didn't wait for him to respond and took off toward the dock. I hadn't worked up the courage to come out here before, but now that I was all the way out in the fresh night air, I didn't know how I'd managed being cooped up for so long with this so close by. It was a typical steamy summer night in Tennessee, but the breeze stirred things and made the air feel fresh, especially compared to the air-conditioned apartment.

As I neared the long dock, I inhaled deeply. I hadn't realized how much I needed fresh air. It was absolutely glorious. I stepped out on the dock, went all the way to the end, and sat on the edge with my feet dangling in the water. I'd never swum in a lake before, and I wasn't too sure I loved the idea of what might be under the surface, but I was half-aware that Seth might be watching me and I didn't want to seem like *that* much of a city girl. The coolish water washed over me up to my lower calves, and I quickly forgot about being creeped out by fish and sighed in contentment.

I propped my hands on the hard surface behind me and

lifted my face. My chest expanded as I took in the millions of stars dotting the black velvet sky. Out here, the trees didn't block my view of the sliver of moon. Out here, it felt like I was on another planet, away from my problems.

Seth was right. There was a peace here I'd never before experienced.

I found myself just sucking in air, filling my lungs, imagining it permeating every cell. Yoga had been a part of my weekly fitness routine for years, but I'd never felt so compelled to yoga-breathe as I was now.

There were boat lights way out on the water, and some of the houses on the shore were still illuminated. Looking to the right, off in the distance, I spotted a large complex that I guessed was the new Marks Hotel.

Yes, there were signs of humans if you looked for them, but I let the gentle sloshing of the water on the dock pilings and the breeze in the trees lull me for several minutes.

I was so lost in the peace that I jolted when a canoe glided toward me from the shore side. It only took a second to recognize Seth, but it showed how relaxed I'd become... foolishly relaxed. Seth was safe, but who else could paddle right up to me?

"You startled me," I said, wondering how he'd gotten the canoe in the water so quietly and quickly. I'd seen the canoe on the boat rack in the yard, along with some kayaks and paddleboards.

"Sorry about that." His voice was soothing and low. He eased the boat up alongside the dock and held on. "Do you canoe?"

I let out a quiet laugh, because I was so far from *canoeing* that it struck me as odd that he used it as a verb. "I haven't, no."

"Want to?"

I looked it over carefully. Seth sat in the seat in the back, leaving the empty one in front of him. It looked like he'd added pads to the front bench, and the other seat had a back, giving extra comfort, as if maybe he spent a lot of time in this canoe. There was a small light on the back end. I glanced out at the dark water to see if anyone was close enough to get an eyeful.

"We won't go too far," he said. "Just far enough to feel like we're in the middle of nowhere."

"The end of this dock does a pretty good job of that."

"It gets better. Trust me."

The other day, when I'd made the decision to spend the week in the garage apartment, I'd vowed to stay put, stowed away inside. Safe. But the late hour, the cloak of darkness, the reassuring calmness of this man had lulled me out.

I glanced up at the little balcony where I'd been watching a slice of the world for three days. Though I could only partially see it through the lush trees from here, it looked lonely.

It would be smarter to walk back up the stairs into my hideaway. Though I was feeling pretty secure that no one would recognize me tonight, in a canoe, on the middle of the lake, that kernel of anticipation Seth Henry seemed to generate deep inside of me told me there were other dangers out here.

I met his gaze, easy to see because he was only a couple feet away now. With a single nod, I got to my feet and stepped closer to get in the boat.

CHAPTER 8

SETH

When Everly had apologized for interrupting my peace, I'd been stunned silent. Her assumption that she was bothering me couldn't have been further off the mark, because when she'd signaled from her balcony, it'd sparked something in me that was way out of proportion to what would be an appropriate response. When she'd come down those stairs, I'd been more than a little surprised—and way too happy to see her.

Before I could reassure her that she wasn't interrupting anything, she'd hurried to the dock, leaving me sorting for the right thing to say. I wasn't a big talker, didn't feel the need for excess chatter. What I was big on was saying the right thing at the right time, and tonight I'd been slow on the uptake.

An average guy would've followed her over to the dock, sat down a couple of feet from her, and reassured her she wasn't an interruption. Either I was shooting for above average or I was inordinately stupid when I'd gone the canoe route instead.

As she'd deliberated whether to join me in the boat, my pulse had pounded with the hope that she'd agree.

Now I kneeled close to the center of the canoe and held on securely to the cleat on the dock. I extended my other hand to help her in.

"You'll want to go slow and keep your body down so your center of gravity is as low as possible. Less chance of rocking the boat and capsizing."

Her eyes widened, and she looked for a second like she might reconsider.

"Once you're in, you'll feel more secure. Wait a second." I leaned toward the other seat and grabbed the life jacket from under it, then handed it to her. "Can you swim?"

Everly nodded. "It's been a good long time, but I imagine it's like riding a bike."

"I always wear a life jacket in this thing. Just to be safe."

"Does it tip often?"

"Only when my asshole brothers show up and tip it on purpose."

"Do they do that often?" She looked over her shoulder as if worried they might pop out.

"Not for a good decade at least. It's safe, Everly. I used to be a certified lifeguard, and a lot of that's like riding a bike too."

She took the life jacket and stuck her arms through it. I didn't know who had used it last, but it was too loose, and I directed her in tightening the belt as small as it would go.

I stretched my arm a little farther in her direction. Finally, she took my hand in a quick motion, and you'd think I'd be prepared for it after waiting so long for her to decide.

I was not fucking prepared for the charge that zipped up my arm and settled in my chest. Her gaze whipped to meet mine, as if she'd felt it too.

I was a man of science, not whimsy, and on some level, I realized that must have been my imagination. Reinforcing my hold on the dock—and maybe my equilibrium as well—I nodded at her, encouraging her to step over the side of the canoe.

She kicked off her flip-flops, and then, with an audible inhale, she put her first leg into the center of the boat, making the canoe wobble and her gasp. I tightened my grip on both the dock and her hand.

"Take it slow and squat low once you get your other leg in. I've got us."

She held on to my hand for dear life, and sweet Jesus, I did not hate it.

"You need a bigger boat," she said quietly. "I don't think I'm a fan of this one."

But she didn't veer from her course, and with another inhale, in came her other leg, and she lowered herself quickly, as I'd suggested. The canoe rocked wildly for a couple of seconds but calmed down as soon as she did.

Everly blew out a loud breath, and I couldn't help but notice she still clung to my hand.

"Are you afraid of the water?" I asked.

She shook her head. "More of what's in it."

I let out a low laugh. "Fish. No man-eating ones, or woman-eating ones for that matter. People swim in the lake every day. The chances of this thing tipping are almost nothing because the wind is calm and the water's protected, but if we did, you'd be okay. You've got a life preserver and a lifeguard and the dock is right there."

"Yeah," she said on another exhale. "Sorry. This is all new and I'm being a wimp."

Then she let go of my hand, and while I was happy she felt confident enough to do that, I didn't want that to be the last time I got to touch her.

She moved slowly to the bench seat and sat on it, facing me. Now that we were out from under the shadows of the trees, I could see her more clearly. Her pretty eyes were wide, as if she still expected Jaws to take a bite out of the boat. Her hair was free, tousled, hanging down her back, and though she'd been breathtaking with her fancy do when she'd arrived Saturday night, I liked this look even more.

"Maybe sometime I'll take you out in the bigger boat you mentioned." I pointed to the twelve-passenger sporty blue and white deck boat in the slip on the other side of the dock. "This one's quieter."

"That's important," she said, seemingly to herself. "Am I supposed to have an oar?"

I hid my grin. "Canoes and kayaks have paddles. Row boats have oars. But I've got this tonight. The point is for you to relax and get out of the apartment for a while with no one discovering you."

She studied me for a couple of seconds. "Thank you." Then she shot me a hint of a smile that awakened something deep inside of me.

Ignoring the strange sensation, I eased us away from the dock, picked up my paddle, and dipped it into the water. There was only the slightest ripple to the lake tonight. The air was thick with humidity, so the breeze was a relief even at this hour. Since it was Tuesday and almost midnight, it was quiet, the majority of the homes on the shore dark. Perfect time to take Everly out for a little escape.

I wondered when I'd made her isolation my problem. Probably about ten minutes ago. Something about her determination to not intrude along with a thread of loneliness so blatant that I'd picked up on it even before she'd descended the stairs. What the hell had happened to my keep-to-myself tendencies? I used to think I was the smart guy, but life had proven that wasn't true many times over, tonight included.

Without a plan, I headed out about a hundred yards and veered to the left, which would take us past McNamara Marina and Henry's Restaurant. Both were closed and deserted. The marina's slips were well lit, and our dock was illuminated by dim solar lighting along the length, but I didn't even see a single of the McNamara brothers out and about.

"That's our restaurant," I said as we glided even with it, still quite a ways from shore. I let up on the paddling.

"It's an A-frame. I love that." Her eyes sparkled in the darkness.

"My grandma chose that style back when she opened it, before I was born. When my grandpa died, she wasn't sure what to do with herself. She always said the only thing she was good at was cooking, so she decided to cook for other people."

"Is she retired?"

"She passed away a few years ago."

"I'm so sorry."

I smiled around the sadness that inevitably arose at the thought of the sweet woman my brothers and I owed so much to. "Thanks. She offered the restaurant to us four grandkids if we wanted it. She didn't want us to feel chained to it. Holden and Cash and I took her up on it."

"But not your sister?"

I shook my head. "Hayden had earned her interior design degree right before that. Up until last year, she still worked the bar on weekends in the summer, along with her design business and a retail home decor store in Nashville. She was conflicted about letting go until she got pregnant."

"She had three jobs?"

"Two of them full-time plus. Zane and Harrison are the best things that could've happened to her. They changed her priorities."

Everly was studying me again. "You love your family a lot. I can tell you care about what's most important to them."

"Of course." The comment struck me as odd. It made me curious about her family. I'd read a lot online, but I gave almost no credence to any of it and had the compelling need to learn more about Everly Ash from her. "Have you talked to your family yet?"

The second the words were out, she stiffened, and I regretted bringing her down.

"That's none of my business," I said, shaking my head and picking back up on the paddling.

"It's okay." She went pensive for a few seconds. "I've texted my parents. I know I need to talk to them but I'm dreading it."

Her words aroused even more curiosity. I knew how difficult it was to think you'd disappointed your parents. I couldn't help but wonder though if her parents were disappointed. It appeared she'd merely done what she'd had to to prevent a lifetime of unhappiness.

"Why are you dreading it? You think they'd choose Team Trey over their own daughter?"

"God, are they doing the team thing in the media? Making people choose sides?" Her eyes squeezed shut and she pressed her lips together as if she couldn't stand it.

Damn, I could be insensitive. The press was indeed referring to Team Everly and Team Trey, and though I'd mostly kept my distance from the "news" stories since my original binge Saturday night, I'd seen enough to know that the teams were lopsided thanks to the media positioning Everly as the bad guy. Obviously they had no clue what the real story was, and too many "journalists" figured that gave them license to make one up. Whatever got the most clicks. I vowed at that moment to not click a single other article about Everly or her situation.

My thoughts must have shown on my face, because Everly said, "It's fine, Seth. I've no doubt I'm being painted in an ugly, heartless way and that the whole world is taking Trey's side. I kind of don't blame them. I ditched him on our wedding day." She paused, looked out over the dark water, and inhaled. "I wish I could say it doesn't bother me, but there's nothing I can do about it. Although I'm sure my publicist would argue that point." She muttered the last to herself.

"Not talking to her either?"

She shook her head and her dark hair rustled around her face. I'd slowed way down on the paddling, so we hadn't gotten far, which was fine. I wanted to keep us close to home.

"I'm being a coward," she said.

"Sounds like you just need time to yourself."

"It turns out time to myself hasn't made facing the people I'm supposed to be closest to any easier."

I stroked the paddle through the water, using a C stroke to keep us going in a straight line, even though I didn't have a destination in mind. Having no idea what to say, I kept my mouth shut. I didn't want to make anything worse by saying the wrong thing again.

"I've been doing a lot of thinking the last couple of days." She let out a quiet laugh. "I mean, not much else to do when you can't turn on your cell phone."

"Did you figure anything out?"

"A few things." She went silent.

"You don't have to talk about it if you don't want to," I said even as I itched for her to say more so I could understand her better.

"I've spent so much time alone I want to. If you don't mind. My friend Drea went back to work yesterday and hasn't had much time to talk. She's probably sick of listening to me anyway."

"Was she the getaway car girl?"

"She and her saint husband."

"I don't mind. Listening," I clarified. "If it could help."

"I don't know if anything can help, but I know I could go out of my mind if I just keep circling around the same thoughts. So if you mean it…"

"I mean it. Tell me what you've figured out."

CHAPTER 9

We'd glided beyond the Honeysuckle Inn now. The shore was wooded for another mile or so before it opened up to a bunch of older homes that weren't part of the town of Dragonfly Lake. It was peaceful here, quieter than any other stretch, as it was one of the longest undeveloped parts of the shoreline. I stopped paddling, rested the paddle along the inside of the canoe, and let us drift where we might. And waited.

"Have you ever taken a long look at yourself and not liked what you saw?" she asked.

It was my turn to laugh, though I felt the opposite of humor. "Oh, yeah. Been there. One star. Do not recommend."

She half grinned, seemingly absorbed in her thoughts. Then she drew in a deep breath and blew it out into the steamy night air. "I'm not proud of any of this. Just putting that out there right now."

"Okay." I dipped my hand in the water to cool down, trying to imagine what she was going to reveal.

"I've been letting my parents and my team run my career and my life," she said.

I hadn't expected that, but somehow I wasn't shocked either. "Your team being…?"

"My manager, my publicist, people at the label. My mom is my assistant, officially, but I've given her more power than you'd probably ever give a regular assistant. My dad. Have you heard of Eddy Ash?"

"Confession: only when I looked you up online that first night. And just so you know, I believe about five percent of anything I read online or in the media. It said your dad is a music producer? Big name?"

"Huge name. Objectively speaking, he's truly a genius at what he does. He's worked with countless artists, some of the biggest names out there, and some of them became big names because my dad is that good."

"So you were born into music royalty." I'd read something of the sort but taken it with a grain of salt.

"Luck of the draw. I know a bajillion artists would kill to be Eddy Ash's daughter. I'm grateful, because I've learned so much from him, musically and otherwise."

I watched her, waited. "It sounds like there's a but."

Everly frowned and started running her finger up and down her opposite thumb, watching the movement in her lap. "No matter how I say all this, I'm going to sound like a spoiled, ungrateful brat."

"Not going to judge you," I said, already knowing I'd likely take her side regardless.

"I've always sung. Like, my parents say I was born singing and that's probably only a slight exaggeration. Growing up, I was surrounded by the music industry. My parents' social lives revolved around so many VIPs, from artists to record label presidents to the most elite managers and talent agents. I was named after the Everly Brothers because my mom was a superfan. I hung out in the studio when my dad was working. It was all very normal to me, you know?"

I nodded. I was fascinated by every word coming out of her mouth.

"I recorded my first songs when I was a teenager."

"Did your dad produce them?" I had the urge to go home and research the crap out of the country music industry just so I could understand her life better.

She shook her head. "When my dad produces someone, it has the potential of mega success. He has stories of so many artists he took from nobodies to household names. These days, he can basically choose who he'd like to work with. My mom, especially, was always very careful with my career. While she was all for me performing and singing locally, she and my dad had an agreement that they didn't want me to be a 'child star.' It was more about gaining experience. Learning the ins and outs of the business. Honing my voice. They had an agreement that my dad wouldn't produce me until I was at least twenty-one."

"That sounds wise," I said, thinking that a lot of parents would be more inclined to push their kids into the spotlight too early. "Were you in agreement? Or did you want more?"

"I was fine with it. I just liked to sing and write songs and be involved in music every day. I liked school and didn't want to be tutored or treated differently. The career, the stardom? They were secondary for me."

"And now here you are."

"I... feel like I drifted here. Let my parents build it all for me. Everything." Her voice went husky and lower.

"You're the one with the talent." I might not know a thing about the music industry, but in the past three days, I'd listened to every song Everly had ever recorded, and there was no debating that she was incredibly talented. The Sweetheart of Country Music moniker fit. Her voice ranged from sweet and angelic to full and passionate and everything in between.

She nodded briefly. "I'm grateful. Yes, I've worked hard, really hard, but I also know I was blessed with an inborn talent, and I thank the universe for that every day. But I've been molded into what my parents thought I should be molded into. I've let myself be molded, led, directed, whatever. I've never stopped to think about it. Just… rolled along."

"Did they push you into marrying Trey Gilbert?"

Everly's attention was still locked on her lap, her eyes averted. This urge that was bubbling up in me to comfort her, convince her she didn't need to be embarrassed… it was powerful and foreign, and it scared the hell out of me, yet I couldn't deny it. The only thing that kept me from touching her, an arm or a hand in support, was that we were in a canoe and there were a few feet between us. I was adept at not tipping a canoe, but the wobbling that bridging that gap would cause would likely stir up Everly's uneasiness again.

The *hoo-hoo-hoot* of an owl sounded from the woods on the shore, and Everly whipped her head in that direction.

"Great horned owl," I said, glancing toward the trees but knowing we'd never spot him in the dark.

She stared off that way for a few seconds. I was sure she wasn't going to answer the question about Gilbert, but then she said, "Trey and I went on our first date for the publicity. My team, particularly Rebecca, my publicist, cooked it up, along with his publicist, after we'd been photographed at a party together and speculation went wild. It was exciting, so I didn't fight it. And the attention we got from the media, overwhelmingly positive, snowballed every time we appeared together. Our fans loved it, and I'll admit, it was a little heady. I liked Trey. My parents liked Trey. They *loved* the PR. It did great things for my career, things you can't pay for. My social media accounts exploded and I started getting invited to everything. At the time, I was excited to come out from my dad's shadow. Looking back, I think I went directly from my dad's to Trey's."

"You're a lot better-looking than Trey. Trust me." I grinned. as if I were joking, but I didn't see how Everly could ever be in someone's shadow. Even here in the night, in the middle of the dark lake, when she was feeling down, she had a sparkle to her personality that was undeniable.

She shook her head, as if that couldn't be true. This woman, a big star, came across as one of the most modest and humble people I'd met.

"We recorded a duet, a love song, and maybe I got swept up in it all a little bit," she continued. "It hit number one, my first time at the top of the charts. My dad threw us a party, and it was crazy how much attention we were getting. We kept dating, very publicly, I might add, because you can't buy the kind of good PR we got. And there were feelings there. An attraction. We had a lot in common just by virtue of being in the same profession. Before I knew it, he proposed."

"I bet your parents were ecstatic. It was like one royal faction uniting with another," I said. Though I hadn't previously been up on the Ashes or Trey Gilbert's career, there were articles and photos everywhere.

"It's so ridiculous when I think about it now. So embarrassing that I wasn't more deliberate with my decisions. I didn't see it at the time, but now I think I said yes because it's what was expected."

"You've spent your lifetime doing what's expected, it sounds like."

She closed her eyes and rubbed her forehead with one hand, as if ashamed.

"That's not always a negative thing," I said, wishing I could stop making her feel bad with my ill-thought-out comments.

"I see now that I need to make decisions for myself and not everyone else. I need to think about what I really want instead of trying to give everyone else what they want for me. Hindsight is twenty-twenty and all that."

"You're right about hindsight."

"I need to take control of my life, but I don't even know what that looks like. I've been so dependent in so many ways… just… singing, working…" She trailed off and shook her head again. "I have to stand up to my parents and make them understand. They've never meant me any harm."

"Probably the opposite?" I guessed.

Everly nodded. "That makes it even harder. I don't want to hurt them."

"I get it." God, did I get it. My story might've been totally different from hers and happened ages ago, but listening to Everly's situation brought it all back, aroused the emotions I'd been shutting out for years. The fear of disappointing my parents. The regret for messing things up.

"So I've been working up the courage to somehow convey all of that to my parents, then tell Rebecca to do whatever's necessary to make things die down instead of chasing after publicity the way we've been doing for the past year. And at some point, I hope Trey will call me back so I can apologize and we can have a real conversation."

"That's a lot."

"It is." She blew out a breath as she stared toward the center of the lake. Then she let out a self-effacing huff. "I'm so sorry to lay all of that on you. My God, you must think I'm a total head case."

"Not in the least. It sounds like no one had bad intentions, just that things got rolling and gained momentum until you applied a hard brake."

She grimaced.

"Better a hard brake now than later, right?"

Instead of answering, she eyed the wooded shore again. I

kept my gaze on her and thought I spotted a glint of moisture in the corner of her eye. That was my cue to give her an out from the topic. Though I could handle tears—God knows I'd been through half a million with my sister, Hayden—I didn't want to be the one instigating them if I could help it.

"Are you ready to turn back?"

She blinked hard, then swiped at one eye. "Sure." She forced a smile and looked directly my way. "This time I'd love the shore tour edition. Like, what was that place we passed with the long decks?" She pointed toward the last development, a few hundred feet behind where we'd come to rest.

I picked up the paddle and maneuvered around to head home. "It's our historical inn, nearly a hundred years old, called the Honeysuckle Inn."

"A bed-and-breakfast?"

"More like a lodge or hotel, I guess. It's quaint but, last I heard, needed some work. I'm not sure how it will compete with the new Marks Hotel down that way." I pointed to the west side of the lake at the luxury hotel my sister-in-law, Chloe, had had a big part in creating, back before she'd decided to work full-time with Holden and Kemp in their brewery.

"That looks impressive," she said of the Marks. When we floated closer to the Honeysuckle, she said, "This place is cute though. There's a wing going out from either side? You can hardly see them through the trees."

"Those are the guest rooms. The common areas are in the center. All of it with a great lake view."

Most of it was dark now. The two things that place had going for it were the views and the lack of lodging in Dragonfly Lake. We'd always been a vacation spot, but it seemed to get busier and busier every year. That was one of the reasons Marks International had invested in our town for its latest property.

I kept paddling, and soon we were long past the inn and

coming back on the few businesses that were inside the town limits and located directly on the water. Priority had always been given to residential zoning on the shore, with only a patch here and there of commercial. That's one reason the property Henry's Restaurant was on was so valuable, and the same with the brewery. We owed our "luck" to our grandma's foresight in buying each one long ago, before land values were astronomical.

After a scan of the nearby businesses to ensure no one was around, I took us closer to shore. "That's my brother's Rusty Anchor Brewing Company tucked in next to Henry's. Opening next month. They're planning a beer garden right there." I pointed to the treed area between the building and the shore. "We'll serve their beer at Henry's, and Cash is creating several entrees using it. There won't be seating inside the brewery itself, but you can sit in the beer garden and order from a limited Henry's menu out there."

"Are you keeping the trees?"

"As many as possible."

"I wish I'd still be here to see it when it's done."

"You can stay longer, you know. You paid for a month." And I was certain she could afford to pay for as much as she wanted.

"I wish my life would allow that but… all the things…" She exhaled a shaky breath. "I need to talk to my parents."

"Maybe it would help to decide what you want to do first. That gives them less opportunity to sway you."

She nodded, rubbing her thumb again. "You're probably right."

"Probably?" I said, feigning outrage and making her smile.

A few more good strokes of the paddle and we reached my dock. I eased the canoe alongside it in the same place I'd picked her up, next to her abandoned flip-flops.

"I'll get out first and then I can help you," I told her.

"Please. I seem to not have sea legs."

I climbed onto the dock and turned to help her. The canoe floated a little farther away, and I bent down to grab the edge just as Everly tried to stand. Before I could offer advice or even reach out to her, the boat wobbled, she lost her balance, and she went over the other side with a shriek.

CHAPTER 10

I tried so hard to catch myself, but that boat and this body had other ideas.

As I fell toward the water, I knocked my lower leg on the edge of the canoe, and then, with the grace of a pregnant hippo on a balance beam, I flopped into the water. Pretty sure my arms were flailing every which way, and I smacked the surface with one of my shoulders on the way in.

Thanks to the life jacket, I didn't submerge far and my head popped up right away, so no drowning today.

Before I could process another thought, there was a crash in the water about a foot away from me. I think I screamed again as I tried to see what was about to off me, and then Seth's head popped up and he grabbed me under my elbows, his eyes wide and full of concern.

I couldn't help it. A laugh burst out of me. I was less than five feet from the dock, even closer to the stupid canoe, I'd told him I could swim, and I was wearing a life jacket. And this incredible man had dived in to rescue me.

"You're okay?" he asked, still holding on to me.

"I'm fine. Well, I think I ripped half the skin off my leg but otherwise I'm okay."

Since he was supporting me, I dared to stretch my uninjured leg downward to see if I could touch the bottom, and I'll be honest, I had mixed feelings about whether I wanted to. I still had some reservations about what was in this water. I had to admit, though, it felt refreshing. It wasn't what I would call cool, but it was a relief compared to the thick, humid air. My foot didn't touch anything, and I decided not feeling the questionable bottom was a relief, particularly since Seth was holding on to me and I didn't even need to tread water for the moment.

"We'll check your leg out. I'm sorry I lost my grip on the boat, Everly."

As my heart rate gradually slowed closer to normal, I nodded. "All good. It's hot out anyway," I said with a smile. It slid right off my face, and I gasped and jolted my leg away as I felt something move close to it. "What was that?"

"Relax. That's me." Seth's voice was low, calming. Whiskey-smooth. The timbre of it awoke something deep inside of me, and I suddenly became aware of how close his face was to mine, how big his hands on my arms were, what a strong and vibrant man he was. It stole my breath in an instant, and my heart hammered for an altogether different reason.

"If you're sure," I said, keeping my voice down, "and you're not just saying that to stop me from panicking because there's a big, fat fish circling before the kill."

He chuckled. "You smell sweeter than anything the fish in this lake like to nibble on." As soon as he said it, his expression went serious, as if he hadn't meant to let something so personal slip out.

Our gazes met. Locked. My breath caught in my chest again as I froze, knowing on some level that I needed to look away but too wrapped in this man's spell to do so.

I didn't know how many seconds ticked by before he snapped out of our intangible moment, but he inhaled and put a few extra inches between us.

"We should get out and tend to your leg."

"Yes," I tried to say, but my voice didn't work right. I cleared my throat and noticed he still held on to me, as if he was afraid my life jacket and I would sink if he let go.

Though I shouldn't be, I was okay with that.

Seth kicked underwater, moving us closer to the dock. "It's a little high, so I'll lift you. That'll be easier than swimming to the ladder."

I nodded, afraid to try to speak again, not wanting him to figure out those few intense seconds had shaken me.

As he guided me by my elbow, the truth smacked into me: the most dangerous thing in the lake wasn't some kind of fish or reptile. It was this man.

"Ready?" he asked when we were next to the dock, and I nodded.

He moved behind me, and the next thing I knew, his hands were at my waist, beneath the bottom edge of the life jacket and my shirt. He hoisted me up so I was halfway out of the water, and I gripped the edge of the dock and lifted myself until my arms were straight. I pulled one knee up and climbed out with the grace of a fish flopping on the shore.

I half rolled to a sitting position, water dripping off me from head to toe, and brushed my drenched hair out of my face just in time to witness Seth propel himself up onto the dock unassisted. I was close enough to see the ripples and firmness in his biceps. I looked away quickly, but not fast enough that my mouth didn't go dry.

Something about him… I'd never had a reaction quite like this to a guy, and didn't it figure?

There had never been a worse time for me to be attracted to someone. I was a runaway bride, for God's sake, *less than a week ago*. My head was a mess, so full of self-doubt and questions and fears. Not only that, I was public enemy number one in the media—I didn't need to plug in to know that. So sure, why not be attracted to a random guy in a small town who was kind enough to dive into questionable lake water in the middle of the night to "save" me?

I looked away as I sucked in the biggest breath I could, then blew it out. Watching a very fit, good-looking guy flex his muscles while he was dripping wet was not advisable, so I focused on the marina in the distance, noticing two guys out on one of the docks as I took off my life jacket. They seemed rowdy and loud, although I couldn't make out what they were saying. Then one of them shoved the other into the water and I gasped.

"Sounds like the McNamaras," Seth said, unworried, as he came up to a squat and squinted in that direction. "Six brothers run the marina. That sounded like Dex, or maybe Jagger. They're a wild bunch."

The one who'd gone into the water climbed out and took off after the other guy, so I guessed it was all in fun and no one would be drowning from those docks tonight either.

"Oh, shit," Seth said, drawing my attention back to him. He'd slipped off his life jacket and tossed both of them to the big boat.

He was looking at my leg, and at that moment, I became aware of the pain again. I glanced down to see blood running down my wet leg in dark rivulets.

"We need to look that over, clean it up, see how deep it is." He stood and extended his hand to help me up.

On some level, I knew I should ignore his hand and get myself up, but I ignored that inkling because not only did I like his large, strong hands but I also could use the help to avoid looking even clumsier than I already had.

His fingers grasped mine, giving me the illusion of being safe and protected. He might keep me from tumbling back into the water, but I feared it would be way too easy to fall in other ways, detrimental ways.

Once I was standing, Seth said, "I'll get the canoe out and we can go to the house to clean that up."

"I can clean it in my apartment."

He picked up the paddle he'd set on the dock and fished the boat closer with it. "There aren't any bandages or first aid items in there. I'm betting you didn't throw those in your bag before you left, did you?"

That was almost funny. I frowned, realizing as I glanced down at that cut again that he was right. I at least needed some antiseptic to clean that sucker.

"A Band-Aid would be great. Thanks. Can I help with the canoe?"

He'd slid the paddle into it and was bending down at one end, getting ready to lift the whole thing out. He nodded toward the opposite end.

I bent down carefully and took hold of the end, and together we pulled it out of the water and onto the dock.

"Thanks." He went to the middle of the canoe, and before I knew what he was about, he hefted it up over him and walked along the dock toward the shore.

"Can I… do something?" The last bit I let trail off because it was obvious he'd done that a thousand times and had complete control. I was a little bit in awe.

I slid my flip-flops on and followed him up the dock to the shore. By the time I caught up, he had the canoe on the rack. I stood there trying not to be impressed by his ease of toting a boat on his back.

"How's your leg feel?" he asked as he fastened a bungee around the canoe.

"Like I got attacked by a killer fish."

Grinning, he asked, "Does anyone else know the Sweetheart of Country Music has some sass to her?"

"Of course not. That wouldn't be on brand, would it?" I

smiled too, but I couldn't deny there was a thread of irritation at what I'd let my life become—basically driven by branding and publicity.

He walked closer to me, tugged lightly on a clump of my wet hair, and said, "For what it's worth, I like it. Come on. I'll clean that cut."

When I started walking up the paved path toward the back of his house, he fell into step beside me and rested his palm on the small of my back. There was a quiet confidence in the action that absolutely did something for me. That and the *for what it's worth, I like it* comment.

Was he flirting with me? I hadn't had many men flirt with me or had that many relationships because there were always layers of protection around me, whether an actual bodyguard or just my team, my parents, whoever. I rarely went anywhere alone.

With Trey, we'd never been flirty. We'd started out talking as colleagues, discussing music and other artists. When our publicists had insisted we go out again, we'd talked a lot, done the getting-to-know-you thing, but flirtiness hadn't been a part of it. I'd liked Trey—I still *liked* Trey—but I'd never felt this underlying buzz, like there was a charge zipping through me, with him.

We went up the steps to the back deck, which extended the entire length of the house. There was a covered section surrounded on three sides by the house itself, and the whole deck was filled with comfy-looking outdoor furniture—love seats with thick cushions, side tables, a big square ottoman, a dining table that could seat at least eight—plus a fireplace on one side.

"You'll have to excuse the mess," Seth said as he opened a door to the house and we walked into the kitchen. "I'm remodeling. Started upstairs and I had to empty out the rooms while I worked, so there's stuff everywhere."

When we stepped in, a burst of cold, air-conditioned air

hit, and I shivered from being wet. I slipped my shoes off, not wanting to track footprints everywhere.

A large yellow cat sauntered in, peered up at Seth, and let out a soulful meow.

"This is Chaos, one of my two roommates. The demanding one."

I bent down and held my fingers out for the cat to sniff. He approached me, sniffed my hand, and apparently approved, because he rubbed his head against my fingers in a self-petting motion, making me smile. "Hey, Chaos. That's a big name to live up to."

"Ironically, he's a lazy bastard who mostly sleeps," Seth said.

I rubbed his chin, then stood.

"You were working late tonight," I said to Seth. "I heard you in and out of the garage a few times."

"I hope I wasn't too loud."

"The noises made me feel less alone," I said, realizing once the words were out of my mouth how revealing they were. I rushed to cover them. "So you're redoing the upstairs?"

"The whole house eventually. I'm teaching myself what I don't know how to do, so it's a slow process. Hold on a second. I'll get us towels to dry off."

He left the room, and I checked out the place he called home. The kitchen was large, with a lot of counters, an island, and a breakfast nook with a full-sized table. The appliances were stainless and newer than the rest of the finishes, and the vibe was homey and inviting. A coffee machine and a toaster were the only appliances on the clean counters. I wondered where the "mess" from remodeling was, because it wasn't in here.

A loud *thunk* sounded right behind me, and I whirled around to find another cat, nearly as big as Chaos, black with golden eyes. He seemed to have jumped down from the top of the refrigerator.

"Well, hello," I said, trying to slow my heart rate. "Seth doesn't do average-sized cats, huh?"

"That's Mayhem," Seth said, returning with towels and a first-aid kit. "He fancies himself lord of the fridge and sleeps even more than Chaos."

I laughed and leaned down, hand out, but he rubbed up against Seth's legs, keeping his eyes on me.

"He's a big baby." Seth gave Mayhem's ears a thorough scratching. He straightened and handed me a thick, plush chocolate-colored towel as both cats strutted to a feeding area and sat pear-shaped, waiting for their dinner.

"Dinner's late, isn't it, guys?" Seth served up two bowls of stinky cat glop and poured a cupful of crunchies into two more bowls.

I dried my arms and legs, dabbing carefully around the cut, not wanting to get blood on the towel. Then I wrung my hair into it. I was sure I still looked like a drowned rat, but at least I was no longer dripping.

"So you're teaching yourself to remodel," I said, baffled. "You couldn't find anyone to hire?"

"I have a friend with a construction company. He'll help me when I get to some of the tough stuff, but I like figuring things out, learning. It makes me feel like I've accomplished something."

I took a look at the kitchen again. "This room too?"

"This room is what started it. It's dated. Tired." He grabbed a paper towel and got it wet under the faucet. "I figured if I start upstairs and work my way down, I'll know what I'm doing by the time I get to the kitchen. Have a seat." He motioned to a chair. "Let's see that cut."

I sat down and held my leg up, frowning at all the fresh blood.

"You wanted a new kitchen, so you're remodeling the whole house?" I laughed. "And learning to do it yourself along the way. Do you do anything the easy way?"

"My family would say no. What about you?"

With a self-deprecating laugh, I said, "I've been letting everyone else direct my life since I was born, so I'd say I tend toward the easy way."

"Maybe the low-conflict way, but something tells me your career hasn't been easy, even with your parents' ins."

I thought about that, knew I was a hard worker, but I felt so icky and embarrassed by the way I'd been living that the hard worker part was overshadowed in my head. I didn't want to bore Seth more with any of it, so I didn't respond.

I held my breath as he gently dabbed the paper towel around my wound. Once it was cleaned, we could see the gash was about three inches long. It was more than just a surface scratch but not so deep I'd need stitches, or so Seth said.

"You have a lot of experience with things like this?" I asked, gritting my teeth as he swiped some antiseptic over it.

"Living here for half my life, yeah. My brothers, sisters, and I—and all our friends—spent our summers outside, in the water, rough-housing. There were more than a few ER visits and hundreds of first-aid situations."

As he doctored my cut, I questioned him about his family and friends and growing up on the lake. His childhood seemed full of adventure and fun and a carefreeness I wasn't familiar with. He made his family sound chaotic and loving and noisy in a good way. About as far from my childhood as you could get.

Don't get me wrong; my childhood was fine, overall happy, and privileged in a lot of ways. I definitely couldn't complain, but I also couldn't help wondering what it would be like to have a big, close family.

And living on the lake... Even though Seth had spent his high school years in Nashville, his formative years had been in this house, and then he'd returned after grad school. The peace I'd found here in the past three days, close to nature with all the beautiful scenery, was a respite like nothing I'd ever found even with all my traveling. Having this as your full-time address? Part of me was intrigued by what that would be like.

"You're set," he said once he had my leg cleaned, disinfected, and bandaged. He was still bent in front of me, picking up the wrappers and paper towels from the floor. The cats had devoured their food and sauntered out. "I'll send some bandages with you so you can change it once or twice a day."

"Thank you. Mind if I use the bathroom? Then I'll get out of your way."

"You're not in my way. Tonight's been fun." He rested his hand on my knee, gazing up at me with a warm, genuine smile that had my heart doing a little flip. "Through the living room, straight across the hall, you'll see the bathroom. The hall's a disaster area, so watch your step."

I headed through the living area, which had a large stone fireplace and a full wall of windows on the lake side. When I stepped into the hallway, I spotted the powder room across from me, front entryway to the left, and both sides of the hall to the right lined with boxes and things that must be from upstairs. As I rushed into the bathroom, a guitar propped up on end caught my eye. I'd waited too long to relieve myself as it was, but I'd take a peek at it afterwards.

When I'd finished in the bathroom and washed and dried my hands, I took a couple of steps down the dim hall to the guitar. Without turning on the light, I could tell it was nothing special, just an older, no-frills acoustic, but the impact of seeing it was powerful and unexpected. It'd been nearly two weeks since I'd done anything musical, what with all the wedding prep and craziness, then the wedding day that wasn't and the aftermath. More importantly, it'd been forever since I'd pulled out my own acoustic guitar and just played for no reason other than to soothe myself or maybe play with a tune or some lyrics that came to me.

Seth walked into the hallway, probably wondering what I was snooping out.

"Sorry," I said before he could say anything. "The guitar caught my eye. It's been too long since I've played mine. Do you play?"

He laughed self-consciously. "I try. Or I used to. Been a while for me too, but I don't really have any talent. Just taught myself for the heck of it."

"It's been years since I've just played for the heck of it. I miss it." I hadn't realized how much until that moment. Maybe it was just that it reminded me of home, of my life before it'd gone off the rails.

Seth picked it up. A tennis racket stacked behind it tumbled over and he righted it. Holding the guitar vertically, he plucked the E and A strings and they were way out of tune. "Needs a major tuning."

"There's an app for that."

"And I bet you have it on your phone."

"I do," I said, grinning unapologetically.

Still holding the guitar, he stepped closer to me. "You can borrow it while you're here if you'd like. I mean, I'm sure it's like a garage sale special compared to what you're used to, but it plays music. Once it's tuned."

I grasped the neck of it, suddenly itching to get it in tune and strum a few chords.

Seth didn't immediately let go, so I looked up at him at the instant he moved closer to me.

"Are you sure?" I asked, just above a whisper.

With one hand still right above mine on the guitar, he used his other to brush my hair back from my face.

"Would playing make you happy?" he asked, his voice also hushed.

I nodded, because my mouth had suddenly gone dry with

the awareness of his closeness, his whisper of a touch on the side of my face.

"I'm absolutely sure."

He lowered his head toward mine and my heart thundered.

He was going to kiss me. I knew it even as he seemed to move in slow motion, as if to give us both the opportunity to stop it if we wanted to.

I didn't want to.

By the time his lips were a breath away from mine, I thought I would die from anticipation. I stopped breathing, lifted my chin slightly, in case he was looking for a sign from me.

Kiss me. Please.

He closed that last inch of space and brushed his lips over mine in a tease, twice, a third time. Then he closed his mouth over mine at the same time he wove his hand through my hair and pulled my face closer, all uncertainty gone.

I was overcome by the essence of him, his scent, his taste, his heat, the demand of his lips on mine. When his tongue swiped at me, I opened to him and realized I'd lifted to my toes, throwing myself fully into the kiss. My blood went hot and a needy ache pulsed deep inside me.

Still holding on to the guitar for dear life, as if maybe it could ground me, I lifted my other hand and cradled his sandpaper-rough jaw, reveling in the sheer masculinity of that, of him, of the way he was making love to my mouth. In my twenty-nine years, I'd never been kissed like this, to the point of wanting to surrender myself in every way possible. To a man I'd met three nights ago. On my supposed-to-be-wedding night.

That thought froze me, brought me out of my lustful stupor and back to reality. I pulled back from the kiss, ending our contact, breathing hard, heart pounding. I dropped my hand from his face and let out a shaky breath then lowered back to my heels.

He stared down at me with sexy, heavy-lidded eyes, looking lust drunk too. Seeing the effect I'd had on him did nothing to cool me down, but the little voice in my head screaming about *bolting bride* and *basket case* and *three nights ago* was enough to kick up a spike of anxiety and regret.

I took a step back, still gripping the guitar but barely aware of it, my body nowhere close to recovered from that kiss even though I never should have let it happen.

"I better go," I said, my voice coming out lower and thicker than anything resembling normal.

I ripped my gaze from his, turned, and hightailed it across the living room, through the kitchen, and out the door I'd followed him into. It wasn't until I stepped off the bottom step to angle toward my garage refuge that I realized I'd left my flip-flops. I didn't care. I just needed to get behind the safety of my closed, locked door before he came after me. Stopped me. Talked to me.

I sprinted up the steps, let myself in, and closed the door. Only then did it hit me that Seth hadn't even tried to chase after me.

Which was, of course, totally for the best.

CHAPTER 11

SETH

Kissing Everly Ash last night was a boneheaded move.

I hadn't planned it. Obviously hadn't thought it through. In spite of being wired to self-deliberate everything, I'd just... done it. I wasn't sure I could've *not* done it.

It was like I'd momentarily lost my ability to rationalize, and my body had gone in toward her tempting lips of its own accord. And then the softness of her mouth, the little gasp she'd let out, the touch of her fingers on my cheek, as if she couldn't get enough of me either... I'd never been so twisted up by a simple kiss.

When she'd run off, I'd stood there in the hallway, my world spinning and my body pounding with need. By the time I'd come out of my stupor and gone to the kitchen to find her, she'd been halfway up the stairs to her apartment.

I hadn't gone after her because I hadn't trusted that would be the right move. Though my brain had been disconnected, there was some part of me that had known being alone with her in her apartment or, for that matter, in my house or the yard, wasn't wise. Not with the way I'd been dying to touch more of her baby-soft skin.

It was just after one p.m. now, and I was standing on the dock at Henry's Restaurant, getting some vitamin D and fresh air. My humble office back behind the bar area was usually my safe haven, my hideout, as Holden always accused, but today it was suffocating to be stuck in there with my thoughts. Every single last one of them was about Everly. Focusing on my job was impossible.

When I realized I was gazing beyond the marina toward my own dock, remembering that moment in the water with her when we both froze and time seemed to stop and I'd been about this close to kissing her, I shook my head and walked back toward the Henry's outdoor dining deck.

It was high summer season, and today's weather was ideal for lake time, which meant our waterfront deck was filled to capacity even though the lunch hour was past. Unable to stomach the thought of returning to my office, I went by the beverage stand where we kept pitchers of ice water, tea, and lemonade. I went from table to table, filling glasses, greeting guests, acting like a restaurant owner instead of a single-minded puppy with a new toy.

Only a couple of tables had locals at them, the rest vacationers, but that was typical for June. Most locals knew to avoid the busy times on the busy days, which were pretty much Monday through Sunday. However, Kizzy Estes, Paula Ballantine, and Kona Powers were having what they called their two-martini lunch, which was more likely a four-sea-breeze lunch if I knew them well, and I did. At any rate, they weren't too worried about the crowd or the heat. They had the best spot on the deck, front and center where a breeze came off the water, under an umbrella. Plus the best sea breezes in Dragonfly Lake.

After I'd exhausted refill duty for the time being, I stood to the side and watched for anyone who needed something. Our servers covering the deck—Natalie, Bria, and Sarai—were working their asses off and keeping everyone happy as far as I could see. Which meant I was standing here as useless as an ashtray on a motorcycle. I headed inside to see how service was going in there.

In addition to the five servers who were covering the indoor sections, Riley was buzzing around, making customers feel like a million dollars, as was her way. As far as I could tell, Quincy hadn't yet dropped anything, which she did at least once a week, so I was counting that as a win.

As I scanned the three dining areas from the deck doors, Fire Chief Thomas gestured me over to his table.

"Hey, gentlemen," I said to him and Mayor Constantine. "Did Cash do you right today?"

"As always, my friend. Compliments to the chef," Chief Thomas said. "I keep hearing talk that you're changing up the menu. Is there any truth to that rumor?"

I grinned, because with the look on his face, you'd think we were talking about closing up and turning this into a knitting club. "We've got a new menu coming out in conjunction with the Rusty Anchor opening," I told him. "Cash is working on some new dishes using Rusty Anchor beer. Trust me, they'll be good."

"He better not mess with the smoked pork sandwich," the chief said.

"Or the BLTEA," the mayor said, nodding toward his three-quarters devoured BLT with egg and avocado. Both men got the same thing every time they were in, which was often.

"Noted. I'll pass your requests on to the temperamental chef," I said with a wink.

Cash wasn't a warm-fuzzy kind of guy, but if I knew him,

flattery from these two regulars would be enough to continue to stock the ingredients of their favorites, whether they appeared on the new menu or not. I also happened to know both entrees were on the new menu proofs as of this morning.

"Is this a power lunch where you two plan to take over the town?" I asked.

"Just some prep for the Fourth. Less than three weeks left to get all our t's crossed." Chief Thomas waved his fork to emphasize the last few words.

"Rumor has it the fireworks this year will be bigger and better than ever," I said.

"You know it," Mayor Constantine said. "Always have to do better than the last time. This year we had a private donation to the firework fund." He leaned forward, as if giving me insider info. "Angelica Marks. Owner of the new hotel."

"That's great," I said.

I knew from what Chloe said that it was undoubtedly going to be Angelica Marks's last July Fourth on this earth, if she could even hold on that long. It was a sad situation, for sure, but I applauded her for contributing to our little town. The bigger and better the fireworks over the lake, the more benefit to the Marks Hotel, of course, but I suspected Chloe's former boss didn't spend much time worrying about the company's monthly sales figures as she lost her footing in her health battle.

"You two enjoy the rest of your meal."

I headed off to check on the bar, noticing Holden sitting at the counter, chatting with a guy I'd never seen before. Chatting it up with anyone with a pulse was my younger brother's default, so barely worth noting. What wasn't necessarily the norm was that the guy appeared to be alone and not a local. Our summer crowds were usually made up of families, couples, or friend groups.

Our weekday bartender, Pablo, had the full bar of

lunchers handled, but they were keeping him hopping. I stepped behind the bar and greeted a few people and checked on some drinks at Holden's end of the bar.

"Here he is now," Holden said to the solo guy as I stepped up to them. "This is Seth, my middle brother I mentioned. This is Knox Breckenridge. He's a writer."

The guy extended his hand and I shook it. He was dressed casually in a salmon-colored polo. His skin was not suntanned at all, which marked him as new to the lake. He had a pretty-boy face that ladies would likely be all over, but his smile was nervous, and I wondered what that was about.

"Nice to meet you," I said and flashed my own fake grin.

"You too. This place is great. Food is outstanding."

I noted he'd had the venison medallions and nearly cleaned his plate. "Thanks. Credit for the food goes to our other brother. Are you new in town?"

"Got here yesterday. I'm staying at the Honeysuckle Inn for a couple of weeks."

"He's writing a book," Holden said. "Seth reads a couple of books a week."

"Since I started remodeling my house, I haven't read nearly as much. What do you write?"

Knox let out a nervous little laugh that aroused my suspicion. Low-level, but still, I wasn't in any rush to trust this guy.

"Mysteries. I'm a tech writer, actually," he said. "Financial industry. I've always wanted to try my hand at something less dry, so I'm spending my vacation giving the fiction thing a go. I'm virtually a beginner."

"Good luck with it," I said. "Welcome to Dragonfly Lake. I hope it's an inspiring place for you."

"Thanks. Time will tell." The tips of his mouth twitched upward in that nervous smile again. "I'll definitely be back here to eat, so I'll probably see you again." He put some bills in the bill folder, slid it to the side for Pablo to pick up. "If I don't get to work now, I never will. Nice to meet you both."

We said goodbye as he went out through the door on the street side and I briefly wondered what he was really about. Food critic from a big-name publication? Super-secret spy from our rival town on the south side of the lake? Multibillionaire looking to buy out all of Dragonfly Lake?

I must've had some telling expression on my face as I watched him go, because Holden said, "Quit thinking the worst of him. He's a decent guy."

I just shrugged and tossed the folder to Pablo. I couldn't prove this Knox guy was untrustworthy, but I couldn't prove he was trustworthy either, and frankly, it wasn't my concern. He was just another customer.

"Where's Chloe today?" I asked.

"She went to lunch with Anna and Maeve. To the diner."

"When are you planning to take her on a real honeymoon?"

"We'll go this fall, after the season, after the brewery's up and running. I hate to take two-thirds of the management team away at once."

"Kemp'll handle it. You've hired good people."

"I fucking hope so."

My brother was one of those guys who didn't get bothered by most things, but he was sweating hard about the opening of the Rusty Anchor. The business was his dream, his and Kemp's baby, so I understood, but from where I was standing, they were positioned to kill it. Their beer was already held in high esteem by the locals since Holden and Kemp had messed around with home brewing for years and had never skimped on sharing. From what I'd tasted of the early batches, they'd been able to nail some damn good flavors on a larger scale. They had a fantastic branding guy on board and a solid marketing campaign in the works. Everyone—even non-beer drinkers—talked about the beer garden, where they'd serve beer and other beverages as well as appetizers from Henry's.

I was proud as hell of Holden for stepping up, growing up, and going for it, particularly after he'd done a lot of nothing serious in his twenties. It'd taken him a while to find his path, and now that he was blazing down it, he had purpose like I'd never seen before.

"You've got nothing to worry about," I told him. "Your business plan is on point." I grinned, because I'd helped him and Kemp develop that plan, so of course it was on point.

"I know." Holden wadded up his napkin and tossed it on his empty plate. "And the beer is even better," he threw back at me, his cocky grin in place. "If you're not careful, someone might accuse you of being optimistic."

"Realistic," I corrected as I added his plate to the dish bin to go to the kitchen.

"Predictable. Except..." His brows shot upward and he glanced to the stools to his right, where a trio of early-twenties out-of-towners had just left. No one had taken the Knox guy's place yet. I was suddenly wary as my brother leaned forward.

"What's the story with your renter? You haven't said a word since you ran out of the party Saturday, and now I'm hearing you were canoeing with her at midnight?"

My gut tightened into a knot. Fuck.

"Who told you that?" I grabbed a towel and started wiping down the vacant places at the bar, doing my best not to show how distressed I was by that one question.

Holden let out a chuckle. "Multiple people. You know how it is."

I did know how it was, and that made me want to throw a glass against the wall to shatter it.

I'd had my eyes peeled last night while we were on the water. There'd been no one close to the shore, no one paying any attention to us as far as I'd seen. The only possibility was that someone had spotted us from their window, which narrowed it down to just a few houses between my place and the business district. Probably one of the fucking McNamaras. They never could mind their own business.

"Any idea who started that rumor?" I asked, keeping my voice low.

"You saying it's not true?"

I clenched my jaw, refilled Holden's drink, nodded at Hank and Shirley Moody as Elijah, the host, led them to the dining room.

"It is true," Holden said with zero doubts. "Are you hooking up with your renter?"

I whipped my head toward him, and I swear if there hadn't been a walnut bar between us, I would've grabbed his shirt by the collar and thrown him across the room for being a loud, nosy motherfucker and prying into my business in the middle of Henry's.

Tossing the towel into the bucket of soapy water, I stormed through the doorway to my office and wished for something other than a sliding pocket door so I could slam it. Of course, that would draw attention, so it saved me from myself. Unfortunately, that left the door open to Holden, and God knew he wasn't one to let something go.

"It's okay to hook up with a random vacationer," he said as he sauntered in.

My desk was positioned so I could sit and work and not be within anyone's view out at the bar. I sat down hard in my chair now.

Holden stared at me for several seconds, then slid the door shut. He sat in one of the guest chairs against the wall.

"What's going on, Seth? I'd butt out, but when the whole town is talking, ignoring it doesn't do any good. Whatever 'it' is. You know that."

"Nothing's going on." I said it automatically, knowing damn well it wasn't altogether the truth. There was a shit storm going on in my head if nothing else.

And there was nothing else. There could be nothing else.

Not only did I know better than to get involved with her, for a long list of reasons, but Everly had made her feelings known when she'd run off into the night, literally.

"Were you canoeing last night?" Holden asked, and because his tone was more interested and matter-of-fact than accusatory, I relented. Also because obviously someone had seen us.

"Yes."

"With a woman?"

It hit me—yes, delayed reaction—that if someone had seen I was with a woman, there was a chance they could've identified Everly. That would be detrimental for her.

"With the woman who's renting my apartment," I admitted with the goal of getting the lowdown on the info floating around. If she'd been recognized, the sooner we knew, the better prepared she could be.

The half thought that it would be wiser for her to move on if that happened had my throat tightening unexplainably. Was she haunting my thoughts all day? Undeniably. But I didn't have any permanent ties to her. We'd kissed one time, for fuck's sake. It was a fluke and not going to happen again, even if she did stay for the rest of the week.

Before Holden could ask more, I decided to take the bull by the horns and confide in him. If I didn't let him in, I wouldn't be surprised if he'd snoop, knock on her door, play the friendly neighbor. If he knew the truth, understood Everly's dilemma, he'd be just as dedicated to protecting her identity as I was.

"Can you keep this to yourself?" I asked, my voice low. There was still the din of a crowded restaurant on the other side of that door, but I was ever aware that anyone could knock on that door at any minute.

"You know I will." He pulled his chair to the edge of the desk, his attention fully on me. "Tell me what the hell you've gotten involved in."

"I'm not *involved* in anything. Are you familiar with Everly Ash?"

"Of course." He narrowed his eyes and tilted his head, as if to say, *Wait a second…*

"She's renting my apartment."

His eyes went huge and his mouth dropped open. "Everly Ash, runaway bride. Holy shit, are you her secret lover?"

"Jesus. No. Quit reading the internet. She's hiding out, away from her family, away from the press."

"Okay… and her fiancé?"

"Ex-fiancé."

"He's not trying to track her down?"

"Last I knew, he was avoiding her calls."

"Rumors say he's in the Mediterranean on some yacht, nursing his broken heart."

"Don't tell her that, please. She feels bad enough as it is."

Holden nodded. "So you bought her groceries?"

Dammit. Someone had talked. Most likely Darlene. I knew better than to think everyone would keep their mouth shut, but I'd thought, since three days had passed, maybe I was in the clear.

"She can't go out in public for obvious reasons."

"Yeah. I guess I can see that. So, you took her canoeing? Are you involved with her?"

"I'm not involved with her." I fucking wasn't. Never would be. "When I finished working on the house last night, she came out to talk and said she was going a little stir-crazy being closed in and alone for so long. Spur of the moment, I took her out in the canoe. She got fresh air and a reset." Plus a dip in the water, some first aid, and a fucking kiss I could not get out of my head. But she and I were the only two who would ever know about those.

Holden's brows were sky-high on his forehead, as if none of this was believable. "So Everly Ash, the Sweetheart of Country Music, is living in your apartment for a month?"

"You'd have to ask her how long she's staying." I regretted the words the second they were out of my mouth. "Scratch that," I added in a rush. "Please just give her some space."

My brother studied me for long seconds. My knee bounced in agitation as I tried to sit there calmly, though I wanted to crawl out of my skin.

Finally, he shrugged. "I won't keep it from Chloe, but you know she'll keep it to herself. You can't count on that from the rest of the town, though. The more secretive you are, the more they'll be up in your business."

"I know you're right."

I had to distance myself from Everly. If people thought I was sleeping with my renter, they'd nose around to find the truth. If I left her alone, they'd eventually forget there was anyone there and move on to the next potential scandal.

There had to be no more boat rides. No more inviting her in at midnight, even if it was just for a bandage. No more obvious grocery runs. And absolutely no more kissing her.

"That's some crazy shit. You must've been losing your mind trying to keep it to yourself."

"I'm doing fine," I told him. "Thanks for keeping it to yourself."

Holden nodded as he stood to leave. "You know and I know it's nobody's business. But we also know how that goes over in this town."

"They're like a bunch of vultures circling their prey."

He went to the door and stopped with his hand on the handle. "If you need me to pick up some food for her, let me know."

My shoulders relaxed a degree because I trusted him. Appreciated his offer to help. "I will. Thanks. Shut the door on your way out."

Once the door closed again and I was alone, I sagged into my chair.

I needed to warn Everly that people were speculating. And apologize. And then I needed to stay the hell out of her life—for my sake and hers.

CHAPTER 12

ednesday was the first day since my would-be wedding day that I was starting to feel any kind of okay. Well, okay-ish.

When I'd gotten back to my apartment last night after my great escape, I'd called Drea and spilled it all. She'd kindly reminded me that a kiss didn't have to mean anything, that I was a single woman now and could do what I wanted, and kisses that made my insides melt were nothing to regret. Like a best friend, she'd talked me down.

And then I'd tossed and turned until close to five a.m., when I finally fell into a deep, exhausted sleep. When I woke up late morning, I'd felt somewhat refreshed and, strangely, a little lighter.

It had been bright and sunny all day, and since my balcony was shaded, I'd been able to spend time out there without broiling. Did I long for the sunshine? To stop hiding? I'd be lying if I didn't admit to a little of that, but I was nowhere near ready to risk being discovered. So my private, shaded balcony gave me fresh air and a lake view that was so good for my soul.

With anticipation, I'd picked up Seth's guitar, tuned it, and started playing around on it—with the doors closed to avoid being noticed. I found I didn't go to "my" songs—the ones that'd made me famous. The ones I hadn't been allowed to write for myself. My dad and his people and my team and who knows who else had instead curated the "right" kind of songs written by other people for the Sweetheart of Country Music. The songs were usually about love and crushes, upbeat and hopeful, and, if I was honest, a little shallow. Those didn't feel right today, so I'd played some of the tunes I'd grown up loving, some country, some folk, even some pop and rock.

I wished I had some of my old notebooks where I'd scribbled my own compositions so many years ago, before I'd found any kind of popularity. Before my dad had become my producer.

Had my originals been any good? I didn't know. Had they been superstar caliber? Probably not. My dad was an expert at building stars and I didn't question him. What I was starting to question was whether I wanted to be a star.

All of these thoughts felt like a gut punch, so I hadn't spent too much time on them, instead letting myself get swept away by the music itself. I'd played everything from Taylor Swift to John Denver to Johnny Cash. The music settled something inside of me, took me back, closer to my true self. It made me realize how far from that, from *me*, I'd strayed in the past few years, which was disturbing if I thought too hard about it. That return to my favorites also soothed me like a rainstorm on a Sunday morning when I didn't have to get out of bed.

For the past few days, I'd made sandwiches and frozen pizza for every meal, even though I'd had Seth buy other foods and ingredients when he shopped for me. I wasn't a wizard in the kitchen. Okay, truth, I didn't know the first thing about cooking, so I was intimidated. Add to that my reluctance to turn my phone on long enough to look up recipes, and I just hadn't bothered to cook.

Today, though, I'd decided to search out a recipe on my phone browser to use my chicken breasts before they went bad. I was cooking my very first actual meal—garlic chicken and herbed rice. Yes, the rice was instant, but don't judge. The chicken was real. The prep had taken me a bit because I had to look up how to do certain steps, but now I had chicken sizzling away in the pan, smelling like heaven.

My dinner was just about ready, and I jolted in surprise when my phone rang. It'd been days since I'd heard that sound, and I didn't want to hear it now, but I hadn't yet closed the recipe on my phone and turned it off. My mistake.

The phone was sitting on the kitchen counter next to the sink. I went over to it to check the screen, dreading what I'd see. The only person I wanted to talk to was Drea—and she knew to wait until I called her again.

My mom's name and cell number showed on the screen, instead of my parents' landline that they'd used every other time to leave a zillion messages. I didn't know whether it was because it was just my mom or because I was in a better place today, but I snatched up the phone and took the call, putting it on speaker.

"Hi, Mom," I said, eyeing the chicken on the stove, figuring I could use my dinner as an excuse to end the call soon.

"Everly! You answered! Oh, honey, it's so good to hear your voice."

At the sound of hers, a ball of emotion globbed up in my throat, and for a moment I couldn't speak. I squeezed my eyes shut, fighting tears because I missed her.

"Everly? Don't hang up on me! Please."

"I'm here," I managed. "Hi."

"How are you doing?" she asked, her voice dripping with concern.

I fought to swallow and get myself under control. After a deep inhale, I said, "I'm okay, Mom. Like I told you in my texts." I knew she'd received them because she'd replied every time with a litany of questions about where I was and when I was coming home.

"I wanted to see how you're doing after Trey's stunt with the blonde."

"What stunt?" I frowned and wished I hadn't answered the call. "What blonde?"

"You haven't seen it?" She made a disgusted noise with her tongue. "Not what I expected from him."

"Mom."

She sighed in annoyance, I assumed toward Trey or some blonde. "Someone snapped photos of him with a knockout blonde with huge knockers on a yacht in the Mediterranean. They've gone viral. I can't believe you missed them."

"I don't want to see what the media's saying about me. This is why I'm here," I bit out.

"Where is here, honey? Will you tell me?"

I shook my head adamantly even though she couldn't see me. "I'm safe. I'm fine. I'm by myself—"

"You shouldn't be alone right now, Everly."

"Being alone is exactly what I need, Mom." As much as I didn't want to, I needed to know more about the Trey thing since he wasn't responding to my calls or texts. One of the many things I'd been worrying about was him. I'd never wanted to hurt him, and though I understood that might not be realistic, I'd hoped he would come to figure out I'd done the right thing. No one really wanted to be married to the wrong person, did they? I wasn't his right person. "So Trey and the blonde? He's got someone new already?"

"I don't know what that boy is thinking. I think it's a publicity stunt. Your dad says revenge or recovery."

I closed my eyes, fearing my dad could be right.

As I paced to the balcony doors, closed now to keep the AC in, I imagined seeing my ex online with another woman, and it hit me that the main things I felt were concern for his emotional state and irritation that this could drag my name down further with "he's over that bitch" type headlines. What I didn't feel was jealousy. A big part of me hoped Trey would find his right person.

I'd have to unpack all of that later.

"Where is Dad?" I asked because I'd noticed all the calls were from her. All the text replies were from my mom, even when I included both their numbers on my messages.

"Working, of course."

"How upset with me is he?"

"He's… not happy, Everly. The media, of course, hasn't hesitated to drag his name through the mud right alongside yours, and he's taking some guff from a couple of record label guys who know you're supposed to be in the studio soon."

That hit me all kinds of wrong, and I scowled. "He'd rather I marry the wrong man than get a little bad PR?"

I had no doubt his "bad PR" was nothing compared to what they were saying about me. I know, I'd brought it on myself. It just stung that my dad seemed more worried about himself and his career than his own daughter.

"You know how your dad is," my mom said. "Men and their egos."

"That doesn't make it okay!" I snapped.

My mom was quiet for a few seconds, maybe stunned because I never snapped at her. Now that I thought about it, I never said anything negative about my strong-willed, over-bearing father.

She blew out a breath. "I guess we're both struggling with everything, honey, and you haven't talked to us about *anything*. We'd like to understand what happened."

Afraid my chicken would burn, I went back to the stove,

flipped the burner off, and moved the pan to a cool spot. Since I had my mom alone, I would try to explain a little to her, because her point was valid. I hadn't told them a thing other than I was sorry, I was okay, and I needed to be alone.

"I'm not in love with Trey, Mom," I told her. "I love him in some ways, but not the way I want to love the man I'm going to spend the rest of my life with."

She was quiet for a few seconds. "I didn't realize. You two seemed to get along so well…"

"We got along. It's just… That's not the only thing marriage is about, right?"

"It's not. I just assumed you and Trey had it."

I blew out a breath, pacing again. "I messed up, Mom. I was along for the ride, I guess. With all the publicity and the fan craziness, it sort of turned into a runaway train, and I basically just held on without stopping to think too hard."

God, I felt like an idiot. Still. I probably always would. Most people could make a pretty huge life mistake the way I had, and things would eventually die down. Thanks to my career, I worried I would always be known as the runaway bride or the girl too stupid to realize she wasn't in love with the guy or even the heartless bitch who broke Trey Gilbert's heart. If I *had* broken his heart. Based on what my mom said, he might be doing just fine.

"I guess I can see how that could happen," she said. "The media took to you two early on."

"The media took to us before we were a thing," I reminded her. "Everyone loved us together so much. More than I loved us together once I took time to listen to my heart. I'm so sorry, Mom. I know it was a lot of money—"

"I'm not worried about the money."

"I can pay you and Dad back for everything."

"We can talk about that later, when you come home. When are you coming home, Everly?"

There was a part of me that wanted nothing more than to

run home, wrap myself up in a hug from my mom, and pretend like none of the past year had happened. That was the side of me that had gotten me in trouble, though, that drifting, bury-my-head-in-the-sand part. And now that I'd recognized the problem, I couldn't allow it to continue.

"Not for a while," I said vaguely.

"You can't hide away forever, hon."

Maybe not, but I could sure as heck hide away for now. I knew the second I exposed myself to the outside world, both by plugging in online and by venturing out of my physical hiding spot, it would be harder to hear what I was starting to recognize as me, my voice, my thoughts and feelings. Now that I'd realized I'd shut me out for so long, I was determined not to let it happen again. And while my dad's reaction broke my heart, it also pissed me off—and made me see this was how it'd been for too long.

"Try to understand, Mom." I sucked in a deep breath, separating my feelings toward my dad from what I felt for my mom. "You and Dad have done everything for me. In a good way but also in a bad way. I'm twenty-nine! I've never lived away from home—"

"You're not going to move out permanently, are you?"

I suspected I needed to, but I wasn't even thinking long-term at the moment.

"I'm just trying to get through the week right now," I told her. "But I need to start making my own decisions. I'm not blaming anyone but myself, but I need you to understand—I need to be more independent."

"We just love you so much, Everly. A parent wants to give their child the moon and the stars—"

"And you have, Mom. You've given me so much. Done so much for me. I'm so lucky to have you." I meant every word, but it'd also become crystal clear that I couldn't let them continue in the same roles. I didn't know what that looked like yet, but I needed to figure it out.

There was a knock on the door, and my heart started thundering. No one came to my door except Seth.

"Was that a knock?" my mom asked. "Who are you with, Everly?"

"I need to go, Mom. It's probably food delivery," I lied. "I'll talk to you soon."

I ended the call before she could say more, then exhaled, closed my eyes, rubbed my heart to ease the ache of missing my mom. Then, as another soft knock sounded—it wasn't like I could not be there and Seth knew that—I went to the door, coaching myself to be cool and avoid thinking about last night.

I looked through the peephole, and when I saw him, I had an involuntary full-body reaction. He was so good-looking, it was like he had a direct connection to my hormones.

After a deep breath in to try to level my damn self, I opened the door.

CHAPTER 13

SETH

Not only did I owe Everly an apology—who the hell did think I was to kiss Everly Ash?—but I also needed to warn her someone had seen us out on the lake last night and literally everyone was trying to figure out who I'd been with.

And then I would fade to the background and leave the country singer to recover from her breakup. Even though she hadn't been in love, even though she was the one who'd slammed on the brakes, it was obvious she was going through rough times. I was her landlord and needed to be nothing more, for her sake—and, yeah, mine too if I was honest.

That was the goal, and then she opened the door.

As she stood there in cutoff shorts, a tiny pink tee, and bare feet, her dark hair tousled and down around her shoulders, her lips naturally light pink, her cheeks rosy, her eyes both expectant and unsure, I didn't see her as Everly Ash, famous country singer. I saw her as an alluring but troubled pretty woman I wanted to kiss again.

I shoved the thought down, but everything I'd planned on saying drained out of my brain and left me stumbling to form words.

"Hi," I finally managed.

"Hi." A shy smile tugged at her lips. She opened the door wider to let me in, not needing to remind me that the less time I spent standing outside of the apartment door the better.

Before I'd stepped all the way in, the aroma of food hit me. My brows went up and my mouth watered. I'd worked later than usual tonight, meeting with Holden, Chloe, and Chance Cordova, the marketing person at Rusty Anchor, so we could go over the campaign in the works for the grand opening, which the restaurant was intimately entrenched in, from the look of the new menus to the digital ads for the town app to the full-color print ads for regional travel mags. I hadn't taken the time to eat dinner yet.

"You said you didn't cook," I said, glancing across the room toward the stove as she closed the door behind me.

"I don't." She shrugged and grinned more fully. "I can't make any promises about how it tastes, but you should stay and have some."

I straightened and reined myself in. "I don't want to intrude. I came by because I need to talk to you about a couple things."

"Okay." Her smile disappeared and she gestured toward the table, indicating we would sit there, then closed the mini-blinds on the balcony doors, shutting out the world. It was still light outside, so it wasn't likely anyone could see in, but caution was wise.

We sat on opposite sides of the table. "What's wrong?" she asked, looking concerned.

"Nothing's wrong. I wanted to tell you that someone apparently saw me out on the lake with you last night—"

"What?" Her voice was panicked.

"Not *you*. They didn't recognize you. Just saw that I was with a woman." I blew out a breath and admitted, "Around here, that seems to be generating high interest."

"You aren't seen with women very often?"

I shook my head and blustered on. "Like I said, no one knows it was you, because if they'd recognized you, the entire town would know by now."

"Okay," she said on an exhale, nodding.

"Everything's okay," I reassured her. "Your secret is safe."

"Okay. Thanks for telling me."

Her phone, still in her hand, buzzed with a notification, and her expression changed to one of alarm. She powered it down nervously and set it aside.

"My mom called right before you got here," she explained, frowning. "I answered."

"How did that go?"

She inhaled, exhaled, smiled, and grimaced all within a couple of heartbeats. "It made me homesick, hearing her voice."

"Are you thinking of going home?" The thought made it hard to breathe, and when she shook her head, my relief was… more than a landlord's would be.

"It's just… she's my mom, you know? I miss her even if I know I need to be here right now."

"Voices can definitely be evocative. Especially a mom's voice."

After my mom died, I'd found an old voicemail from her I'd inadvertently left on my phone. It was the most inconsequential message, just twelve seconds long, asking me to call her when I could because she had a question. When I'd re-listened to that message, though, heard my mom's voice again, it had kicked me into a powerful bout of grief even months later. I'd eventually deleted it, but not for a couple of years. Everly's situation wasn't the same, but suffice it to say,

I understood what a loved one's voice could do on a visceral level.

Everly nodded, her eyes closed, as if she was holding in emotions. "She of course wanted to know where I am, when I'm coming home, the usual stuff, but she also told me about a photo of Trey and some blonde woman. Have you seen it?"

Narrowing my eyes and resisting the urge to whip out my phone and hunt for it, I shook my head. "I've made a point not to read any of the media crap about your situation. Well, after the first night, when I was trying to find out more about my mysterious renter."

"Same on not reading anything. I haven't peeked a single time, but I have to admit to being curious. It's not like Trey to pick up strangers and flaunt them. Which tells me he's either fine and moving on or he's not okay, and that's the last thing I want for him."

"It might take a while."

Losing a woman like Everly would leave the wound of a lifetime. Doing so in the public eye would make it worse. I almost felt bad for the guy. Or I had before the news he was making a spectacle of himself and some other woman, which would do nothing positive for Everly.

It said a lot about her that she was concerned about the guy she'd left at the altar. This woman might have had a lot handed to her by well-meaning parents, but she wasn't self-centered the way I'd expect. It would've been a hell of a lot easier to walk away if she was, but here I sat.

Everly's eyes darted to the stove, then to me.

I liked to think I was quick on the uptake sometimes, so I said, "If the offer's still good, why don't we plate up some food and you can tell me more about your call."

She was sliding down off the chair back as she responded. "Offer's still good, as is the warning about my untested cooking skills."

I started to get up, but she gestured to stay put.

"I got this. My first dinner guest in my own place." She grinned self-consciously, then went to the cabinets, pulled out two plates, and served up the food. "If it sucks, we'll order pizza," she said as she set the steaming plates on the table.

She added silverware and napkins that Hayden had stocked the place with, then sat across from me again.

Once I had my first bite in my mouth, I nodded, savoring the garlic and other seasonings and the tenderness of the chicken. "It doesn't suck. Are you sure this is your first time?"

With a quiet laugh, she said, "You're sweet, Seth Henry."

"Not sweet, just honest."

We ate for a few minutes, discussing her dip back into music. I waited to see if she'd bring up her mom's call or her ex again.

When she still hadn't halfway through the meal, I asked, "So how was the rest of your mom's call? And what about your dad? Was he there too?"

Her entire demeanor changed, her shoulders sagging, expression saddening, then turning to a scowl as she finished chewing.

"He wasn't there," she said finally.

There was something there that was even more upsetting than her mom, I suspected. "Want to talk about it?" I asked as I scooped in another bite of herbed rice.

Everly set down her fork and pushed her plate away. She'd made it through half of her chicken and some rice. With a gusty exhale, she rubbed both hands over her face, then shook her head.

"I'm so disappointed in my dad." She bolted off her chair and went to the open bottle of wine on the counter. "Would you like a glass?"

I hesitated, thinking I should skip it to avoid dimming my faculties.

"Don't make me drink alone." Everly brought two stemless glasses to the table, set them down, and filled them more than halfway, deciding for me, making me smile.

"I wouldn't want to do that." I picked up a glass.

Everly sat back in her chair and took a sip or three. "The longer I'm away, the more I can see how I've been a pawn for my dad. My mom said he's upset."

"Because you haven't come home?"

She scoffed. "Because the media has thrown his name into the mess with mine."

I stopped chewing the food in my mouth and gaped at her. "So he's mad at the media?"

"Maybe that too but he's upset with me, that I did something that's getting negative coverage." She let out a caustic laugh. "Karma's a bitch. He's always been all about the PR Trey and I could generate, for ourselves but if he got a mention in there, you can bet he basked in it."

I swallowed my food and put my fork down. "Would he prefer you marrying a guy you don't want to marry over getting a little bad publicity himself?"

"It's not just me who thinks that's insane?"

"Not just you." I couldn't fathom a parent who'd put his career before his kid. Yes, I'd been blessed with loving, sane parents, and I was grateful. I knew others weren't as lucky, but this one was still tough to wrap my head around. "Has he always been like that?"

Everly ran her finger around the rim of her glass pensively, her eyes narrowed. "The more I think about it, I don't remember ever getting him negative publicity before. Not anything major. It's mostly been positive over the years."

A couple of articles I'd read that first night came to mind —feel-good stories about the father-daughter connection between the renowned producer and the up-and-coming singer. Talk about damn good publicity for the man…

"It sounds like he's benefited from your career then," I said carefully.

She laughed halfheartedly. "Eddy Ash has never needed me or my career for his success. He was already making a name for himself before I was born. He's got a gift."

"Then this latest thing in the media shouldn't do much damage to him." Unlike what it could do to Everly.

She shook her head. "His career will be fine. He's practically legendary. I think it's his ego taking the hit."

I didn't know the man from Adam, but I suspected she was spot on.

"All my life, I've been aware that the media was hovering, just waiting for something to pounce on. That's how I was raised. I was protected, had layers around me until I was an adult, and then I still had some protection and more experience." Her finger stopped on the glass rim, and she lifted the glass and took a gulp of wine. She set it down and studied the golden liquid for a few seconds, then her lids lowered momentarily before opening again. "I've spent my whole life doing the right things, making good decisions… meeting my dad's expectations."

"Not rocking the boat," I said.

"Until now. I literally fell out of the stinking canoe." I held back a grin because her frown deepened. "They say true character doesn't become evident until hard times. If that's so, I don't like my dad's true character." She swallowed, her voice full of emotion.

I couldn't help myself. I reached across the table and put my hand on hers. "That's a lot to figure out." I got the impression she'd just worked her way through the truth in the past few minutes.

"Yeah," she said, obviously lost in thought. She used her other hand to take another drink, not a dainty one, and I had the passing thought that whiskey might be more appropriate for the occasion. "My mom doesn't help matters. She caters to him, coddles his ego, cushions things for him. She tried to write this off as men being men."

"Oh, hell no."

"Today, for the first time, I called her on it," Everly said, sitting up a little straighter. "Pretty sure I shocked her."

I squeezed her hand. "Good for you."

She met my gaze then. "Thanks. It felt good, actually. I need to do that more often."

"You do." I kept my voice light, aimed to come across as supportive and not judgmental. I sure as hell was in no position to judge anyone. And as much as I needed to keep some distance here, I wanted to be the friend Everly needed. She didn't appear to have an overabundance of people she could trust.

After another drink of wine, Everly pushed back from the table. "Did you get full? There's more rice if you want some."

"I'm good. Either that was beginner's luck or you've got some inherent cooking skills. Thank you."

We both stood and took our dishes to the sink. Everly started rinsing the plates off and setting them to one side.

"You cooked. I can do the dishes," I said, taking hold of her upper arms from behind and scooting her over to make way for myself in front of the sink.

"I can do them later."

"I'm sure you can."

I opened the cabinet beneath the sink to get the dish soap. As I stood, Everly eyed me with her head tilted.

"What?" I asked.

"It's just that I've never known a man to insist on doing the dishes."

"You cook for me and I'm going to do something for you."

"How about you wash and I'll dry?"

"Deal."

I plugged the sink and ran hot water in, added soap, and found a sponge. I was midway through scrubbing the first plate when Everly, who was scooping leftover rice into a storage container, spoke.

"I must seem like such an idiot to you," she said quietly.

"Uhh, no," I said, blindsided. "Why would you say that?"

She took the rice container to the refrigerator, then returned to my side, which was all of three steps away in the compact kitchen. Picking up a dry towel and taking it to a plate, she shrugged. "I've basically let my dad control my life like a naive little girl."

"You trusted him. He's your dad."

She nodded but I could tell how troubled she was.

"I don't know him, but maybe he didn't have bad intentions? Maybe he wanted to help you?"

"I've always thought so. But was that for me or was it for himself and his ego? And why didn't I step away from them when I became an adult?"

"Maybe you weren't ready. Being a famous singer seems like endless work and countless decisions."

She met my gaze, surprise in her eyes, as if not everyone figured these facts out. "Actually, yes."

"Staying with your parents gave you one less decision to make."

"Easy way out," she said with a hint of self-blame, which I hated to see.

"Whatever part your parents have had in your career, you've got a hell of a successful one, right?"

"It depends on how you define success."

"It does," I allowed. That was an interesting response. "How do you define success?"

"Oof," she said animatedly. "This just got too deep. Let's talk about something else."

"Like what?" I'd finished the last of the dinner dishes and all that was left were the pans, so I started in on those.

"How was your day today? You went to work?"

"I did. This is our second-busiest month of the year and today was no exception."

"It was a beautiful day, so that makes sense."

"Rainy days are sometimes worse because people stay off the lake and come to the restaurant instead."

"So you win no matter what the weather's like."

I nodded. I took the dry pans from the counter in front of her and hung them on the wall rack. "How was your day before your mom's call?" I asked, leaning against the cabinet as she wiped the stove clean.

"Really good, actually. Thanks to you."

My whole system went on alert. Was she talking about last night? Had that kiss stuck with her too?

"Your guitar," she added as an afterthought. "I didn't realize how much I missed… well, music. It's been such an inherent part of my life since I was born."

"Listening? Playing?" I was still itching to know more about her life. About her.

"All of the above. My mom listens to music all the time. Wherever she is in the house, there's music playing."

I could just imagine how big her parents' house was. I pictured her wandering through a mansion as a little girl, trying to track down her mom based on where the music was coming from. "And you?"

"I don't put other people's music on as much, but I usually have a song—or twelve—running through my head. Sometimes mine, sometimes others'."

"What kind of music does your mom listen to? All country?"

"All the time," she said, smiling. "She was a big fan even before she met my dad, or so she says. What about you?"

"Country," I said.

"Like, contemporary stuff? Classics?" she probed.

I let out an embarrassed chuckle. I wished I could say I'd always been the biggest Everly Ash fan on the planet, but I wasn't going to lie. Before she'd been hidden away in my apartment, I'd heard her name, had heard her songs at the restaurant without knowing who the singer was.

"My brother says I'm in a rut. I listen to Eric Church a lot."

She set down her towel and faced me. "Eric Church is incredible. I'm a big fan."

I pulled my phone out and opened my music app, where my only playlist was Church's songs. I hit play, and it was already on shuffle, so a random song came up—"A Hell of a View."

"Love this one," she said, and her shoulders started swaying.

Without thinking it over, I set the phone on the counter and held out a hand to her. She lifted questioning eyes to mine.

"Dance?" I asked.

Looking surprised, she smiled and took my hand. The song was somewhere between slow and fast, so I guided her over to the open space in the living room. I kept her hand in mine and put my other one on her waist. Everly's hand landed on my shoulder, and we moved to the beat. Our bodies were a few inches apart, and it could pass for casual, but suddenly I wasn't feeling casual.

She was still smiling, looking up at me, looking fucking irresistible. I held her gaze, took in her beautiful features, pressed her image into my memory to savor again later.

"You can dance," she said after the second verse.

"I can keep the beat. There's a difference."

She wrinkled her nose as if to disagree. As the chorus started again, she sang it to me, and the dance that already had me on sensory overload turned… extra. There was no other word for having this gorgeous woman in my arms, singing to me about having nothing to lose.

I was mesmerized. Captivated by every note of her evocative voice, every sway of her tempting body.

The song and the moment were over way too fast, but then, as if the universe was either looking out for me or setting me up for a fall, the distinctive intro notes of one of

Church's ballads played. I gave her a full two seconds to pull away and end our dance. She didn't do it.

I drew her closer and dropped my other hand to her waist, slowing our tempo to match the song.

"Another good one," she said as she rested her hands at the back of my neck.

I wasn't sure who initiated it, but our bodies pressed against each other, putting us chest to chest. I rested my chin against her temple and breathed in her honeysuckle scent, my eyes closing as I got lost in her, the music, and the moment.

"Eric Church is such a vibe," she said after a couple magical minutes, drawing me out of the spell she'd put me under. "It fits you."

I let her words sink in and tried to make sense of them. "I'm a vibe?"

"You're chill." I could hear her smile in her tone. "Even-keeled. There's a lot going on inside"—she tapped my temple, then my chest, then put her hand back on my neck—"but you keep your emotions in check."

I put enough space between our faces that I could meet her gaze. She wasn't wrong. As I peered down into her smiling green eyes, my heart stuttered and my breath was too shallow. I swallowed. Weighed whether I should speak my thoughts at the moment. Tried to convince myself not to. "My emotions don't seem to be in check right now." My voice was rough, husky.

"Yeah?"

"I told myself I wasn't going to kiss you again after last night."

Her eyes darted to my lips, almost like a dare.

"And...?" she said in barely more than a whisper. "What did your self say back to you?"

"It's pushing pretty hard for a kiss." I froze, not daring to blink or exhale, watching her for any reaction. Her irises got larger, and then she glanced to my lips again, and that was answer enough.

I closed the space between us until my lips were on hers. I meant to keep it light and easy, but the instant our mouths touched, fire raged through my veins and I wanted to devour her. I tilted my head and grasped the back of hers, kissing her insistently, my tongue teasing her lips, then plunging into her mouth when she opened to me.

In the next second, Everly pressed her body into mine and met every ounce of need that pounded through me with an urgency of her own. Our tongues twisted and dueled as I lowered my hands to her ass, pulling her against me, letting her feel that I was hard as granite. She arched into me needfully, a moan escaping her even as our kiss deepened.

Eventually it hit me that the ballad had ended long ago and another two or three full songs had played, though I couldn't have told you what they were if you'd paid me. As another song started, I skimmed my fingers over the bare skin on her back between her tee and her shorts, then dipped them below the waistband, relishing the softness of her flesh.

There was just enough capacity for rational thought left in my brain that I realized I needed to reel it in before this flared completely out of control. I brought my hands up, cradled her cheeks, and broke the contact of our mouths, mine hovering an inch away from hers.

"Ev…"

She kissed me again, as if she hadn't heard me.

"Everly," I tried again.

"Mmm."

I put a couple of inches between our bodies. She dropped her hands and clasped her fingers to the belt loops on my shorts, holding me close as she pressed another short kiss to my lips. Her eyelids rose partway, treating me to a languid, lust-filled leer, and I knew I had to be the dumbest man alive to be pulling away from that, from her.

"I like you," I managed. "I respect the hell out of you. And I know you're going through a lot right now."

Her lips flitted over mine again, three quick touches, and then she smiled up at me.

"Everly, we should stop."

CHAPTER 14

Seth's words caught me off guard because his actions until right now said anything but *we should stop.*

My body was aching for him, so it took a few seconds for me to rein myself in enough to think straight. I put a few inches between us and looked up into his eyes, assessing. What I saw in those heavy-lidded milk-chocolate orbs was heat. Desire.

"Do you *want* to stop?" I asked.

He let out a shaky laugh that said even more than his words. "Of course I don't want to stop but—"

"I don't want to stop either."

I went up on my toes again, ran my hands up his well-defined chest on top of his polo, then wound them around to his nape and furrowed my fingers into his hair as I kissed him. The growl that rumbled from deep in his chest confirmed that he was one-hundred-percent with me. Thank God. I'd never *needed* someone the way I needed Seth.

We kissed and touched and caressed, the songs starting and ending in the background nearly unnoticed. I slipped my hands under his shirt and relished the heat of his skin, explored the ridges and dips of his abs, his chest. When Seth did the same and trailed his big hands beneath my T-shirt, up my sides, then slipped a finger beneath the bottom edge of my bra, every cell in my body seemed to wait for him to move that hand higher. He massaged me, kneaded the underside of my breast, teased me.

Breaking the contact of our mouths briefly, I whipped my tee over my head and tossed it on the floor. I reached behind me and unhooked my bra, then shed it and threw it aside as well. With my upper half bare, I faced him, watched the look on his face as his eyes roved over me. There was a half second when fear rushed in. I'd never been this forward before. Never been the aggressor. Never trusted someone I'd known for such a short time enough to share myself with him.

"You're beautiful," he breathed out then held a hand out to me. My fear slipped away in an instant. I took his hand and he pulled me back into him.

He ran his palms up my bare back, kneading his way upward from my waist. Our mouths found each other again, and I caught his head and pulled him in. When both of his thumbs rubbed over my nipples, I gasped out a shallow breath and arched into his touch, my head falling back.

"I need to taste you, Everly," he said into my ear, his breath a whisper that made me shiver.

"Please…"

He bent, took my breast into his hot mouth, and swirled his tongue over me. He flicked it over my nipple, and a pulse of need zinged directly to my female parts deep between my legs. The ache inside of me intensified and I moaned again. I'd never been a moaner, but with Seth I couldn't seem to help it. He drew out reactions from my body I hadn't known were possible, particularly with my shorts still on.

I wanted him to need me as much as I needed him, so I undid his belt, then unbuttoned his shorts. I could feel how hard he was, but he seemed to hold himself tightly in control. My mission became to make him lose that control, to drive him to come undone, the way I was absolutely certain he could do to me.

"Wait," he breathed out as I was about to slide my fingers inside his underwear.

My eyes popped open in question.

"Are you sure about this? You're vulnerable right now…"

My body throbbed with need. There was no question in my mind.

"Sex doesn't have to be emotional," I said. Something I never would've said before tonight, but apparently Seth Henry changed everything. "I trust you, Seth. I want you. Do you want me?"

"You know I do."

"What if we just leave it at that?"

He peered down at me for the longest seconds of my life, and I waited, tempted to persuade him with another kiss or by slipping my hand downward and wrapping my fingers around him.

Finally, he lowered his head toward mine, closing the inches in slow motion, making my heart pound harder with every second that crawled by. "Far be it from me to argue," he said.

At last, his lips were on mine again, his tongue plundering my mouth, the scent and taste of him filling me, driving my hunger for him higher.

I grabbed his belt loops and yanked his body closer, then unzipped his shorts and pushed them down his thighs, letting them drop to the floor for him to step out of. I eased his shirt up to his neck, and he pulled it off. Then I dove my fingers under the waistband of his boxer briefs, dying to wrap them around his erection that'd been pressing against me, teasing me. When I touched the velvet skin, he sucked in a breath. He'd been teasing my breasts, and his fingers came to a halt as I stroked down his length.

He retaliated by unbuttoning my shorts and getting them and my underwear off me in no time flat. Moments later, we both stood there, naked, hands roving, mouths connecting again.

"What do you like?" he asked between kisses as he rubbed a thumb over one of my nipples again.

"I've… never had anyone ask me that before." I wasn't that experienced—I'd been with two other guys in my life—so I didn't know how to answer.

There was a low growl in his throat, and then he said, "I'm asking."

I was pretty sure I'd like just about anything he could do to me, but I said, "I don't know. Try to find out."

He lowered his mouth to my nipple and swirled his tongue, sucked me into his mouth, and had me clinging and arching into him again. That connection to the hollow deep inside me, calling out for him, was like a cord of sensitized nerves that could only be soothed with his touch. He kissed his way to the other breast and gave it equal attention, until I wanted to pull him to the floor and climb on top of him and impale myself.

"Do you like that?" he asked, looking up at me with curiosity and so much desire in his eyes.

I let out a shaky laugh and said, "If you can't tell how much I like that…"

"Making sure." His lips tipped upward in a knowing smile. His voice had gone so low and rough that it added another dimension to my need for him. He resonated with every single one of my senses.

After another swipe of his tongue around my nipple, he kissed and nibbled his way down my abdomen. He dipped his tongue into my navel and peppered below it with kisses. With every millimeter lower he went, the ache at my center intensified. I ran my fingers through his hair, caressing his head, encouraging, begging in my mind for him to hit the spot that was aching for his touch.

He did exactly that with the tip of his tongue for about two seconds, then I felt his breath whispering over my needy skin. It drew a whimper from me, and then his mouth was back on me, tongue twirling gently, teasing and tantalizing but not giving me exactly what I was craving.

"Do you like that?" he asked.

I shook my head once, biting my lip. "It's torture. I need more."

"More, huh?" he rumbled. "That can be arranged." He took my hand and tugged it downward. "I can do my best work down here on the floor."

Grinning and totally on board for his "best work," I went to my knees, then eased onto my back with his urging, right there in the middle of the living room floor—and I didn't care a bit where we were.

Seth spread my legs and lowered his mouth to me, nearly sending me to the moon in no time flat. He was thorough and generous with his attention and didn't leave a single inch of me untouched, and though he wasn't teasing now, he seemed to know exactly how to prolong it, keeping me climbing higher, reaching, arching into his face unashamedly.

Then I was tumbling, gasping, moaning, making sounds of exquisite pleasure that I'd never uttered before. My orgasm went on for countless blissful seconds, contractions of ecstasy stretching out, and I wondered at the magic this man could wield. I'd had orgasms before, but this was so next-level that I wondered what he could do if he was inside me. I wasn't sure I would make it if he tried to show me at the moment.

As I came down from the stratosphere and slowly back into my right mind and my physical body, my chest heaved and my body went limp. I was thankful he'd pulled me to the floor beforehand because there was no way I'd be able to remain standing through that euphoric, rapturous assault.

Seth was pressing gentle, tender kisses to my inner thighs, my hips, my lower abdomen. I eventually lifted an arm and caressed his head, loving his light touch now and his attentiveness. Once I could speak, I managed to say, "That."

"That?" he repeated, peering up my body to meet my eyes.

I nodded. "I like *that*."

His laugh was a quiet rumble that I felt from his chest against my legs.

Slowly, supporting himself with his hands on either side of me, he made his way up my body, skimming his lips here and there, giving me goose bumps and shivers I wouldn't have thought possible after the orbit I'd just come down from. I felt his hardness settle in against my belly, reminding me not all of us had just come apart.

He kissed up the side of my jaw, then said into my ear, "There's a slight problem."

My brain was working on a low setting, trying to puzzle out what he was talking about.

"What?"

"I don't have any condoms."

That *was* a problem. "I thought most guys carried one in their wallet."

"I'm not most guys."

That pretty much summed up why I was with him tonight, but it didn't solve the issue. Then I remembered…

"Just a second." I sat up, then stood slowly, hoping my blood had fully returned to my limbs. I went into the bedroom, opened the nightstand drawer, and grabbed the box.

On my way back to the living room, I opened it, laughing quietly. I tossed a foil packet to Seth and then lay down next to him, savoring the picture he made there, all stretched out with not a stitch of clothing on. His long body was toned muscle from shoulders to calves, and I wondered briefly what he did to stay in that kind of shape.

"Banana flavored?" he asked, grinning.

"Other options are apple, orange, and strawberry." I laughed. "Drea stuck them in my suitcase as a joke for my honeymoon. I found them when I unpacked and thought it was an ironic, unfortunate joke. But now…"

"Be sure to thank Drea for me. *If* you tell her about tonight."

"If I could send her flowers without giving my whereabouts to the world, I would."

I stretched out next to him and rolled on my side, nestling my body close to his and rubbing my breasts against his chest. He pressed into me, pulling me closer with a hand on my butt, then kissed me again. Rolling me onto my back, he leaned partway on top of me, giving himself room to run his hand up my body, kneading my breast and then toying with my nipple until I felt that spear of desire shoot straight to my core again. Already.

Reaching down, I wrapped my fingers around his length, ensuring he was very much still turned on to a level of ten, judging by the rock hardness I discovered. "Condom?"

He got it from wherever he'd set it down and handed it to me. I went up on my elbows, tearing open the packet as he continued to lavish his attention on my breasts.

"Mmm." I couldn't deny my reaction to what he was doing, but it was his turn for some pleasure. "Roll to your back," I managed, holding up the condom.

He took his sweet time, licking and sucking one breast, then the other, before doing as I said. I sat up and straddled his thighs, then rolled the protection down his dick, noting that the condom was stretched tight. When I glanced at Seth's face, he was watching me, his hands propped behind his head, his lids heavy with lust, his lips in a dopey half grin. Because of me.

That gave me the last bit of courage I needed, and I crouched over him, took his tip in my mouth.

"You don't have to…" he said.

Grinning, I replied, "I have to at least taste the banana."

He laughed, then sucked in his breath as I took him farther into my mouth. "And?" he asked, sounding like talking was a struggle.

"Tastes exactly how I'd imagine—a cross between a tire and Laffy Taffy." I lowered my mouth to him again, loving that he sucked in his breath and then moaned.

"It's not… going to take much," he said. "This sexy brunette got me pretty ramped up already."

"Mmm," I answered around his shaft, and he groaned again.

A few swirls of my tongue and a couple bobs of my head, and he grasped my head and tugged me upward. "Ev, I want to be inside of you."

I wanted that too, as my body was pulsing with need for him again. I stretched out over him, and in a blink, he'd rolled me to my back and climbed over me, then sought out my mouth with his. He made love to my mouth with his talented tongue, then I felt his tip at my opening and I opened myself to him, guiding him with my hand.

The friction had my eyes rolling back in my head. He went slow, giving my body a chance to adjust to him. It didn't take long, and then I needed him to move. I ran my hands over his ass and drew him even closer, winding my legs around his thighs, arching my body up to his.

He moaned as he pulled out slowly, driving me mad in the most delicious way, then shoving home again and making me cry out at how good it felt. His thrusts got faster quickly, and as he looked down at me, his mouth fell open with desire.

"You… feel… incredible," he said to the timing of his thrusts, and all I could do was let out a sound of pleasure that didn't come close to resembling a word.

His movements sped up, his need clearly intensifying, building along with mine, which amazed me. I wasn't a multi-orgasm kind of girl, or so I'd thought, but I was on the verge of begging him to send me over.

We moved as one, with me clinging to him, both arms and legs, as he pumped into me and robbed me of the ability to think. My focus narrowed to our connection, our one-ness. I wanted this to last till eternity at the same time I needed to explode and find that sweet release.

"God, Ev, not going to last…"

Neither was I, but I couldn't even manage the words.

In the next seconds, I tumbled, the tingles starting in my core and shooting through my blood just as he thrust into me harder, stiffened for several seconds, then went lax on top of me. I kept contracting around him, milking him thoroughly, savoring every second, and hopefully making that evident with the sounds coming out of me that I again had no control over.

Once I thought I might survive and my body turned to jelly, Seth rolled both of us to our sides with a growl. He sought out my lips and gave me the sweetest, tenderest kiss, like a silent thank you or maybe a hallelujah. Or maybe that's just what I was feeling.

Another song started, making me realize that the music had never stopped, even though it hadn't registered in my brain. My head had been too busy exploding in a thousand really good ways.

"The Eric Church vibe just totally changed for me for the rest of my life," I said, grinning.

"In a good way, I hope?"

"Sexiest music ever now."

"I suspect that had nothing to do with the music."

I loved his low, intimate voice that made me think it was just for me. Maybe it was right now, and right now was all that mattered.

"So… I'm hoping you liked *that*," Seth said.

I laughed quietly, sluggishly, so content and satisfied. I didn't know when I'd felt this safe and happy. "I liked that."

"Me too. A lot."

We lay there kissing, caressing each other, talking about nothing important for a while, then Seth went to use the restroom. When I looked around, I realized it was dark outside. The only light we'd left on was the one over the kitchen sink. I sat up, bare as the day I'd been born, and tried to figure out if I should pull my clothes on or stay this way. I wasn't ready for Seth to leave yet, but I didn't know where he was in his head with this. With us.

Without thought, I wandered to the freezer, took out the pint of mint chocolate chip cookie ice cream, and helped myself to a spoonful. Before I could put the container away, Seth reappeared, still naked and making no move toward his pile of clothes on the floor. He came up next to me, eyeing my empty spoon with interest. I took the lid back off, scooped a large spoonful out, and held it up for him. He leaned forward and I fed it to him.

"Do you want a bowl?" I asked. "You probably didn't get enough dinner."

"Oh, trust me, I'm very satisfied." His brows shot up suggestively, then he kissed me. I wasn't going to get tired of his kisses anytime soon. He took the carton from me, replaced the lid, then put it back in the freezer, all while holding on to me with one hand, as if he needed to keep me in place.

He didn't.

Tonight had been magical, and I didn't want to rush anything or pressure him, but even more, I didn't want this to be the only time I was with Seth.

"I was thinking…" I started, trying to summon the confidence that had overtaken me during sex. "What if I stayed for the whole month?"

He thought for a few seconds. "The unit is yours. You paid for it. I think more time to yourself would be good."

I nodded, because everything he said was correct, but I was hoping he'd read more into it than just those facts.

"And if that means more naked Everly time," he added, "my vote is a resounding yes."

That. That's what I'd been looking for.

I took his hand, pulled him into me, and said, "Then it's a done deal. I'm staying for the month." Winding my arms around his neck and standing on my toes so our bodies lined up just so, I pressed my lips to his and teased them with my tongue. Seth needed no encouragement to take the reins on that kiss. He lifted me to the counter and burrowed his body between my thighs.

"We could go to the bed," I said, closing my legs around him to let him know I wasn't opposed to *this* either.

"I'm thinking that's the next round. If you're up for it."

"I'm thinking I'll definitely be up for that."

CHAPTER 15

SETH

I woke up in Everly's bed well after the sun came up the next day, a good hour or more later than I usually awoke —I could tell by the brightness of the light filtering through the blinds in her bedroom. We'd finally landed there not long after she'd blown my mind in the kitchen. It turned out we were good together everywhere, whether it was the living room floor, the kitchen counter, or the queen-sized mattress in her room.

As I lay there, I waited for a gut twinge, a pang of regret, a wave of *oh, fuck, what have I done?*

It didn't come.

I hadn't had a relationship since Gail, thirteen years ago, if that farce could be called a relationship. I didn't do flings often. The last time I'd slept with a woman was over a year ago, probably closer to two or three. And that time, when I'd done the gut check—before a wink of sleep—the regret and the *oh, hell no* had been insistent and nearly immediate. Nothing against the woman. I'd met her on a rare guys' trip to Vegas to celebrate Levi Dawson's birthday. We had a fun couple of hours and then she'd wanted me to stay all night, but I'd needed to get the hell out of there. I liked sex, but it wasn't worth the drama or the hassle most times.

Last night had been worth all of it and more. The sex... Maybe if I'd had sex like that before, like a twenty on a scale of ten, it would've been worth the hassle.

It wasn't that Everly incorporated yoga poses or that we used particularly creative positions. It wasn't the background music, because Eric Church wasn't exactly sensual music. I wasn't sure what it was, exactly, that made it so incredible, but after the third time, I'd started to suspect it was just that the two of us had a unique connection. We were in tune with each other. There was trust between us, which wasn't at all the norm for someone I'd met less than a week ago.

Everly stirred a little and rolled closer into me, still mostly asleep I tightened my arm around her and inhaled the honeysuckle scent of her hair for the dozenth time.

I suspected another reason what was happening between us was so good was because we had similar expectations and we'd been open about them. This was for fun. For a month. She'd made no secret about where she was emotionally since I'd met her—not up for emotional ties. That was perfect for me. She knew this was temporary and only surface deep on my side too. I wanted to be a friend—absolutely with benefits—for as long as she was here trying to map out her next moves. She apparently was more than open to the same arrangement.

I angled my wrist so I could see the time on my smart-watch and jolted to attention as reality set in.

"What's wrong?" Everly asked drowsily. She was so fucking cute when she was half-asleep and naked, with the sheet pulled up almost to her shoulders.

Reluctantly, I sat up and rubbed my eyes. "My sister and her husband are meeting me at eight with new furniture for one of my spare bedrooms."

"What time is it?"

"Just after seven thirty."

"Hayden, right? The designer. And Zane?"

"That's right. She picked out and ordered some pieces for me, and they were delivered to her store this week. Today's the only day they could bring them to me. If I don't get out of here, I won't have time to shower before work." I was already going in late because of the delivery, and I was missing out on my morning swim as well.

The night with Everly was completely worth it.

We'd done more than just screw all night. We'd had conversations, some of them deep, lots of them fun, all of them absorbing and entertaining because I liked the hell out of Everly Ash. We'd slept a little too, emphasis on *little*, and today was going to be a rough one. I still hoped to end it back in her bed tonight, but that was probably getting ahead of myself.

I stood and glanced out to the living room to verify my clothing was still in a heap on the floor, and then I looked back at Everly. She was propped up on her elbows, rubbing her eyes, and the sheet had fallen below her breasts. Her dark hair was a tousled mess, her lips rosy, probably from being kissed so much, and even now, looking sleepy and dazed, she made the prettiest, sexiest picture. I burned it to my memory, knowing full well I'd spend many a night summoning that image after she was gone.

In the living room, I pulled yesterday's clothes on, and by the time I'd finished, Everly came in wearing a camisole and short shorts, her hair pulled up to the top of her head in a messy pile. She still looked fresh from bed and made me want to take her right back in there and ravage her one more time.

"I'd offer you coffee and donuts but…"

"Your donut source dropped the ball," I finished for her, smiling.

"I'd like to say someday you could take me to the bakery

but… we're a secret." Her smile was conspiratorial and irresistible.

I went over to her and kissed those alluring lips. You'd think I would've gotten enough of her in the past twelve hours, but no. The intensity of her response told me she was in the same place as me, and our kiss went on and turned hotter.

After a couple of minutes, she said, "Seth. Your sister."

"Right," I said against her lips. "You're staying for a month."

Everly nodded. "We have time." She laced our fingers together and walked me to the door.

I turned to her and pressed a quick kiss to her nose, not wanting to get delayed by another marathon kiss, as I knew I would if I started it. "I'll bring you some dinner from Henry's tonight if you want."

"I'd love it."

"I'll text you some entree options later."

"Sounds good."

I opened the door and glanced to the yard, toward the lake, ensuring there were no boats close to shore, then I stepped one foot out.

"Wait," Everly said.

I turned back to her. She grabbed my hand again and yanked me closer, then stretched up to plant another kiss on my lips.

Groaning and then laughing, I kissed her back, my arms automatically going to her waist and pulling her against me. She laughed too, and when we separated, she'd come outside a few inches, so she ducked back in the doorway. "Have a good day at work. I'll talk to you later."

"You definitely will." I winked and then pivoted and started down the stairs, breathing in the already steamy morning air.

I checked my watch as I descended. I had twenty minutes to feed Chaos and Mayhem and take a quick shower.

For the first time in what seemed like hours, I took in a giant breath and tried to let my brain catch up with my night. I'd gone to apologize to Everly for kissing her. I'd never even gotten the apology out because I'd gotten so wrapped up in her from the moment I stepped inside.

Her openness about the call from her mom and the way her dad was hurting her had drawn me in. How could it not? She was going through a pretty big realization about patterns that had spanned years and years and been a foundational part of her life. I sure as hell couldn't just nod my head, then walk away and leave her alone after that. I hadn't wanted to.

Falling into bed—or more accurately, onto the floor—with her had never been part of my plan, but thank fuck that's the way it'd worked out. I'd remember last night for as long as I lived.

My step was light on the stairs, my mood flying high, and I practically felt like whistling.

I hadn't been looking for a hookup or even anything extra to do with my time, what with the remodeling I had going on, my full-time job, and all the additional to-dos in conjunction with Holden's grand opening for the brewery. But there she'd been, sitting on my steps last weekend. Everly was a gift, something I'd never expected. And all we had to do to make it last a little longer was keep it to ourselves.

I was more than halfway across the yard when I noticed Hayden and Zane at the back door of the house.

"Hey, Seth," my sister called out.

My heart thundered as I wondered what they'd seen—where I'd come from, how distracted I'd been… Shit. I hoped like hell they hadn't spotted Everly hanging out the door, kissing me. Not only would that spoil the secret but Hayden would have questions. Endless, no-boundaries questions.

"Hay Bear," I said to her as I reached the short flight to the deck. "Zane." I went up the three steps and extended my hand to him, trying to read his face, but he was a man of few words, and his face gave away even less.

Zane shook my hand, smiled, and said, "Seth. Good to see you."

"What's up?" Holden's voice came from the driveway as I went in to hug my sister. He was heading toward us since he'd agreed to help us unload the furniture.

"I don't know," Hayden said as our hug ended, and I knew immediately from her singsong tone that I was screwed. Her eyes were glued to me. "You'll have to ask Seth."

Holden jogged up the steps to join us, looking from Hayden to me. "What should I ask Seth?"

"Ask him what's up." Hayden raised her brows at me. "And who the girl he was kissing in the garage apartment is."

CHAPTER 16

With an internalized *fuck*, I turned and went toward the door, muttering, "It was nothing." The door, of course, was locked, and unlocking it slowed me down, but I turned the key and went inside, knowing full well my family would follow me.

"*That* didn't look like *nothing*," Hayden said as she came into the kitchen behind me.

"It could be what he means to say is that it's none of your business," Holden said as he and Zane came in.

I turned and shot him a look of gratitude. Unfortunately, Hayden had never been one to mind her own business well.

"My brother, who hasn't kissed a girl since probably senior prom, is making out with some gorgeous woman in what was clearly a morning-after, thanks-for-a-good-time goodbye kiss…"

"I've kissed plenty of women," I clarified.

"You could see that she was gorgeous?" Holden asked, and I knew he was fishing to find out whether she'd recognized Everly.

"Dark hair thrown up all sexy, slender, long legs…"

In other words, no. She hadn't seen it was a country singer she'd no doubt recognize. Hayden loved celebrity news and had acquaintances in the country music industry because her store was a couple doors down from a recording studio, so this was a relief.

"So this is the woman you hauled ass out of Holden's wedding celebration to rent her your apartment?" Hayden asked.

"We need to get busy on the furniture so I can get to Henry's," I said. It wasn't a lie, but I needed to divert Hayden's attention even more than I needed to work.

She sent a deliberative look at me, and I could almost hear the battle in her head between continuing the third degree or letting it go. Finally, she laid a bakery box on the center island. "We brought muffins from Sugar Babies for you. I ate mine on the way here."

"Of course you did," Holden said lightly.

"I'll grab one after I shower." After they left. I loved my sister and thought the world of Zane, but today I needed them out of here.

"I'll take one now," Holden said as he dug into the box.

"Everything's done in my room?" Hayden asked. It was the bedroom she'd had growing up, before we moved to Nashville, and she still called it hers.

"All done. Ready for the furniture, just like I promised," I told her.

"Let's go look, Zane. I can make sure I still want everything in the same place."

The two of them went through the living room toward the stairs, and Holden watched them go. Once we heard them on the steps, he turned to me and said, in a low voice, "You spent the night with Everly Ash?"

"Who's to say I didn't just deliver her breakfast?"

"You're wearing the clothes you had on yesterday, bro."

I clenched my jaw but didn't say anything.

"You don't trust Hayden enough to tell her what's going on?" Holden said.

"It has nothing to do with Hayden. I don't want to betray Everly's secret to another person. Telling you was bad enough."

"That's fair. But in this situation, it might be the only way to get Hay to shut up about it."

"She's persistent as fuck," I admitted.

My phone buzzed with a message, so I took it out.

It was from Everly.

Your family saw us, didn't they?

I clenched my jaw again. I didn't want to give her anything more to worry about, but I wasn't going to lie. *They did, but they didn't see your face. Holden knows it's you but he's keeping it quiet.*

I'd meant to tell her about Holden knowing last night, but I'd gotten massively distracted.

Hayden came zipping down the stairs with Zane following at a more reasonable pace.

"It looks fantastic, Seth!" she said. "I can't wait to get everything in there."

"You like the floor?" I forced myself to the design topic.

"The color's just the right amount of warmth with the walls and trim, and the wide planks are perfect. I have a rug in mind that will bring everything together."

"We might as well start the fun part," Holden said and headed toward the outside door.

The rest of us went out after him and started unloading Hayden's commercial delivery van. She and Zane took the headboard, and Holden and I carried the chest of drawers. I was halfway down the stairs afterward when Everly texted again.

How much do you trust your family to keep my secret?

Everyone else was ahead of me, so I slowed on the stairs

and typed out an answer with no hesitation. *One hundred percent.*

A few seconds passed before she started typing, and then I read, *Don't lie to them on my account. If you trust them, you should tell them as much as you're comfortable with.*

On the main floor, I stopped in the hallway to finish the conversation while the others were still outside. I didn't want Everly making this decision lightly.

Maybe not the part about the living room floor, she added, ending with a grinning emoji.

Are you sure? I asked, barely smiling at her joke.

I am They're your family, and it looked like they might have seen us.

They did. Hayden grilled me.

I'm sorry, Seth. It was careless of me to kiss you that last time.

I liked that you kissed me that last time.

I heard the outside door open again and Hayden's and Zane's voices, telling me my texting time was up.

Gotta go, I typed. *If you're comfortable with it, I'll tell them and swear them to secrecy. Hayden will be much more bearable if she knows the stakes.*

I am. Talk to you later.

Zane and Holden came through with a queen-sized mattress, and Hayden had a nightstand. I went out to the van and grabbed the last nightstand, then followed them up, where they were arranging everything to Hayden's specifications.

"It's exactly what I had in mind," my sister said as soon as all the pieces were together and placed. "The bedding will be perfect."

"It looks great, Hay. Thank you." I liked it too, but I was distracted.

"I had to get our place on the lake all taken care of," she said, grinning, sharing a look with her husband that I didn't want to think too hard about.

"My favorite nephew still needs a little boy room," Holden said. "Where's Harrison today?"

"Mimi and Papa's house," Zane said of our dad and his mom. "Getting spoiled, no doubt."

"I hope he takes his morning nap," Hayden said. "The stuff for Holden's old room should be in in the next couple of weeks. Until then…"

"I want to talk to you guys before you go," I said. "Let's go downstairs."

"Going in, huh?" Holden asked quietly, bringing up the rear on our parade.

All I could do was nod and hope this was the right decision.

Hayden helped herself to a bottled water from the fridge and looked at me expectantly as I walked into the room.

"Everything I'm about to tell you, you need to keep to yourself," I said, resisting the temptation to glance toward the garage.

"Yes, sir," Hayden said.

"I'm serious, Hayden. There's a lot at stake."

Her brows popped up on her forehead, expression sobered, and she said, "You've got it, Seth. You can tell us anything."

"The woman renting my apartment is Everly Ash."

Hayden sucked in her breath, and her eyes went wide. "You. Are. Kidding me."

"Who's Everly Ash?" Zane asked.

"An incredible country singer," Hayden said. "She just left Trey Gilbert at the altar."

"Who's Trey Gilbert?" her husband asked, and Hayden gaped at him.

"I thought you were getting to know country music."

"Slow learner, I guess." He grinned at her as if he knew damn well his lack of pop culture knowledge was a thorn in my dear sister's side.

"One of the hottest country singers out there right now. The press has been going nuts over this. So she escaped to your rental?" She switched her attention to me with the last bit.

I nodded.

"And you're her secret lover?"

Jesus.

And yet… *now* I was.

"I just met her Saturday night," I clarified. "No one can know she's here. If the media finds out…"

"It'll be like Shark Week," Hayden said.

"Something like that."

"You knew about this?" she asked Holden.

"Since yesterday," he said.

Hayden nodded, and I could see her mind working through all the details. "I love this," she finally declared, looking happy as can be.

"Well, thank God for that," Holden said, tongue-in-cheek.

"I mean, maybe our brother will smile more and lighten up."

"Maybe I will," I told her.

"It only took a little lovin' from the Sweetheart of Country Music."

"Hay," Zane said, shaking his head with a grin.

"You should see her. She's a looker." Hayden's eyes sparkled.

"I did see her."

"From far away. Seth, I think it's great. All of it."

"Thanks. She said I could tell you if I trusted you. Don't make me regret it."

"We won't tell a soul. Before we go, I need to get measurements of the study upstairs and the master bedroom, so that'll just take a few more minutes."

"Seth and I can do the study if you two can do the bedroom," Zane said. "We'll cut the time in half."

"There's a tape measure up there," I said. "Just the room dimensions?"

"Up there, I also need the distance between each of the windows and from the window edges to the walls."

We headed up to do her bidding, talking about Zane's flight schedule for his family's company jet and his son, Harrison. He noted all the measurements on his phone as we measured everything twice and continued the small talk. When we went back downstairs a few minutes later, Hayden and Holden were nowhere to be found. The master was empty, as were the bathrooms, the living room, the kitchen. It was by chance that a movement out the kitchen window caught my eye. I recognized Hayden's back just as she stepped inside the garage apartment.

CHAPTER 17

Not long after I'd texted Seth and told him to level with his family if he wanted to, lyrics started coming to me. Sexy, sensual lyrics. There was no question what had inspired them.

I'd scanned the apartment for a notebook, but of course, there wasn't one. I'd powered up my phone to dictate the words before I lost them, and once the initial word storm was on my Notes app, I downloaded a songwriting app, because a melody was coming with the words. A gift from the music gods, and it'd been so long since I'd tried to compose anything that I was terrified I'd lose it all before I could get it on my phone. My caution about keeping my phone off was waning, but I still kept my ringer silenced.

I'd strummed Seth's guitar as I worked out the tune to go with the lyrics, and it took almost no time at all to get four lines down. It'd taken me longer to figure out how to use the app than it did to create the first verse.

The lyrics were sexier than anything I'd ever written. Not surprising considering I'd been a teenager when I'd last focused on songwriting. In the ten to twelve years since, I'd sung other people's creations and gotten so busy I hadn't taken the time to create.

It felt amazing to create. Even just a single stanza of a single song.

I was strumming it again, singing quietly, when there was a knock on the door.

With my heart racing, I set the guitar aside and crept to the entry, trying to be so quiet that no one would be able to hear that I was in here. When I peeked out the peephole, I saw a woman I recognized as Seth's sister, based on the glimpse I'd had of her out the window when Seth had left. Though I hadn't had a good view of her, her shirt was an apple-green color that was easy to identify.

I debated for about two heartbeats, and in the end, part of what drove me to open the door was curiosity. I wanted to know someone close to Seth. Meeting Hayden would give me insight into him.

Truly, after our night together, he seemed too good to be true. All the more reason to carry on with our intentions of having a fantastic month together and then moving on.

I opened the door about a foot—enough to be welcoming but not enough for people to see in easily if they happened to be around.

"Hi," I said.

"Hi, Everly. I'm Hayden, Seth's sister. I brought you some muffins and wanted to introduce myself. My brother swore us to secrecy." She held out a simple black earthenware plate with a blue rim. It was covered with plastic wrap, and beneath the wrap, two large muffins were visible. "If I'm intruding, just tell me."

"Come in," I said without hesitation. This woman was instantly likable, plus she'd brought scrumptious-looking muffins. She was pretty, with a happy sparkle in her blue eyes, straight brown hair that reached just below her shoulders, and an indulgent smile on her clear-glossed lips.

As if she understood my twitchiness about the outside world seeing me, Hayden hustled through the door and closed it behind her. Grinning, she said, "I feel like some kind of secret agent." Then she extended her hand. "It's so nice to meet you, Everly. I'm a big fan, but that's not why I'm here."

"Does Seth know you're here?" I couldn't help smiling back at her because I suspected I knew the answer even before she confirmed it.

"Not yet. Holden took off and I slipped out while Seth and my husband were upstairs. He's very protective of you." Her brows shot up her forehead.

"He's sweet." *Among other things.* Things I would not be uttering a hint about to his sister. "Want to have a seat?"

"I don't mean to interrupt your morning," she said, "but I know if I was stuck in a tiny apartment and had to stay there alone, I'd be climbing the walls, so I thought maybe a visit would be okay. A secret visit." Her smile was conspiratorial, and I was glad I'd opened the door to her.

I led her over to the sofa, and we each took one end of it, sitting at an angle. "It gets... lonely, for sure. In my regular life, I'm surrounded by people all the time, so I needed the space..."

"I can imagine. You've been through some things lately. Anyone would need time."

Instead of a pregnant pause where I'd feel like she was searching for info on my breakup, she kept talking and changed the subject, as if making a point to *not* pry.

"Is that my brother's old guitar?" She pointed at it.

"He insisted I take it in case I wanted to play."

"And did you?"

Nodding, I said, "I hadn't realized how much I needed it. I've been keeping my cell phone off, so no music, no streaming..."

"You've been completely unplugged, huh?"

"Avoiding mom calls, avoiding the media and the tabloids."

"Understandable. Do you want me to pick up a new phone for you so you can at least play the occasional Candy Crush?"

"God, I miss that game," I said, laughing.

"I don't know how you've survived! I'll get you a phone with a new number and we can figure out the billing details later. Then you can play music and watch your shows and still avoid the bad stuff."

"Don't you live in Nashville though?"

"I do, but it's not that far. Or I can have Seth get one and it'll be faster."

"He's done too much for me already." *Like more orgasms than I can count on one hand, for example.*

Hayden tilted her head and sized me up. "So, something you should realize about my middle brother… He doesn't go out with many girls. Like, ever."

"He hasn't taken me out either." As soon as I said it, I remembered Hayden had seen him leaving this morning. "Who am I kidding, huh?" I laughed softly. "*Technically*, we haven't gone out. Except he did take me out in a canoe two nights ago."

"I'm telling you, that's not Seth's status quo. Any of it."

"He's gone out of his way for me because I'm sort of dependent as I hide away here, trying to be independent." I rolled my eyes at myself. "I don't think I could pull this off without him. My closest friend lives in Washington State. She ordered some things for me online and is shipping them to Seth's, but again… if he wasn't being so kind about everything…"

"Seth is kind and caring and stable and my favorite brother," Hayden said. "He could be all of that without sneaking out of your place first thing in the morning. No judgment," she said in a rush. "I'm just saying, my brother must think a lot of you."

"We get along well." Call me the queen of understatement. "I trusted him the second day I met him."

"Not the first?"

I shook my head. "I didn't trust anyone the day I was supposed to get married. I was terrified he'd recognize me—"

"He didn't, did he?" Hayden asked.

Again, I shook my head, smiling at Hayden's tone, which told me she and her brother likely gave each other a hard time frequently.

"He's so super smart, has an MBA, is a business genius, but when it comes to anything trendy or current, he doesn't have a clue."

"It came in handy, believe me."

"So you finally told him?"

"He came back the next morning after seeing a story online with a photo of me."

"That sounds about right. And obviously there's an attraction."

Now I was pretty sure she was fishing for info, but somehow I didn't feel threatened by Hayden. I'd only met her ten minutes ago, but she reminded me in some ways of Drea, someone to whom I could let out a little of what was in my head and she might shed some insight. She already had. There'd been a couple of moments in the past few days when I'd questioned to myself why Seth was going out of his way to be with me. Was I being foolish to trust him? Was he just after one thing? As an entertainer, I had to constantly be wary about who I trusted for the littlest things, let alone something major like my body.

When I was with Seth, those doubts disappeared for the most part, but meeting his sister, learning that he wasn't one to sleep around confirmed what I'd instinctively guessed.

"There's an attraction," I said, thinking back on the day

he'd brought me donuts for breakfast, when he'd admitted he knew who I was. Even though I hadn't known whether I could trust him at that point, I couldn't deny he was good-looking. So good-looking. And then his kindness… "I'm sure you know I'm not in a place in my life where I could have a lasting relationship. Seth knows that. He's in the same place. I'm planning to stay here for a month, and I hope to spend some of that time with him, having fun. Nothing more."

"I'm all for it," Hayden said. "As long as you're both in the same place mentally. I would hate for either one of you to get hurt."

I shook my head. "I'd hate for that too. We're on the same page."

She seemed to relax a little and nodded.

"So tell me, what does a famous country singer play on an old, beat-up acoustic guitar? I'm thinking 'First Date' wouldn't quite have the same feel."

I chuckled at the mention of one of my biggest hits. "Not quite the same, no." I sobered and said, "I haven't played a single 'Everly Ash' song since I've been here." I made air quotes around my name. "I didn't write the songs I've recorded in the past ten years. Most times, I didn't even pick them."

"Who did?"

"My dad, who's my producer."

"Eddy Ash," she said, surprising me. People in the industry knew him, but I wasn't sure those outside of it did.

"That's him. He's mega-talented, but I've let him have too much control over my career."

"You're mega-talented too, I'd say. So are you a songwriter too, but you just don't get to use those on your albums?"

"I used to be a songwriter. I let it go when my dad started producing me. But today…" Did I really want to tell her this? It felt extremely personal but also somehow important. "Today I started writing a song for the first time in years."

"Yeah?" Hayden looked genuinely excited for me. "And? How did it feel?"

That was an interesting question. How did it *feel*, not how did it *go* or how did it *sound*.

"It felt… kind of incredible. Like, made my blood flow faster, made my heart beat stronger… That probably sounds weird. It made me feel alive. It… gave me hope."

As I stumbled over the words, I realized how spot on they were.

"It sounds like you need to write music."

"Maybe I do." I had time. I'd just committed to staying here for a month. What did I have to do besides think? "It might be fun for a while. I'll have to go back and start working on my next album soon, and I won't be able to use my own songs for that."

"What if they end up loving these songs?" Hayden asked, gesturing to the guitar.

I thought about that, imagined how hard it would be to even get all the right people to listen to any songs I'd written, my dad included. I imagined they might say they liked them but that they were off-brand. I was so sick of hearing about off-brand, frankly. How could I be off-brand for Everly Ash? But that's where my career had gone, and I had myself to blame for it. Myself and maybe my dad. Probably my dad.

"I might just be writing for myself, but that has value too, right?" I said.

"It can. It might fill a space inside of you that needs to be filled."

That resonated so much that I asked, "Are you a musician too? I know you're a designer."

"No. Just a designer, and I own a home furnishings store. I love music but I have no talent whatsoever."

"You seem to know a little about the industry."

"I have friends in it. You might know some of them, actually. Joey Bloom? Tucker Steele and Steele Hearts?

Midnight Moonshine? There's a recording studio two doors down from my store and some of them live in the neighborhood."

"I know Joey and I've met Tucker," I said.

"I'm good friends with Tucker's wife, Gin. She's a producer and a musical genius, from what I hear. If you ever want to go indie…"

I let out an almost-laugh, not really giving the idea any thought. I had a good career, and I was lucky to have it, regardless of how I'd gotten there. Going indie would set me back a good eight to ten years.

"What studio is near you?" I asked, purposely avoiding her suggestion.

"The Hale Street Recording Studio. It's independent but sometimes labels rent it out. It's always busy, with everyone from newbies to some big names. The muffins are from a bakery on the same street."

"I'll have to visit it sometime," I said. In the future. When I was back to my normal life.

"I should probably go. My husband will be ready to head back to the city and my brother will be ready to strangle me. But I'm really glad to meet you." She stood, and I did as well.

"Me too," I said, and I meant it. If I had a different life, Hayden was the kind of girl I could imagine being good friends with. "Thanks for the muffins. If they're half as good as the donuts from Sugar, I'm in for a treat."

"You're in for a treat. But those donuts are to die for too. Maybe I'll get Zane to stop by there so I can take some back with me."

"Life without donuts is sad." I knew, because they'd never appeared on my diet since my dad had hired James as my trainer.

"Truer words have never been spoken," she said. "It was really good to meet you."

"You too. I'm glad you stopped by."

We were at the door now, and Hayden looked hesitant, then she hugged me. "Sorry. I'm a hugger."

"Nothing to apologize for." There was nothing quite like girlfriend hugs, and it'd been a long week since my last hug from Drea. In my normal life, there wasn't a lot of room for girlfriend hugs. Instead, there were handshakes and contracts and, from time to time, fake hugs.

Hayden promised to get a new phone to me soon, and I didn't argue. We said our goodbyes, and I closed the door.

Just the thought of my normal life made my stomach uneasy. Obviously I wasn't ready to go back there yet. I had a lot of things to figure out, like how to handle my parents, how to take the reins of my career, and how to not make another giant mistake like Trey Gilbert.

But for now, I wasn't going to think about any of that. I was going to see about writing the rest of a song. And later, I was going to have dinner with Seth and, if I was lucky, maybe more.

CHAPTER 18

A week after coming clean to Hayden and Zane, I jogged from the Subaru to the front door, through the rain, after a hectic day at Henry's.

I let myself in and wiped the water off my face. Chaos blinked up at me from the back of the couch in the living room. Obviously the rain had prevented him from hearing my arrival.

"Hey, big boy," I said to him.

He yawned, then jumped down and came over to me. My wet legs didn't deter him from swiping against my calves. It was going on seven, which had become my norm lately with the brewery stuff and tourist season keeping me busier than usual, but the cats hadn't adjusted to a later dinner hour. I didn't figure they ever would, as both of those lovable bastards were pretty much always ready to eat.

"Let's go get your chow."

He pranced ahead of me to the kitchen. When I entered, my eyes were drawn to the top of the refrigerator, where

Mayhem peered down at us as if we were his subjects and he was deciding whether we were worth interacting with or not.

When I went to the cat food cabinet, all airs disappeared, and the black thundercat leapt down. I'd just spooned some canned food into their bowls when I heard knocking at the back door. I smiled and my heart sped up because I was pretty sure I knew who that was, even though she hadn't been to my place since that first canoe night.

I'd planned to go over there as soon as I figured out dinner for both of us and got the cats taken care of, like I'd done every night since the first one we'd spent together. With the cats' noses in their bowls—six feet away from each other because they played a stupid his-food-is-better-than-mine game otherwise—I headed to the door and pulled it open, feeling the usual good feelings that seeing her brought.

"Hey, Ev. Come in out of the rain."

She came inside, soaked—including the Seattle cap I'd learned belonged to Drea's husband—and apologizing. "I'm sorry to bust in on you."

"You're not busting in. You're welcome anytime." At that moment, I wondered for the first time why I hadn't invited her here before, beyond the first-aid night, but I let the thought drop.

"I'm driving myself crazy," she said, running her hands up and down her upper arms as if she was chilled in the air-conditioning. "The day is gray, the apartment is quiet, and I can't for the life of me figure out the song I'm working on. I had to get out of there."

"I'm glad you did then."

"I made sure no one was out."

"It's a good day to not be out." I'd resisted the urge to greet her properly for all these seconds so far, but now I stepped toward her, put my arms around her, and kissed her.

"The day is suddenly better," she said, grinning. "Hey, kitties."

I laughed. "Those two are hardly 'kitties.' More like grumpy-ass felines with attitudes."

"Adorable ones." She bent down and ran a hand over Chaos as he went by, his bowl empty already, tongue busy licking his chops. "I'd pick you up, handsome, but I'd get you wet."

It would be dumb to be jealous of my cat, right?

"I was about to change into dry clothes. Can I get you some shorts and a tee?"

"Or you could just get me naked."

I liked this woman so much.

"Come here." I tugged at her wet shirt and pulled her closer, then lifted the shirt over her head. She wasn't wearing a bra, and fuck, that was hot.

I took her breasts in my hands, eager, impatient, as if I hadn't just tasted them this morning. Her skin was so soft, breasts so round and gorgeous. Had I known I'd be treated to this welcome home, I would've cut out of work early.

I locked my mouth over hers and kissed her urgently, my dick rock hard and pressing into her, my blood pounding lower, turning me all caveman as I backed her up against the island. She matched my intensity, our kiss turning urgent. Next thing I knew, Everly had lowered her shorts and underwear, let them fall down her legs, and stepped out of them.

I was still fully dressed in shorts and a polo. As she lifted one of her legs and wound it around me, my clothes were like a fucking prison. I palmed her perfect ass and lifted her. With a writhing Everly wrapped around me, I blazed a trail to the master bedroom and went through it to the bathroom. There wasn't much light, just what came in through the window of the dreary evening, but it was enough to see her milky flesh as I slid her down my body.

With our tongues still entangled, I reached into the shower and turned the water on.

Everly undid my shorts and shoved them and my boxer

briefs off before the water could heat. I helped her by whipping my shirt over my head and dropping it.

She grasped my dick and I closed my eyes, groaning at the exquisite pleasure the slightest touch from her brought. When she tightened her grip and stroked me, I sucked in a breath. I knew what she could do with her hands and her mouth, but I was set on being inside of her when I came.

The room was starting to steam up, which told me the water was ready, and I knew I sure the fuck was. I picked her up, and again, she wrapped her legs around me, opening herself to me, as I stepped into the shower. I pressed her body against the tiled wall, my dick pressed between me and her belly, aching to be sheathed by her.

Fuck. I was *this* close to going in bareback.

"Need a condom," I said into her mouth, and she kept kissing me. I pulled away before I lost my damn mind. "Don't move. Got one right outside."

I bent down and sucked her nipple into my mouth, swirled my tongue until she arched, then released her with a little pop.

Everly's reply was a needy moan as she opened her eyes halfway. The smile on her face was full of need and knowing, probably that I could never walk away from her at a moment like this so I'd be back faster than she could blink.

I opened the door, grabbed my shorts off the floor, whisked my wallet out, and secured the condom I'd put in there a few days ago just in case. We were getting low on the pack in her apartment.

Two seconds later, I had it open and rolled on and was turning back to the sexiest woman in the known universe. She stood exactly where I'd left her, watching me and extending a hand to me. I wove our fingers together, pressed against her, and kissed her. I was trying to slow it down but my dick was having none of it.

Lifting her so her opening lined up with me, I trailed a

hand down and teased her with my fingers, ensuring she, too, was ready. Between the dampness inside her and the needful moan, I got my answer, so I lowered her onto me and dropped my head backward at how fucking incredible she felt.

I tried to rein myself in, because I was primed and ready to explode in no time flat, but I needed Ev to come first. As I slowed my thrusts, biting my lip against the temptation, Everly moved against me insistently, squirming where we were connected, which took some doing considering I had her pinned against the wall.

"Why'd you slow?" she asked, her voice breathy.

"Trying… to make it… last," I managed.

I thrust into her again, and her body started contracting around me. She closed her eyes, threw her head back, and said, "God… Seth… yes…" and then let out a long moan of pleasure that I knew now was her coming apart.

That sound did something to me, as if I'd been conditioned in just over a week to respond to her coming with a climax of my own. With my next thrust, I let go and came hard.

We were silent and still for seconds as we caught our breaths and came back into ourselves. With our bodies still connected intimately, Everly said, "That was…" Her cheeks were flushed, lips swollen, and she couldn't seem to wipe the sated smile off her lips. Nor could she apparently come up with a word that was good enough.

I wasn't about to try. Instead, I nuzzled her neck and growled, long and low, to let her know I was with her.

Several more heartbeats passed, and eventually I lowered her feet to the floor, then kissed her as the water continued to cascade over us.

"I was thinking about you the entire day," I told her. "What we just did blew every hot, sexy thought I had about you straight out of the water."

"Pun intended?" she asked with a self-satisfied grin.

I kissed her again, then grabbed the soap and started sudsing both of us.

A few minutes later, we'd shampooed and soaped each other, and the water turned cool. We got out and dried off, then went to my closet. I pulled a pair of athletic shorts on, and Everly helped herself to one of my T-shirts, which fell to her mid-thighs.

We were in the kitchen, waiting for the oven to warm up for pizza, Everly sitting on the island, looking sex-mussed and gorgeous. The lights were low and warm, the summer storm intensifying outside.

"Do you have some scratch paper?" she asked.

I went to the junk drawer, pulled out a notepad, and offered it to her, along with a mechanical pencil. She bent over the counter, scribbling something down faster than the average man could think. When her pencil paused, she read over what she'd written, nodded as if to a beat a few times, then bit her lip. Her head was tilted pensively, and then she scratched out a word and wrote something else.

I leaned against the counter opposite her and enjoyed watching her even though I didn't know what she was up to.

After a few mores seconds, she nodded once, as if whatever she'd written was right, then realized I was watching her.

"The song I was fighting with all day," she said. "A line of lyrics just came to me."

"And they work?" I guessed.

"They work. For now, at least."

"When am I going to get to hear this one?"

"When it's done. If it's ever done. This one is frustrating, but it's also not letting me move on to something different."

"You'll figure it out and make it amazing. I don't have a single doubt."

Over the past week, she'd written several songs and

treated me to a private mini concert each night. I was no music expert, but the songs were evocative, honest, and showed a lot of what she was going through, with some about searching for herself, looking for her inner strength, and some about opening up to another person.

She said these were just for her, to flex her creative muscle that hadn't been used for so long. They wouldn't be played for anyone else, so I was privileged as hell to hear them. I was also blown away by her songwriting talent. That her father hadn't allowed her to write her own material was a travesty. For being an industry power hitter, he was missing the fucking boat.

The songs Everly was writing, though, were nothing like what she'd recorded in the past—the songs that were, according to her, her brand.

My all-important, godforsaken brand, she'd said.

She was so much more than her dad allowed her to be.

I went around the counter, came up behind her, and said, "Turn the paper over."

"What? Why?"

"So I don't see it until you're ready."

She flipped the paper over. I put my arms around her from behind, my hands running under the shirt, over her flat, sexy belly, and I trailed kisses up one side of her neck.

"Have you ever written a song about a boat?" I asked her.

Everly laughed. "A boat? No. Why?"

"There's lots of country songs about boats."

"Yeah. I don't get it."

"Ever been on a boat?"

"Just a canoe," she said, grinning. "It wasn't my favorite thing, to be honest. Although the first aid afterward was five star."

I grinned too, remembering the first night I'd kissed her. In some ways, it seemed like it'd been so long ago. We'd come a long way since then, gotten intimately comfortable, explored every inch of each other. Our time together was going too fast, and I didn't want to have any regrets once she was gone.

"You need to go on a real boat so you can write a song about it."

"Are you going to take me out on yours?"

"I'm actually taking my family out this weekend. Hayden, Zane, Holden, Chloe, maybe Cash. You should come with us."

"You're doing this in the daytime?" She looked panicked, and I hated that something as normal as a boat ride could instill that kind of fear in her, even though I understood why. The media had too much fucking power over people's lives.

"Some people swear it's easier to get a suntan that way," I joked. "I know it's scary, but we'll just be departing from the dock and then heading into open water, where no one will get close enough to see you. And if you wear a hat and sunglasses, you'll be impossible to recognize from a distance."

She nodded slowly, thoughtfully, considering.

"You need it. You need to get out of that apartment, as today proved, and you need to interact with people who'll protect your identity and don't care what your day job is."

"Which is your family," she said. "I haven't met anyone but Hayden."

"They're all solid. All of them know about you, have known about you"—I'd told Cash the secret the day Hayden had visited Everly's apartment—"and none of them have told a soul. They won't. That's how our family is."

"They sound awesome." There was a hint of longing in her voice.

"You like Hayden, right?"

"I did from the moment I opened the door to her. She's hard not to like."

"And you like me?" I nibbled at her neck again and ran

my hands over her breasts.

Laughing, she leaned into my mouth. "A little too much."

"Then you'll like all of them. Well, except maybe Cash. Depends on his mood, if he goes."

Everly sucked in a breath. "You're sure we can stay far enough away from everyone else?"

"I am. And if you want, you can learn to waterski or tube. Or you can watch. Your call. There's nothing quite like having the wind blow through your hair at high speed over open water."

"Okay," she said, pulling me around in front of her and lacing our fingers together, wrapping her legs around my torso, and peering up at me with a spark of excitement and courage in her eyes. "I want to try it. I trust you, Seth."

Those words carried a lot of weight, I knew, and I relished them.

As the storm raged outside for the rest of the evening, we ate, we played several games of backgammon, we touched and kissed and talked and laughed. When we both started yawning midway through a movie, it was the logical thing to head to my bedroom for the night. We'd always stayed in the apartment—every single night—mostly because I met her there so she wouldn't have to go out and risk being seen.

It wasn't until we were in my bed, tucked under the covers, that it hit me. I'd never had a woman spend the night here. Never had a woman in this bed.

A kernel of uneasiness formed in my gut. I'd leaped over a pretty big line without so much as a thought tonight, and while it might be no big deal at the moment, I was worried about what it meant for the future. Would having Everly here now make it all the more difficult later, when she was gone for good?

Pushing the thought away, I pulled her closer, sought her lips, and set out to blank my mind by getting lost in her body.

I'd deal with the future later.

CHAPTER 19

Maybe I *would* write a song about boats.

We were about three hours into our Sunday on the boat, and I was having the time of my life.

Worth noting: I was swimming—yes, in the deep water—where Hayden and Chloe had taught me the subtle art of peeing in the lake, and I'd conquered any lingering fear of what was lurking beneath the surface.

I'd gone tubing for the first time, paired up with Hayden while Seth steered the boat. He was being endearingly careful to keep us at a distance from everyone else in this giant lake. Now, we were anchored in an out-of-the-way area on the opposite side from the sandbar, which was unofficially known as party central.

While the rest of us got in the water, wearing lifejackets, Holden had stayed in the boat, playing with Harrison, Hayden and Zane's adorable eight-month-old baby. Hayden, Chloe, and I had just decided to get out of the water and get a little sun, while Zane, Seth, and Cash stayed in. They were currently discussing a race to the shore and back.

Hayden hoisted herself up on the back deck, her hair draping in a dripping-wet, silky curtain down her back and her neon pink and yellow bikini looking fantastic in spite of her recently giving birth.

"Wait for me, jacka— guys," Holden called out with a sheepish look at Hayden.

Hayden laughed. "You have a couple months before I start charging you cash for every swear word."

"How are you going to collect that, shorty?" Holden asked.

With a nod toward Zane out in the water, she said, "I got muscle."

"Yeah, I'm not messing with the navy guy," Holden said, and then he lifted Harrison from the shade he'd been under and blew a raspberry on his chubby belly, eliciting a hearty baby giggle. "Here's your mean mama, Harry baby." He handed off the large bundle of boy to Hayden.

Chloe was next to get out, and Holden hurried over to help his pregnant wife. She wasn't showing yet and was still in her first trimester, but apparently Holden had told the whole town their news just minutes after he'd found out he was going to be a dad. There was no denying he was fantastic with kids. He'd volunteered to stay with Harrison while Hayden and Zane swam and had kept the boy amused and busy for the past hour plus.

Holden kissed Chloe once she stood, then looked to me. "Need a hand?"

"You might need to get a dipping net," I joked. However, I climbed out, took his hand to balance on the small deck, then made my way toward the front, where the other two girls had gone.

"That suit is perfect on you," Hayden said just as Holden dove over the side and swam out to the guys.

"You have good taste," I told her. "In suits and donuts."

She'd picked up the bikini—a tiny floral print in navy,

periwinkle, and cream—for me and donuts for everyone this morning, and I was only a little self-conscious that my belly was showing those donuts. Seth had told me more than once what he thought of me in this bikini, and it revved my blood every time, particularly when he'd spoken it directly into my ear in that sexy growl of his.

"I can only imagine how it is to have a trainer plan your diet," Hayden said.

"Like prison?" Chloe asked with a grin.

"That or hell itself," I said as I settled with them on the U-shaped, cushioned bench seats in the front of the twelve-person boat. The bow, I'd been told repeatedly. That one I could remember, but I would never be able to distinguish between port and starboard. What was wrong with left and right? "The diet scrutiny is one of the downsides of my career, I guess. What about you guys? What's the worst part of your jobs?"

"Insane clients," Hayden said without hesitation as she stretched out on the cushion at the very front. Chloe and I took up the other two sides, all of us with our legs up on the bench, soaking up the hot sun. "And paperwork."

"I love the paperwork," Chloe said. "I might be sick in the head."

"My brother's lucky to have you," Hayden said. "He didn't get the paperwork gene either. That went entirely to Seth."

"Holden's the people guy of the Henrys," Chloe said. "Seth is the anti-people guy. Except when it comes to you." She aimed the comment at me as she rubbed sunscreen on her chest.

"We're having fun for now." I couldn't help smiling when I said it, pushing the for now part out of my mind. "So Holden's the social one, Seth's the cranial one, and where does Cash fit in?"

"He's the silent, grumpy one who shows love through

food," Chloe said. She got up and went to the cooler. "Anyone need a drink?"

"Water, please," I said.

"Same," Hayden agreed. "You pretty much nailed our oldest brother in a single sentence."

"Everything I've tried from Henry's that Cash has made has been delicious," I said. "And now lunch today. That was the most gourmet picnic ever."

I'd thought maybe there'd be sandwiches and chips and possibly some cookies. Oh, how wrong I was. The chef had made a bulgur and tomato Mediterranean salad, home-baked pull-apart garlic bread, a ham, potato, and bacon frittata, and to-die-for blueberry bars. Holden had brought some of his home-brewed beer in a variety of flavors, and the two I'd tried had changed me from a "beer is just okay" person to someone who wanted to explore all the flavors and types he and his business partner, Kemp, brewed up.

"We're lucky he took the day off today," Chloe said, handing off bottled waters to both of us and then sitting back in her spot. She wore a one-shoulder one-piece suit in white, sea foam, and teal that looked great on her tall frame. "He works too much."

Hayden laughed. "Not that any of us can talk. We seem to have workaholics in our family. I'm betting you work a lot too, usually," she said to me.

"When I'm not escaping the international scandal I caused, you mean?" I was starting to be able to laugh about it, sort of, among friends, and both these women felt like they could be friends.

I'd only met Chloe this morning. She was quieter than Hayden, but most people were. She seemed smart and welcoming and super in love with her husband. Neither she nor Hayden treated me like a celebrity but rather a human, and that was priceless in my eyes—plus hard to find.

"Hey, ladies," Holden called out from the huddle of men

out in the water. "We need someone to start the race and watch the finish line."

"Boys will always be boys," Hayden said quietly enough that only Chloe and I could hear. To them, she asked, "Where's the finish line?"

"We're swimming to shore, then coming back to the boat," Holden said.

I wasn't a good judge of distance, but the shore wasn't close. "That's crazy," I said to the girls.

Laughing, Chloe said, "They're trying to show off. Bad decision on Holden's part. Zane was in the navy and Seth swims every day."

"And Cash is more fit than him," Hayden agreed. "Line up!" she called out to them.

There was discussion among the guys as they did so, with Holden arguing whether they were even or not, and then Hayden yelled, "On your mark, get set, go!"

The four took off, with us watching intently, and it was quite a show. I'd watched Seth on his morning swims from my balcony—he swam from the dock to a large rock that jutted out of the water a few hundred yards away, then back, usually a couple times, but he didn't go for speed. Now he was going for speed, and he was impressive.

"That's so hot," I said under my breath.

"You aren't kidding," Hayden said. "I've seen Zane in the water before but never like that."

They started out even, but about halfway to shore, Seth and Zane pulled ahead of the other two. I watched in awe of Seth's speed and his smoothness.

"Look at Daddy go," Hayden said to her boy, whose eyes were on the race.

"I know some guys who are getting lucky tonight," Chloe said, and we all laughed.

"What about Cash?" I asked. "Is he seeing someone?"

"Not for years," Hayden said. "I mean, he goes out with

women. Usually women not from Dragonfly Lake, because one-nighters are his thing. He hasn't had a relationship that I know of since his divorce."

"I didn't know he'd been married," I said.

"Years ago for about a minute." Hayden grabbed the baby bag and pulled out a baby-sized floppy hat and settled it on Harrison's head.

"In reality, they were married for a couple of years, right?" Chloe asked.

Hayden nodded.

"What happened?" I couldn't help asking, turning my attention away from the guys, who were too far away to see details. I was trying to imagine the guy who didn't talk much having a serious relationship.

"Karla was an interesting person but not the right one for my brother. I don't think anyone was surprised when it didn't work out."

"I absolutely get that," I said quietly, my mind veering to my ex.

Hayden's attention zeroed in on me. "Thinking about Trey?"

I nodded. "He's a great person…"

"Just not the right one for you?" Chloe asked.

"Yeah," I said on an exhale. "My friend Drea said I would know if he was the right one for me, and I didn't."

"I don't know Drea, but I think she's right," Hayden said.

"I felt bad for doing that to Trey," I said, "until he made it clear he's fine and having a grand time with someone else."

"If he can move on so fast, it confirms you were right," Chloe said, which led me to believe she'd seen Trey and the blond woman online. I still hadn't looked, and it felt good to not live and die by what the media said for once in my life. To not even know what the media was saying.

"Here's to the right decision, even when it's hard," Hayden said, lifting her water bottle.

"Cheers." I clunked my bottle with theirs.

"Cheers," Chloe repeated. "I'm glad you came out with us today. It's good to get to know you better. I know you're important to Seth."

At that, I glanced out at the guys, who were nearing the shore. Even though James kept me in good shape, I was reasonably sure I couldn't swim that far at a snail's pace, never mind at a sprint.

"You two seem… good together," Hayden said, her head tilted.

"I agree. Really good. Are you sure there's not more than 'for now' going on there? I've never seen Seth like this with someone, and I've known him for most of my life." Chloe scrutinized me too.

"He's always aware of where you are and what you're doing," Hayden said.

"In a non-creepy way," Chloe added, making me laugh.

It was easy to laugh when I spent time with Seth—and his family. It was a fun, low-stress time-out from my real life.

"I like him. A lot," I admitted. "But we agreed to the month I'll be here. Neither of us wants more."

"He sort of seems like he could want more," Chloe said, and Hayden narrowed her eyes thoughtfully and nodded.

"No," I said with a little laugh, trying to reassure them. "I can't see how that could ever work out. He's entrenched here, and I have to go back to the real world, well, my real world and get back to work." My stomach dropped at the thought, but I didn't have to think too hard about that right now. I still had two more weeks.

"Tell us more about your real world," Chloe said. "I mean, I know Nashville. I lived there until a few months ago. But are you doing a new album soon, or what's the plan after your time here?"

"I'm under contract to record another album before the

end of the year. We'll be picking songs when I get back, getting organized, and we'll start recording in September."

The thought of going through songs my dad had hand-picked for me to narrow down gave me a sick feeling in my gut. Or maybe it was just all the food I'd eaten and followed up with swimming. Wasn't there a rule about not swimming after you ate?

I was pretty sure that rule was a myth, and I was fairly certain that my nausea was caused by my thoughts. I needed to figure out what to do about that situation soon and figure out a way to get my dad to let me put a couple of my own songs on my album. But not today. Today was for fun and sun and… a boat.

"It sounds fascinating," Chloe said. "I know so little about the music industry even though I was right there next to it for so long. I have to admit that I'm loving the small-town life though."

"The small-town life or my brother?" Hayden asked with a knowing grin.

"Holden's the main draw. You know me too well," Chloe admitted. "And I just want to throw this out there, Everly: if you'd told me a year ago that I would fall in love, get married, and move to Dragonfly Lake, I would've told you you were insane. And now here I am."

"Happy as a clam and a mama to be," Hayden said.

Chloe nodded once emphatically. "So just keep an open mind. Like your friend said, if Seth turns out to be the one for you, you'll know."

"I'm glad you and Holden got together after all those years," I said. They'd told me the story of how they'd been friends since they were little, had gotten married for business reasons, and finally realized they were meant to be together. "Seth is exactly what I need right now, but we're both dedi-cated to ending it when I leave. No long-distance stuff, no two-cities commute, no ties. That would put too much pressure on what we have right now."

Hayden tilted her head again, as if she didn't believe me.

"Really. You can't argue that I'm in the right headspace for a real relationship," I said with a laugh. "I'm a hot mess and all the other things the press is saying."

"You're none of the things the press is saying, except maybe confused," Chloe said kindly. "But I get it. You can't think about the future right now. It sounds like you're still processing the past."

"Exactly," I said, grateful for her understanding.

As the guys approached the boat at full speed, with Seth in front, Zane close behind him, then Cash a ways back and Holden on his tail, I tried to yank my mind back to the present. I had to admit, only to myself, that there was a big, flashing section of my brain that was thinking *if only things could be different… If only Seth and I could have a future…*

CHAPTER 20

Call me a simpleton but I loved full-day boat outings with my family. Even with Holden's gotta-talk-to-every-damn-body take on life, Hayden's chattiness, and Cash's grouchiness, it was good to get out on the water with them, and one of these days, I hoped our dad and Faye could join us too.

Today had been like any other boating day—except not. Today had been more. Having Everly by my side, as she got to know my siblings and their spouses, receiving a private smile from her from time to time, was exhilarating. It was another one of those memories that would be bittersweet once she was gone, definitely a day I wouldn't forget anytime soon.

All of us but Cash had come back to my place afterward and grilled burgers and brats. Cash had insisted on going into Henry's to help with dinner service, even though Zinnia had it completely under control. If it wasn't the heart of summer and ninety-five degrees today, everyone likely would've stayed for a fire in the pit, but Hayden and Zane had headed home after dinner to get Harrison to bed, and Holden and Chloe left shortly after.

Everly and I had showered, spent some quality naked time together in my bed afterward, and had ventured out to the deck to look at the stars. Once she was settled, I went back in to forage for snacks and wine.

I returned with a large bowl of buttered popcorn—real butter at Everly's request—and two glasses of her favorite white. As I approached her there in the darkness, I couldn't help feasting my eyes on her like I always did. An odd look crossed her face for an instant as I set the popcorn on the table and handed her one of the glasses.

"What was that?" I asked.

"What was what?"

"That look. You had a thought, and it wasn't all sunshine and light."

She popped a few kernels of corn in her mouth and chewed, closing her eyes in bliss for a couple seconds. "Mmm. Butter is the best." I let her finish chewing her food, wondering if she would answer my question or not, vaguely thinking her trainer, James, needed to lighten up about two hundred percent on her diet.

"I can't figure you out," she finally said as I took a swallow of the sweet wine that was growing on me.

"I'm pretty much an open book," I said lightly, even as I had the thought that I absolutely wasn't. Hadn't been since grad school.

"Why aren't you married or hooked up in a long-term relationship or otherwise happily involved? You're literally one of the kindest, sweetest guys I've ever known. You're scary smart, successful in your business, and you get along well with your family, who's awesome, by the way."

Laughing, I said, "Are you done?"

Everly didn't laugh back and didn't return the lightness. "You have an endearing protective side, and you're unselfish and humble and funny as well. Like, seriously, where's the disconnect? What are your flaws, Seth?"

Oh, hell. I blew out an attempt at a laugh, but my insides tensed up. "I have plenty of flaws, Ev." *So many fucking flaws.*

"I haven't seen them yet," she said, glancing over at me.

I didn't meet her gaze. I couldn't. Because I was anything but the perfect picture she was trying to paint.

"How have you made it to almost forty without any serious relationships?" she persisted.

"I'm only thirty-seven," I corrected, "which is closer to thirty-five." Was I trying to divert? Maybe. Probably.

I set my wine down on the table, my gut churning. Most days, I buried shit deep and played one hell of a game of denial, but with Everly, I felt like a fraud and a dishonest son of a bitch.

"Did you have a girlfriend in high school?" she asked.

"A few. Nothing serious." I was only half paying attention to the Q and A. I'd broken out in a sweat. My heart had sped up, and it felt like something was compressing my lungs, until I blurted out, "I had one in college."

Her brows shot up in surprise and a smile tugged at her lips. "A girlfriend?"

"What I thought was a serious relationship."

Her smile disappeared. "Oh? It wasn't?"

Fuck. I couldn't believe I was going to do this, but something compelled me to be honest with her the way I hadn't even been honest with my family.

"It… wasn't." I forced myself to take in a full breath and bent forward, resting my elbows on my knees, because I couldn't stand to see her expression as I revealed how badly I'd fucked up in the past. "Her name was Gail. She was my professor when I was in grad school."

"In New York, right?" Everly showed no hint of astonishment that I'd gotten involved with my professor, and I suppose, since I'd been a grad student, that could almost be excused, almost seen as not a slipup in ethics. Almost but not quite, but that was the least of it.

I nodded. "It was my last year of school when I was assigned to her for a graduate seminar. There were a lot of one-on-one meetings required, and the attraction was instant." I cringed to think about it now. "Long story short, we got serious. I thought I was in love. I thought she was in love. Until the beginning of the next semester, when her husband found out about me."

Everly gasped. "Did you know…?"

Shaking my head, I said, "She'd neglected to mention she was married. We were careful and discreet, I assumed because of her job."

"It wasn't quite because of her job, huh?"

"Not exclusively, though she ended up losing it anyway."

"God, Seth. I'm so sorry."

I sat back and looked up at the night sky, not really seeing the speckled canvas of stars, feeling sick at my stomach. "That's not the worst part," I managed.

She whipped her head toward me.

"It turned out she was pregnant. Early stages. She hadn't told me or her husband before he found us out."

The night sounds of the insects seemed to get louder, more emphatic, as they were the only sound for several long seconds while Everly apparently let that sink in.

"Whose baby was it?" she finally asked in a quiet voice.

I swallowed hard on any of the feelings trying to awaken. "It was mine."

"So you're a dad?" she asked tensely.

I ran my hands down my legs, thighs to knees, my eyes locked on my fingers. "She lost it a few weeks later." I swallowed hard, seeing nothing. "Shortly after her husband killed himself."

"Oh, my God." She grabbed my hand.

I leaned forward again and coached myself through some

deep breaths, reminding myself of all the truths I'd figured out in counseling in the months following the worst time in my life.

You didn't know she was married.

You were not responsible for her decisions.

You were not responsible for his decisions.

You were only responsible for your decisions, and you didn't have all the info you needed to make the best ones.

That's what still killed me, that I was so fucking naive and foolish.

"Nobody here knows," I said once I could breathe again. That was the one redeeming thing about the entire nightmare. While the local media back east had been all over the story and ruined Gail's and her husband's lives and done me no favors, it hadn't gotten back to Dragonfly Lake.

"Your family?" Everly asked, and I shook my head. "A good friend? Like Nick or Levi or someone?"

Again, I shook my head. "I had a counselor in Nashville for a few months. That's the only person I've told the story to. The entire college town knew, thanks to the press, and that was godawful enough."

I felt her studying me, though I still didn't meet her gaze. Instead, I closed my eyes, wondering why the hell I'd vomited all of this out tonight.

"That's why you have such a distrust of the media," she said.

"They don't give a thought to the people whose lives they're affecting with their 'stories,' whether they're true or not."

"No, they don't." When I expected her to distance herself from the train wreck that was me and my past, she rested her head on my shoulder and squeezed my arm.

I greedily took the comfort she was offering, a little stunned that she'd accepted my story so easily.

"It must've been awful," she said after a while. "All of it.

And to think you went through it alone…"

I didn't reply. She'd nailed it. Except *awful* didn't really do it justice. But it was all in the past, and that's where I intended to keep it. "This is one of the reasons we could never go public with us. Why we can only be short-term and private," I said. "The media will be all over any new man you're seen with."

"That's true," she said quietly, pensively. "I wish I could say otherwise, but…"

I nodded. "I can't let my past get out. For my sake or yours."

"I get why you don't want to relive any of it…" She trailed off, like there was something else she wanted to say.

"Go ahead and say it."

"Say what?"

"Whatever you're thinking. That I'm a bad person, that I'm an idiot, that we should stop seeing each other now."

Everly let out a quiet laugh. "Really? I hope you know me better than that."

I hoped I did too, but I was feeling damn vulnerable after spilling all of that, and while I didn't think I was a bad person, I still, all these years later, felt deep shame for being so naive and clueless at twenty-four.

I let out a shaky exhale, feeling drained like I hadn't in years. We'd been in the sun all day, with lots of swimming, and that could drain a guy on a good day, but this was an emotional exhaustion on top of it that took everything out of me.

"What I don't understand," she said quietly, "is why you didn't tell your family, Seth. You have a good one. You and your siblings seem supportive. I get the impression your parents would've been understanding too. How could you weather such a big, tragic time by yourself? *Why* did you?"

"I'm just a lone wolf," I tried lightly.

She wasn't having any of it.

"It's good that you went to counseling. I bet that was hard."

"It wasn't a picnic."

Elizabeth Guernsey had been a no-nonsense, intuitive, and intelligent therapist who'd helped me stop blaming myself for Gail's husband's death and the loss of what would've been my child. I'd be so much more screwed up if I hadn't gone to sessions with her for over a year.

"I was a mess for a long time," I told her. "All of this happened in late January of my last semester of grad school. I stopped going to classes and never finished my MBA." Even now, I burned with shame, because everyone who knew me believed I had an MBA.

"You never told anyone? Not even your parents?"

I gazed off toward the dark lake, shook my head. "How could I tell them any of it? I was humiliated. I didn't want them to be ashamed of me."

Everly laced her fingers with mine and leaned into me again. "They wouldn't be ashamed. They love you."

"Maybe they wouldn't, but I was ashamed enough for everyone. I'm supposed to be the smart guy. Throughout school, that was me, the smart kid. In my family, I was the brainiac. So how could I so majorly derail my life by being so dumb? Why didn't I figure out Gail was married, for fuck's sake? I was ready to pop the question to her after I graduated. I thought we were so fucking happy. How could I miss so much?"

"She was deceptive and manipulative is my guess."

"I knew better than to get involved with a professor. One who was eight years older at that. If there was a definition of someone who's foolish in relationship stuff, you'd find my picture."

"Seth, you were twenty-four and in love."

"Was I though?" I asked. "Can you be in love if you don't actually know the other person?"

"You can sure think you're in love."

"I might be book smart, but when it comes to relationships, I'm the dumbest dumb ass alive. That's why I avoid them."

"We all make mistakes in relationships. Look at me." She shook her head. "You don't have a monopoly on that at all."

I managed to yank myself out of my angst and embarrassment enough to consider what she said, and I supposed there was some validity to it. Poor judgment could be labeled a "mistake."

Her mistake had resulted in an uproar of the public, not even limited to country music fans, I'd bet, since people felt entitled to judge celebrities for every little thing. My mistake had resulted in a man's death, the loss of a baby, the loss of a job, and the loss of every ounce of my confidence when it came to romantic relationships.

There was no question that my mistake had much more detrimental, literally life-and-death consequences, but we *had* both screwed up when it came to love.

"I guess I see your point," I conceded.

What I couldn't help noticing was that Everly was coming out of her mistake with grace and self-growth. I'd come out of mine with fear, shame, and the opposite of growth, kind of a shrinking into myself.

"You should tell your family about your past, Seth," Everly said quietly, rubbing my forearm in a slow, soothing motion.

Everything in me tensed at her suggestion.

"I've met them," she continued. "They love you. They'll accept your past, your mistake, whatever you tell them, with love and understanding. If one of them were to tell you a similar secret, would you turn them away, stop loving them?"

"No," I said begrudgingly, because I understood the point she was making, and on some level, I knew she was right. "Of course not."

"Same goes for them. They don't care if you made a mistake. They sure don't care whether you finished your MBA. The biggest contention they'll have is that you didn't tell them before now. Didn't lean on them for support when you were going through hell."

Now, all these years later, I could sort of see what she was saying.

Did telling my family my secrets appeal to me? Not in the least. The thought of it made my gut knot. My instinct was to shut it all down and never speak of it again.

But there was a voice in my head hollering about what a coward I'd been, was still being, and there was a part of me that wanted to try to turn some of that around, as Everly was doing with her own crisis. She made me want to stop running from myself. Made me want to be a braver person.

I leaned forward, my elbows on my thighs, and ran my hands over my face, suddenly feeling hot all over. I felt Everly's hand on my back, running gently up and down it, and something about her touch gave me courage. After blowing out a breath, I nodded. Kept nodding as I worked up the guts to fully commit to doing what I needed to do.

"Yeah," I finally said into my hands, then I straightened, nodding again. "I'm going to tell my family."

Everly took my hand and squeezed it, leaning her head on my shoulder again, offering the silent support I needed—more than I ever could've guessed.

"Only my family though," I added. The thought of everyone else finding out any of it was unbearable, and maybe it said some messed up things about my ego or my pride, but having people find out I never finished my MBA was at the top of the list of embarrassments. Maybe because I'd gone along with the mistruth for so long. I hadn't ever set out to lie about it, but I absolutely let people believe what they wanted, and back then, everyone wanted to believe I got my MBA.

"Only your family," she said. "It's not anyone else's business."

"And that's why you and I can't be together in public."

"Exactly," she said. "I mean, that and the fact that I'm the runaway bride who screwed over country music's favorite son. The double scandal would kill people." Her voice had lightened, and her grin was irresistible and contagious.

"We make quite the pair, huh?" I said with a halfhearted grin.

"We kind of do." She brought my hand to her lips and pressed a kiss to the back of it. "I have a feeling you'll be a little relieved once you've told your family."

I tried to imagine feeling anything but nauseated and shameful but couldn't do it, so my only response was a shrug.

"If it's just your siblings and their spouses and your dad and his wife…" she started, then hesitated until I looked over at her. "I'll go with you if it'll help. Moral support?"

I finally looked her in the eye, gauging whether she was comfortable with that. While she'd met my siblings and in-laws, it would be another layer to meet my dad and Faye. As committed as she was to maintaining her privacy, this was more than a small deal, and fuck if her offer didn't make me grateful as hell.

"You sure?" I asked.

"You trust them as much as your brothers and Hayden, right?"

"I do." There wasn't a doubt in my mind they'd keep Everly's identity secret. "It might be better if we don't let on that we're… involved."

"I agree. I'm up for it, Seth. If you want me to be."

I pulled her onto my lap so she was straddling me and ran my hands hungrily over her soft-skinned thighs and up to her hips, drawing her into my body. Cradling her cheek, I kissed her. "I want you to be," I whispered, "and I'm going to show you how much right now."

CHAPTER 21

I t was a huge mistake to meet Seth's dad and his new wife.

I liked them both. Too much. I didn't want to become more attached to Seth in any way, and meeting these people who were so important to him had the potential to strengthen my attachment.

It was Thursday night, and the whole family had gathered at Seth's house. We'd briefly discussed letting Holden and Chloe host instead, but apparently their neighbor, Loretta Lawson, didn't miss anything, and she'd likely see us coming and going. In the end, we decided even if I went with a minor disguise, it wasn't worth the risk of the gossipy woman figuring out who Seth's "mystery woman" was.

After a busy day at work, Seth had ordered pizza to keep it simple. The nine of us adults had devoured it, sitting at the long dining table on the back deck. Hayden and Zane had brought Harrison, of course, and the crowd-favorite little guy had burned through a jar of green bean mush, a jar of some kind of meat mush, and some plain cooked pasta.

Faye North Henry, Seth's new stepmom and Zane's mother, swore her grandson was taking after his daddy by eating so much. I had no idea what was normal for an eight-month-old, but he was admittedly irresistible and had been passed around from uncle to uncle. There was a part of me that loved watching Seth with the baby, but that was just some kind of hormonal, biological reaction that I needed to ignore.

Seth had repositioned the outdoor table so that one end was protected in the alcove that was surrounded on three sides by the house. That way, if any neighbors tried to steal a gander, they'd be hard-pressed to spot me on that protected end.

Though we'd finished dinner, as well as gourmet cookies from Sugar, we remained at the table with drinks. Seth had spilled out everything about his grad school relationship and subsequent disaster, and unsurprisingly, his family was accepting and understanding.

Hayden had been momentarily outraged that he hadn't confided in her when it was happening, which surprised me not at all, but when Seth had explained how humiliating it would've been to disappoint his little sister, she'd backed down. Holden had taken the story in stride, commiserated with Seth, and that was that. Like, not an issue at all and with an unbothered next topic attitude, which I was learning was how Holden was.

Cash was an interesting guy, a hard-to-know guy. He'd been sitting next to Zane all night, and though both men were quiet types, they had a bond I guessed must be due to their military tie. When Seth had revealed his secrets, Cash didn't say much, but I happened to see a flash of sympathy skitter across his face, which made me suspect he wasn't as badass or grumpy as he wanted people to think.

"Dad?" Seth said when there was a pause in the discussion. "You're quiet."

"He's always quiet these days," Hayden said, her voice full of affection.

"Now that he doesn't have to kick Holden's ass every other day," Cash added.

The sixty-something man smiled, his skin crinkling around his eyes. "Seventy percent of my gray hairs were caused by this one." He nodded to Holden. "But look at him now. The first of my sons to get his act together, find a good woman, and give me another grandchild." He winked at Chloe. "You're the best decision he's made yet, my dear."

"I can't argue with that," Holden said, taking his wife's hand in his. "You really had no idea of anything Seth was going through back then?"

"How would I know?" Mr. Henry said. "Seth didn't communicate a whole bunch while he was off at school. It took your mom a good year to get used to having him so far away, talking only once a week, if that, but we knew he was doing what he needed to do. We thought he was happy."

"I was for a lot of the time," Seth reassured.

The words were overridden by a shadow of regret that crossed his face, but I, sitting right next to him, might've been the only one who noticed. I gave his wrist a subtle squeeze under the table, determined to maintain the front that he and I were only friends. We'd let the siblings know that would be our story. Thankfully the topic hadn't come up once the senior Henrys arrived. I didn't like to deceive them, but we couldn't exactly tell them we were having casual sex with an agreement of no future.

"If you'd told us you were just short of your MBA, we would've been just as proud of you," Mr. Henry said. "I still am, son."

Simon Henry was one of those kind, quiet types who I could tell was a supportive and nonjudgmental father. I couldn't imagine him ever trying to steer any of his kids' careers or lives in the direction he wanted them to go. After spending the past two hours with him, I'd say he was the quintessential opposite of Eddy Ash.

According to Seth, Mr. Henry had had his years, as they were all growing up, when he'd dished out discipline and consequences as necessary. He wasn't a pushover, but watching him now, with his grandson Harrison on his lap, I could tell the man was a teddy bear.

"You're awesome, Seth. We all know it," Hayden said lightly but sincerely. "This changes nothing."

"I may be the new girl here," Mrs. Henry said, "and I've only known you for a few months, Seth, but you're a remarkable young man I'm proud to call my stepson."

"Thanks, Faye," Seth said. I sensed that, because he was more formal with her, he was striving to be polite, but if anyone else at the table had called him remarkable, he likely would've brushed it off.

I wished I could make him see how remarkable he was. Maybe later, when we were alone, in bed…

Wrong moment for those thoughts, I told myself.

Seth's stepmother was one of those genuine, gentle, understanding women who you instinctively knew upon meeting also brooked no trouble. When I learned she'd raised five boys, Zane included, I was sure of it. It was clear she and Mr. Henry were totally in love, and it did my confused heart good to know that kind of connection was possible even later in life. Theirs was the kind of bond I longed for someday. The kind I hadn't had with Trey.

"I appreciate you telling us now," Mr. Henry said. "Hope it brings you some kind of relief to know we don't think any differently of you."

"You're still the badass business brains behind Henry's," Holden said.

"Piece of paper saying you graduated doesn't mean squat in the real world," Cash piped up.

"I'll second that," I said, earning a little upward twitch of Seth's older brother's lips.

"No MBA for you?" Cash asked me.

"Not even an undergraduate degree. I dropped out of the Belmont School of Music after a year and a half."

"You seem to be doing okay for yourself," Holden said with a grin.

"Okay or freaking amazing," Chloe added.

"As is Seth," I said, looking up at Seth, willing him to see the truth in what we were all saying to him.

Little Harrison, who'd been contentedly bouncing on his grandpa's lap and occupied by a teething ring with hippos and bunnies on it, let out an unhappy cry. Every head at the table turned his way.

"What's wrong, baby?" Hayden cooed, looking ready to leap to his rescue.

Mr. Henry wrinkled his nose. "You smell like a sewer, my little man. Phew."

Harrison cranked up more loudly, getting both his lungs into his wails.

"Harry baby, is Grandpa being mean to you?" Holden asked as he stood, then went around to the boy. "Come here. Let's go get rid of the poo." He lifted Harrison high above his head, which made the baby's cries pause for a couple of seconds and his eyes go wide. Holden sniffed, frowned, and said, "Phew is right. What are they feeding you that you smell like that?"

Harrison's cries lessened as Holden kept up a running commentary in his nephew-spoiling voice on their way inside the house. "Diaper bag is where?" Holden called out.

"In the living room, by the sofa," Hayden replied. To Chloe, she said, "I never thought I'd see the day when Holden would volunteer for diaper duty."

"He can't wait to be a dad," Chloe said.

"He'll be a good one," Mrs. Henry declared. "He's incredible with Harrison and even Calvin and Jasper and Wyatt. Those are our other grandbabies," she said to me.

"Calvin and Jasper are Mason and Eliza's boys," Hayden added, "and Wyatt is Gabe and Lexie's son. Speaking of Lexie, did you decide what mural you're having her do in the nursery, Chloe?"

"We did." Chloe's enthusiasm rang through her voice. "We'll have a forest and a lake and lots of colorful dragonflies."

"I love it," Hayden said. "That crib and changing table in the light wood will be perfect then."

And just like that, the discussion of Seth's tragic, life-transforming secret was set aside, in a good way. To me, it said these people were here for him when and if he wanted to talk more about it, but they weren't fazed by it. Sympathetic, yes. Concerned about what he'd gone through, without a doubt.

While the rest of the table discussed due dates and whether any of Zane's brothers and sisters-in-law would be adding to Faye and Simon's grandchild count, I studied Seth from the side, watching for signs of remaining angst. He laughed with the others, stayed engaged in the discussion, and seemed lighter somehow. Less burdened, and weirdly, I felt less burdened for him, when I hadn't even been aware of the depth of my concern for him.

Before Holden could return with Harrison, Chloe stood, gathering her and Holden's plates. "I'm going to check on those two. I wouldn't be surprised to find them both asleep on the couch."

"Oh, I would," Hayden said. "Harrison's our little night owl. He'll be up for a couple more hours minimum. My brother, on the other hand... Yeah. You should go check." Hayden stood as well and gathered her dishes.

Seth and I stood to do the same just as Mr. Henry asked Seth about the house remodel. Next thing I knew, the men had escaped to the garage to look at some new saw Seth had purchased, because power tools, I guess?

Hayden, Chloe, Faye, and I gathered in the kitchen, cleaning up, though there wasn't much to it besides storing what little leftovers there were, disposing of pizza boxes, and putting plates in the dishwasher. Hayden disappeared for a couple of minutes to the second floor, where we could hear Holden playing noisily with Harrison.

"I'm so glad you were here tonight with Seth," Faye said as she rinsed plates.

"Same," Chloe said. "You're good for him, Everly."

"I'm just thankful he's finally been honest about what happened," I said, ignoring the *good for him* comment completely, hoping she remembered the front that Seth and I were only friends. "I can't imagine not telling anyone."

"Simon says Seth has always been one to solve his own problems," Faye said. "He keeps things to himself, more than is healthy. I'm with you, Everly, really pleased that he felt like he could confide in all of us." She placed the last plate in the washer, straightened, and, finger pressed thoughtfully to her chin, gazed into the distance. "What he must have gone through… That poor boy… Only twenty-four years old, hundreds of miles from home, and what a tragedy."

"I can't imagine," Chloe said.

"Your bond with him must be quite strong for him to finally open up," Faye said. The words were uncomfortable enough, but the knowing look she gave me told me she suspected Seth and I were more than friends.

"We talk a lot," I admitted, then laughed. "He's a saint to spend time with me. My first week here, I was a hot mess and climbing the walls from so much solitude on top of all the drama." I leaned over to put the rest of the silverware into the dishwasher, appreciating the excuse to hide my face for a few seconds. "He didn't have to give me the time of day once the rental agreement was taken care of."

"He's a pretty good guy," Chloe said.

"He is, but I'd wager there was more to it than innate goodness," Faye said, again with the knowing look that made me squirm like a tough, prying interview with a reporter.

"We…" I grabbed the sponge from the back of the sink and wiped at a dollop of pizza sauce on the counter. "We're spending a lot of time together while I'm here, but when I go back to Nashville in a week and a half, that'll change."

"When you go back to Nashville in a week and a half, we're doing lunch," Hayden said as she walked back into the room. "Like, weekly. My brother may be a commitment-phobe wimp, but I don't plan to lose touch with you."

"I'd love that," I said truthfully. "I haven't had a lot of opportunity for true local friends since Drea got married and moved to the West Coast."

"I know the brewery keeps you busy, Chloe, but you're invited too. And you, Faye, of course."

With a laugh, Faye said, "You don't need your mother-in-law crashing your girlfriend lunches, but you know I'll lunch with you anytime."

"I'd love to see your store, Hayden," I said. "Seth says you have some great pieces."

"Yeah? Are you in the market for anything or just want to see what we do at Henry Interiors?" Hayden raised her brows, her face warm and anything but pressuring.

"Just curious," I said as Chloe soaped up the dishwasher then closed it. "Actually…" I hadn't thought this all the way through, but I blurted out, "I might be in the market. I'm" —*breathe, Everly, you know this is the right thing*—"I'm going to move out of my parents' house."

Hayden clapped her hands together, enthusiasm etched on her pretty face. "Ooh. First time?"

After another big inhale, I admitted, "First time. Long overdue but… still scary." I glanced at Chloe and then Seth's stepmom and saw nothing but warmth in both of them, so I relaxed a notch.

"Well, we can help that be less scary," Hayden said. "This is big! Are you thinking of buying a house or renting something?"

I had the money to buy whatever I wanted, but… "Renting. Baby steps." I laughed nervously.

"Moving out can be exciting," Faye said, "and you have this design expert at your disposal." She nodded toward Hayden.

"No design charges," Hayden said. "I just love helping people make their nests, and your first one is super important."

"I'll go along if you want company," Chloe said, "but I bow down to Hayden's skills. She's a design genius."

"I still have to break the news to my mom and dad." Over the past week or so, although I hadn't spoken to my mom again nor heard a word from my dad, it was becoming clear as day that I needed to make some drastic changes in my life.

"Surely they'll understand?" Faye questioned, and of course she couldn't imagine what my domineering parents were like because she didn't seem to have a domineering bone in her body.

"Probably not," I admitted, "but this is something I have to do."

"Absolutely," Chloe said.

My mind was spinning now that I'd said the words out loud, committed on it to someone other than myself. "Also… could you give me the contact info for that indie producer you know, Hayden? Tucker Steele's wife, I think you said."

"Gin Verdinelli, or Steele now. Yes. She's a wonderful person and apparently a musical wizard. Are you looking to go indie?" Her perfectly arched brows shot up her forehead again and her eyes sparkled.

"I'm under contract with a label. I have to be back in the

studio this fall," I explained, "but I was hoping to maybe play around with some of my originals. A side thing. Just for fun," I reassured them. "But I'd pay Gin full rates, of course. If she has any interest in doing this."

"I don't know Gin personally," Faye said, "but any producer would be crazy not to want to work with you, hon."

"You're sweet," I told her. "I guess I'll find out." I hoped the laugh I let out covered my nervousness.

Hayden had her phone out, and my own phone—the private one she'd had Seth get for me—dinged with a message. "Gin's contact info. Tell her you got it from me. And if you're ever open to a private audience when you're working with her, sign me up."

"Thank you," I said; however, the head spinning was not slowing down. But in a good way, mostly. Was there trepidation about talking to my parents? Yeah, I couldn't deny that. But now, with these three women cheering me on, I was also more than a little excited to take steps toward independence. Better late than never, right?

"So moving out, starting a side indie project for fun, you've got some big things going on," Hayden said.

I laughed out an exhilarated exhale. "Yeah. I guess I do now. You're the first people I've told—besides Seth."

"It's all going to be good," Chloe said. "And look at it this way, on moving day, you've got bunches of strong Henry and North guys who can help you."

"Yeah," I said, trying not to let my smile waver.

By that time, just a few weeks in the future, my time with Seth would be over. But maybe we could keep in touch until I found an apartment. Especially if I started looking now.

And maybe, if he helped me move…

For the first time, I started to wonder if there was a way we could make this—us—work for longer than just a month. Scary question, that, but as the men rejoined us, it was one I couldn't dislodge from my head.

CHAPTER 22

Dragonfly Lake was turning out to be good for my soul in so many ways.

Three weeks ago, when Drea's husband, Tim, had suggested it, I'd been full of doubts and fear and shame and confusion. Now, with less than a week until my apartment lease ended, I'd turned a corner and was starting to see how I'd gained so much. Self-confidence, clarity, a really hot temporary boyfriend, and—something I'd never in a thousand years expected—girlfriends.

Hayden, Chloe, and I were on my balcony, the two of them flanking me but not so much for strategic reasons as that's just how we'd landed when we'd come out here nearly an hour ago.

It was July Fourth, and from what I'd seen from afar and heard about, this small town did the Fourth up right and then some.

According to Seth, the population had tripled overnight, with tourists, vacationers, weekenders from Nashville, Memphis, and Chattanooga, and residents alike out and about, eating, sunning, boating, shopping. While a lot of businesses in other cities closed down for the holiday, Dragonfly Lake's downtown was open, hopping, and raking in the money.

I'd had to fight the urge to put on a disguise, walk downtown, and explore to my heart's content. Hayden had told me there was a paper store, a bookstore, a yarn store, a gift shop, a souvenir shop, plus my new favorite bakery, and apparently much more. I longed, more than I'd ever longed before, to be a "normal" person and wander around without having anyone recognize me, talk to me, take my photo, stalk me, or stare at me.

Seth had worked at the restaurant for most of the busy day, then he'd come home and we'd had a private cookout with Holden, Chloe, Hayden and Zane on his deck again. His dad and stepmom were spending the day with some of Faye's boys and their wives and children at one of Gabe North's vacation rentals on the other side of the lake. They'd be missing the sunset boat parade on this side, but we'd all see the same fireworks show they put on from the center of the lake once it was fully dark.

"Boats should start coming in fifteen minutes," Hayden said excitedly. "I wish Harrison was awake, but we pay for it whenever we mess with his sleeping schedule." Her son was inside, sleeping in a playpen in my bedroom.

"He'll love it even more by next year," Chloe said, her hand skimming over her own still-flat belly. "Plus this gives you a little break. Everyone tells me those will be invaluable."

"Everyone is right!" Hayden said with conviction.

I was looking at the list of boat entries for the parade on the town app. "So Holden and Seth are technically competing tonight?"

"They are, for the first time," Hayden said. "There's a personal category and a business category for best decked out boat. In the past, we all worked together on the Henry's one

—well, I helped until I didn't, thanks to being pregnant and spread too thin. Now that Holden's doing a Rusty Anchor boat, they're head to head."

"God help us if one of them actually wins," Chloe said. "We'll never hear the end of it."

"That's not hard for me to imagine," I said, laughing.

I hadn't had this kind of quality girl time since... I wasn't sure when I'd actually been able to pull it off. Maybe in high school with Drea. Before my life really got out of control with music and career. Yes, I loved certain aspects of my life, but this, the unquestioning support, the easy understanding, the unwavering acceptance, the bond with women I genuinely liked and admired... This was everything.

Well, almost everything. I couldn't deny I was counting the minutes until Seth would come back to watch the fireworks on the lake, and then, hopefully, we could make our own fireworks in his bed.

"I'm so glad we did this while the boys fight it out." Chloe raised her can of soda. "Cheers to us."

"I love you girls," Hayden said, lifting her wineglass.

I'd spent much of the past three weeks overwhelmed with emotions, and here I was again, drowning in them. This time they were good ones—gratitude, affection, belonging. "I'm so damn glad I met you two," I said, my heart full.

As we tapped our beverages together—I, too, was having wine—my phone sounded with a notification from Drea. I swallowed a sip, then pulled it out, because I knew she was planning to spend the Fourth with friends of theirs, and I wasn't expecting to hear from her now.

It was a text message that got my adrenaline pumping.

Trey just texted me because he's been trying to get ahold of you all day on your other phone.

My old cell phone, which I still kept turned off but checked daily for messages. Except today. I'd been otherwise occupied, between watching the heavy lake traffic, writing a song inspired by the intense desire to be anonymous in a crowd, and cooking out with Seth's family.

Did he say anything else? I typed to her.

Nothing. Just wanted to know if there was a better way to contact you. Very distant and "professional."

I blew out a breath, sent Drea a distressed emoji, then told her I'd call him and thanked her.

"Bad news?" Hayden asked.

I looked up to find both girls watching me and realized my body language reflected all the stress pumping through me. "Trey texted Drea, wanting to get ahold of me," I said.

"Your ex?" Chloe asked, reminding me she wasn't a diehard country music fan, which was something I loved about her.

"Hooo, yep," Hayden answered for me. She studied me for another couple of seconds. "Do you think you should call now?"

"I've been wanting to talk to him since I bolted, but… it's the Fourth of July. The parade starts in a few minutes." That might've been a stall, because when you got down to it, talking to Trey was more important than watching some lighted-up boats glide by, at least to me at this moment. I'd been waiting too long to apologize and try to set things right.

"Go," Chloe said. "Call him."

"If you don't, you're just going to wonder all night," Hayden said.

Without a word, I nodded and stood. "Sorry to interrupt the party."

"Please," Hayden said. "This is important. Chloe and I will just sit and eat cookies."

I gave them a halfhearted smile and walked inside. I grabbed my old phone from the end table, unsure if I wanted Trey to have my new number. It all depended on how hostile he was to me.

Since Harrison was in my room, I went in the bathroom for some privacy.

Sitting down heavily on the closed toilet, I went to my contacts, stared at Trey's photo for a few seconds, thinking how odd it was that now, after everything we'd gone through together, I felt like I was about to call a stranger.

Enough of the nerves and hesitation. I'd been waiting for this for weeks, for better or worse. I hit the button to connect to him.

"Everly," he said after a single ring. I couldn't decipher much from his tone.

"Hi, Trey. Drea said you were trying to track me down. I usually check my messages more often but—"

"I know," he said. "Holiday. Happy Fourth." With that came an uneasy laugh, which was better than anger, even if it was puzzling.

"Thanks. You too. This is weird," I said.

"It is." I heard him blow out a breath as I worked up the courage to say all the things I'd been intending to say. Of course he'd catch me on an off day, when I'd nearly given up ever hearing from him again. It was tough to get my head in the game after two glasses of wine.

I took in a fortifying breath, sat up straighter, playing with the fringe on my cutoff shorts, then went for bust. "Trey, I'm so sorry to leave you the way I did." My heart raced and I felt suddenly overheated. "I..." *Come on, brain. You what?* "If I'd admitted to myself we weren't right for each other before that day, I swear I would've spared both of us the embarrassment..."

"I was pretty upset," he said with another nervous chuckle. "But I've had a lot of time to cool off and figure out you did exactly the right thing."

"Wait... what?" I leaned forward, propped my elbows on my thighs, and wondered what I'd missed.

"It would've been nice if we'd figured things out before

our wedding day," he continued, "but what you said in one of your messages, that we weren't right for each other, not for a full lifetime…" Several seconds passed. "You were spot on, Everly. It took me a while to see it—"

"But you do?"

His laugh now was less nervous, more genuine. "I do." He cleared his throat. "The reason I can see it… Hell. This is hard to say to you." He hesitated for a couple of seconds. "I met someone when I was in Croatia. There was an instant connection. I don't know how to explain it to make it believable, because I don't think I'd believe it if it didn't happen to me."

"Okay…" I sat up, intrigued, relieved, so freaking curious. Was he talking about the blonde woman who'd been all over the media? Someone else?

Trey took an audible breath. "I assume this won't hurt you, based on, well, everything," he said with a half laugh, "but I'm in love, Everly. Like, I can't exactly explain, but what we had, like you said, it was nice, companionable, comfortable. This is different."

"It's more," I said, thinking of the way Seth made me feel.

"Yes. Like you and I weren't right for each other, just like you said, but because of you, when Tihana came along, I could feel the difference."

"Tihana, huh?" I said, smiling. "Pretty name."

All I wanted for Trey was for him to find happiness, and looking back, that was definitely not going to be with me. Not in a bubbly, happy, in-love way. Not like the lightheartedness and joy I could hear in his voice when he responded, "Yeah." I could hear it all, and I found myself nodding.

"I'm happy for you, Trey."

"You're not upset?"

With a little laugh and a shake of my head that he couldn't see, I said, "I'm the one who left you on our wedding day. I'd thankful you don't seem to be upset with me."

"I can't be. I'm… Hell, Everly. In a way, I'm grateful to you for being brave enough, smart enough, whatever it was that made you put the brakes on. It took me a while to see it, but I'm indebted to you."

I exhaled, and all the worry and guilt where Trey was concerned slid right out of me in that breath.

"Anyway, I wanted to let you know what's going on before the rest of the world. Tihana and I haven't released a statement yet, but she's coming back to the US with me."

"Wow."

"I know it must seem stupid fast—"

"Only you and Tihana can decide that, Trey. You know the media will have a heyday."

"I know. They already did when some asshole managed to get a photo of us out on a private yacht."

So it was the blonde. I wasn't surprised to learn that what my mom had made it seem like, what the press had painted it to be—a revenge fling with a woman with large breasts—was inaccurate and purely conjecture based on literally a single second in time that was captured by a camera.

"I haven't seen it, but I've heard. I'm sorry they tried to cheapen a relationship that seems to mean the world to you."

"She's perfect for me. I believe that everything happens the way it's supposed to, though I sure as hell couldn't see that on what was supposed to be our wedding night." He laughed again. "Life is funny. I'm glad you were in mine, Everly, and I hope you still will be on some level. I have no ill will toward you, and I'm sorry it took me so long to reach out and let you know."

"We both needed time to figure stuff out."

"Yes. And shame on me for not even asking before now. How are you doing? You seem to have found one hell of a hiding place. I'm glad, for your sake."

I smiled easily when I said, "I'm actually doing okay. I've met some good people where I'm hiding."

And now that I knew Trey was more than okay, I

suspected I could let go of a lot of my remaining angst. I still had to deal with my parents somehow, sometime, but not today.

"I'm really happy to hear that," he said.

I laughed. "You're just plain happy, Trey, and I'm happy for you." I ran my fist over my heart. "Thank you for calling. Thank you for being a good human."

"Likewise, Everly Ash. We were a hell of a chapter in this book called life, and I wouldn't edit that one out."

Laughing again, I said, "Sounds like you have some song lyrics there. Minus my name."

He laughed with me. "Maybe I do."

"I'm really glad you're getting a happily ever after."

"Thanks, Everly," he said. "I'm hoping for the same for you, my friend."

"You take care, Trey. Good luck with the media."

We said our goodbyes and ended the call.

When I stood in front of the bathroom sink, filling the cup with water for a quick drink, I was taken aback to see tears filling my eyes. After a couple of seconds, it hit me they weren't sad tears. They were relief. Happiness for Trey. Maybe even… hope for myself?

Maybe my parents would never understand what I'd done. Maybe the fans never would. But the ones who really mattered were me and Trey. Based on everything I'd just heard in my ex's voice, there wasn't a single doubt left in my mind that I'd done the right thing.

I drank some water, dabbed at my eye makeup, then headed out to rejoin the girl party of three.

As I retook my seat and held my glass up for a refill of wine, Chloe said, "Just in time for the parade. Look, they're heading this way."

Hayden side-eyed me, as if deciding whether she should ask about the phone call.

"It was good," I said preemptively, and I couldn't help smiling. "Trey's good. We're good. He doesn't hate me."

"That's awesome news," Hayden said. "Wow. I can see your relief in your eyes, your smile."

"Truly," Chloe added.

I nodded.

"If you girls can keep this to yourselves, I'll tell you more. Some of it will be common knowledge soon, but I'd rather that not come from us."

"Of course," Hayden said.

"Given," was Chloe's response.

I told them briefly why Trey was so okay with everything, how content and ecstatic and in love he'd sounded.

"So the woman in the photos…" Hayden said.

"Tihana. Apparently the love of his life."

"And you're okay with that?" Chloe asked.

"So okay with it," I said and meant it with every fiber of my being.

The first boat in the parade—the sheriff's boat, with a big, lit-up star like a badge, plus red, white, and blue lights everywhere—was drawing even with our balcony, and behind it were countless boats against the coral and pink sunset sky.

"This is awesome," I said, taking everything in, savoring the bone-deep relief from Trey's call as well as the solidarity and friendship of these two women, the warmth from the wine and the July evening. "Happy Fourth, girls."

We tapped beverages again. As we did, I noticed a kayaker in the water, just far enough out that they would clear Seth's dock as well as the others along this section of the lake. Watching the parade from a kayak was a smart idea, I thought.

Then, all the thoughts in my head were sucked out in a mind-blanking panic when I saw a camera flash from the kayak and realized it had been pointed at us.

CHAPTER 23

SETH

The morning after July Fourth, I woke up in Everly's bed, registering the tension before I'd even cracked my eyes open. We'd stayed at her apartment, not wanting to risk the mystery photographer getting another glimpse of her if he or she was still lurking.

I had my arm around Everly, spooning her from behind, as if I could protect her from all the things that could hurt her, but what an illusion that was.

I hadn't been here last night when someone potentially got a photo of her. Even if I had been, would I have been able to keep her safe from discovery?

Would she be discovered, or were we losing our minds with worry for nothing?

Easing away from her, I reached to my side of the bed, picked up my phone, and unlocked it. When I rolled to my back, my heart rate elevated as I checked for texts, skimmed the Dragonfly Lake social app, social media, and then went to my browser and did a search for news on Everly to see if her location had been discovered.

There was nothing.

Not even on the Dragonfly Lake app, which normally was the hub for any and all gossip. I went back to that and scanned the posts again, more slowly this time, to make sure I hadn't missed anything.

Apparently Dex McNamara had gotten into a fight with a tourist on the square, Hadley Ballantine was seen leaving the public beach of her own free will with an unidentified male before the fireworks show was over, and Sebastian Dumay and his partner, Patrick Wiggans, had adopted a puppy, showed him off during the boat parade, and then taken him home well before the fireworks began. Also, that Knox Breckenridge guy had watched the fireworks show with none other than Loretta Lawson and Dotty Jaworski. No doubt the two sixty-somethings had loved every second of attention, both from the questionable dude in his early forties, who even I could admit was a looker, and from the rest of the town. In fact, I'd put money on Loretta being the one who'd spread the word.

There was more gossip, but none of it included Everly's name, and since I didn't spot any of Henry's employees, none of it concerned me, so I clicked out of the app and made the rounds on my phone again.

Still nothing.

I finally let out a long exhale, daring to believe Everly's privacy was safe for the time being.

Everly rolled over to me, wound an arm around my middle, and snuggled into my side. I closed my eyes and tried to savor the moment, but it was a battle not to let reality in—she was going back to Nashville in a handful of days.

I tried not to give that truth any space in my brain, but I'd been spending every spare moment I could with her, telling myself I'd catch up on everything else once she was gone. Ignoring the fact that once she was gone, it was going to hurt like a motherfucker.

I'd grown some feelings for her; of course I had. But I still knew it would be for the best for us to say goodbye when she went back to her "real" life.

"Have I been found out?" she asked in a concerned but sleepy voice, her body tensing up again like it had been last night when I'd gotten here after the parade.

"I've looked everywhere online," I said. "Nothing yet."

"Surely it would've hit already, right?"

"I'd think so. If someone was trying to find you and got a photo of you, it would only take seconds for the whole world to find out."

She rolled on top of me, her legs straddling me, hair hanging down on my chest as she bent closer, slowly moving in for a kiss. I let my phone fall to the mattress beside me and growled impatiently, running my hands over the gorgeous globes of her naked ass.

"Mmm. You're impatient this morning," she said, grinning like a she-devil.

I pulled her face to mine and kissed the hell out of her tempting mouth. When we came up for air, I said, "I'm impatient every morning when it comes to you."

"I know," she said with a laugh.

"You love that about me."

"I sure don't hate it." She hovered over my mouth again for a second, her beautiful eyes gazing into mine, connecting us beyond the physical level somehow, making something in my chest dip and swirl. Then her lips were on mine again, and every thought in my head faded to nothing as she grasped my throbbing dick, hurriedly rolled a condom on, and lowered herself onto me, connecting our bodies and our breaths so we were more like one person than two.

An hour or so later, we'd sated ourselves and drifted back to sleep, more relaxed than the previous twelve hours. When I checked the time, it was a few minutes before my seven a.m. alarm would go off to make sure I got my ass to work on time. My daily swimming habit had been put on hold because I wanted to spend every moment of every lazy morning with Everly while I could. It was another thing I'd get back to after.

While my dark-haired beauty snoozed on, I perused my phone again to make triple sure there was nothing about her whereabouts. There was nothing, and I released my breath, then pulled up the Henry's schedule to see who was working today. Another thing I'd let slip—normally I knew the day before who was scheduled. These days, I checked the schedule before going in.

Before I could access the schedule, a message came in from Nick.

I think your secret is out, bro. Or should I say Everly Ash's secret?

Fuck. My heart seemed to skip a beat before racing into overdrive, and I bolted upright, forgetting to ease away from Everly.

"What's wrong?" she said in a sleep-roughened voice.

Reeling myself in, not wanting to alarm her until it was necessary, I said, "I don't know yet." Then I typed a reply to Nick.

What are you talking about?

As I waited for him to answer, I paced out of the bedroom, into the living area, thinking on some level that I would hide my distress from Everly.

I'm at the diner with Gran, Nick texted. *Everyone's chattering about Everly Ash being your secret renter and your secret lover and how she must've been hiding here since bolting from her wedding. How much of it's true?*

I ran my hand through my bedhead hair, thinking through my options here. Normally, Nick would be one of the first I'd level with. I trusted him. But he was sitting in the middle of a bunch of gossip-hungry townspeople who'd probably already guessed he was texting with me.

"Seth?" Everly came out of the bedroom wearing one of

my T-shirts she'd latched on to and taken from my place. The sleeves went to her elbows and the bottom reached to her mid-thighs, engulfing her. I loved the way she looked in my shirt. Loved knowing she had nothing underneath. "Is it out? Does everybody know?"

I inhaled slowly as I took in the alluringly rumpled sight of her, and the thought flitted through my head that this was it. Everything between us would be different going forward. I wasn't sure how, didn't have time to think that through, but it was something I just *knew*.

I wanted to soften the truth, protect her, but in the end, that would do more harm than good. "I'm trying to find out. I suspect they do."

Everly expelled a breath, then nodded. My phone vibrated with another message from Nick.

Can I assume your silence is confirmation?

Son of a bitch. I tried to think of what to do, how to handle this.

I guess you can assume what you want but that doesn't neces-sarily mean it's true, I punched out on my phone.

Hey, this is me, Nick replied. *I'm not the enemy. I wanted to give you a heads-up about what's going down here.*

Everly was at my side now, reading our conversation, and I let her. She needed to be as armed as possible.

If I don't tell you anything, you can't confirm anything, I typed to Nick. *I'm on my way there. I'll handle it.*

"I'm going with you," Everly said, rushing into her bedroom. By the time I got to the doorway, she'd whipped off the tee, and damn if I didn't wish like hell we could just burrow in here together for another day or another year.

I yanked my mind from her killer body, picked up my shorts from the floor, and pulled them on. "That's a bad idea. Then your secret really will be out, Ev. Think this through."

"I've thought it through. It's time." She took out clean clothes from a drawer. "There's no way around it, Seth.

Someone knows. Someone has proof, so even if I continued to hide, it wouldn't work. There won't be any privacy." She came over to me, went up on her toes, and pressed a quick, distracting kiss on my lips. "I know from experience that the best way to handle it is to come forward with grace. So that's what I'm going to do."

"I might be able to convince everyone it wasn't you…"

"I don't want you lying outright. Look, I appreciate that you want to fix this for me, but I have to start solving my own problems. I'm going to take a two-minute shower, throw on some clothes, a hat, and some sunglasses, and go to… Where did Nick say he was?"

"Dragonfly Diner. I'm going with you."

"Not in the shower, you're not, or it won't be two minutes." She kissed me again, then whirled around and headed to the bathroom, clean clothes in hand.

As much as I wanted to make this problem go away for Everly—and if I was honest, for me too, because dammit, I wanted my last four days with her—I couldn't help but be proud of her for stepping up and being determined to face this herself. I'd be by her side the whole way. If my connections to the people in this town could help her at all, I'd be all over it.

With a glance at the time, I called to Everly in the shower, "I'm heading to my place for clean clothes, then I'll take you to the diner."

CHAPTER 24

Within ten minutes, Seth and I were in his SUV, heading toward downtown Dragonfly Lake.

Downtown, it turned out, was only two blocks from his house. There were cars parked everywhere, and he drove slowly around the square, made up of Hummingbird Drive on three sides and Main Street on the fourth, looking for a place to park.

We'd decided not to walk in spite of how close it was so there'd be less chance for people to notice me ahead of time. Though I wasn't in disguise, I was in semi-under-the-radar mode in cutoffs, a Maren Morris concert tee, flip-flops, my/Tim's Seattle ball cap, and some everyday sunglasses, as opposed to giant ones that hid half my face.

My secret phone, as I'd started to think of it, dinged with a message from Chloe.

Morning, Everly. I hate to be the bearer of bad news, but I think your secret's out. Holden and I are at the diner and everyone's talking. She ended it with a frowning emoji.

Nick already warned us and we're on our way, I typed to her.

"See if we can join them," Seth suggested when I read him Chloe's message.

Do you have room at your table for two more?

You bet. To the left of the door, along the windows. We just ordered, so we're not far ahead of you.

We'll be there soon, I told her.

Sitting with them would allow us to avoid waiting conspicuously for a table and causing a stir. I hoped we could just walk in nonchalantly, sit down with Seth's family, and have an uneventful breakfast, but mostly I knew better than to expect that.

I was going into this knowing full well I would be recognized, and I was as prepared as I could be.

Or I would be by the time we walked in the door.

This lack of parking spaces was working to my benefit, giving me more time to brace myself and get my public "face" on.

"There's the bakery you love so much," Seth said, pointing, and I glanced over in time to see the sign for Sugar and its colorful, irresistible window display.

"Someday I want to go there," I said. Maybe that someday would be today, because in a few more minutes…

I turned my attention to the rest of the shops we were driving by, attempting to get my mind off what was coming. There was a big hardware store on the corner, City Hall, the pizza place we'd ordered from in the past, a bar, and there was the bookstore I'd heard about, among at least another dozen mom-and-pop-looking shops.

In the middle of the square was a gazebo, and scattered around the block-sized green space were open grassy areas with old-fashioned wooden picnic tables, beds of all colors of blooming flowers, and sidewalks winding through it all.

"Your town is adorable," I said, wishing I could climb out and explore it.

"This is the first time you've seen it in daylight, isn't it?"

I nodded as he pulled into a diagonal spot, my mind going to the scene ahead.

"You don't have to do this," Seth said once he'd stopped the car.

"I'm going to. And I think we should make it known we're just friends." It was more for his sake than mine, as I was sure I'd already been raked over the coals by the media in every way possible during the past month. There was no sense in Seth having his past dug into, privacy invaded, and all the things that would go along with the general public finding out we'd been more. What was the point, anyway, when our "more" was due to end in a couple of days? That thought caused a knot in my gut even more so than this upcoming public appearance. "Ready?"

"Whenever you are," he said.

When I nodded, he got out. As he came around the front toward my side, I gathered my nerve, then opened the door myself and met him on the sidewalk. We walked in silence, and I had to stop myself from reaching for his hand.

We crossed Main Street and headed to the entrance of the Dragonfly Diner. Hand-painted on the front window was a large, vibrant turquoise-blue, apple-green, and amethyst-purple dragonfly, wings spread in flight, with words trailing its body in a spiral that listed some of the things they served.

"So cute," I muttered.

"There's Holden and Chloe." Seth pointed, and I saw them through the window once I stopped admiring the artwork. Chloe was facing us and smiled and waved.

When Seth opened the door for me, I directed my gaze to Chloe and Holden, smiling like I wandered into the Dragonfly Diner every day of the week to meet friends. Holden was facing this way, and he grinned warmly but didn't stand or make any kind of commotion, which I appreciated. He didn't need to though. I could hear almost-whispers as we walked through, including my name. I could feel people's eyes on me with every step I took. I could also feel Seth right behind me, flanking me protectively, and that helped me breathe.

I slid into the booth next to Chloe, who squeezed my forearm affectionately and said, "You made it," in a normal voice and then leaned in to my ear and whispered, "Are you holding up?"

"Hey," I said warmly and nodded, sensing that two-thirds of the eyes in this place were glued to me. "Thanks for saving us spots."

"Happy to," Holden said, then nudged Seth with his shoulder. "What's up, bro?"

"We're hoping for pancakes," Seth said, which we hadn't discussed, and yet he'd still pretty much nailed what I was in the mood for. Over the past few weeks, my love for sweet desserts had been revealed. I didn't know how I was going to go back to James's food and regimen, but I knew I needed to because my waistband was a little tight.

But not today. Today I needed pancakes or waffles or something with mass quantities of sugar and carbs to get through the next hour.

"Good morning, Seth and friend." A tall, slender man with curly dark hair slid up to the table with a coffeepot and a welcoming smile as he looked me in the eye. "It's a pleasure," he said to me, then added quietly, "I'm a mega fan."

"Oh," I said with my public smile. "It's nice to meet you…"

"This is Patrick Wiggans," Seth said. "He's worked here for ages."

"Twenty-two years, since I first moved to town," Patrick said as he filled both mugs with coffee and then gave Chloe a warmup.

"Might as well own the place by now," Holden said. "You work more shifts than anybody."

"I love starting my mornings at the DD," the enthusiastic

server said. "Your usual ham, cheese, pepper, and onion omelet today, Mr. Seth?"

"At the risk of throwing you off," Seth said, "I'm thinking the maple nut pancakes for a change."

Patrick's brows shot up as he wrote down Seth's order. "Strange things are amiss," he said with a laugh. "And you, beautiful?" He winked when I met his gaze, and I got the impression he'd avoided using my name on purpose, in case it could dissuade someone from recognizing me.

"I've heard good things about your chocolate chip pancakes from Hayden," I said, assuming—correctly, it appeared by Patrick's knowing nod—that the server knew the whole Henry family.

"Miss Hayden usually gets a side of ham for protein."

Knowing this was one of my last "free-choice" meals, I said, "I've been dreaming about some bacon."

"I can make your dreams come true," Patrick said without missing a beat, then he picked up the coffeepot and moved on.

Before I could say anything about how awesome the server was, a little girl approached our table, or me, specifically, with big brown eyes, determination, and nervousness all over her face.

"Hello," I said, managing that professional mix of friendly but not too. It was an even finer line with kids.

"I was wondering if I could get your autograph, please?"

"Sure," I said. I tried to be gracious with fans and rarely said no to autograph seekers, even though, in a place like this, it meant there could be others following this little cutie.

Then again, if the majority of the grown-up world hated me, maybe not.

I took the Dragonfly Diner napkin from the girl and the pen she provided and set them in front of me. "What's your name, sweetie?"

"Jessica." She edged closer to me, watching me intently.

"That's a pretty name," I said and spelled it out loud to make sure I got it right. Jessica nodded.

"You're the youngest Lowenstein daughter, aren't you?" Holden asked with his typical irresistible warmth.

Jessica nodded enthusiastically.

"Your daddy comes to Henry's Restaurant," Holden explained.

"I know," she said, making the rest of us laugh. "I love your songs, Everly" she said as I scribbled a short message and signed my name.

"Why, thank you. That means a lot to me, Jessica." I handed her the signed napkin. "Do you have a favorite song?"

"Umm, I like 'Brown Eyes' the best." She grinned wide, gazing up at me with what I'd come to know as star-struck eyes. Just like always, it made me slightly uncomfortable, but I hid it.

"That's one of my favorites too."

"Jess," a woman a couple of tables over called. "Come on back, honey."

Jessica looked at her mom, then hesitated long enough to look back at me and say, "Thank you!" Then she trotted off to her family's table and I exhaled, smile locked in place, as Holden and Seth both waved at Jessica's parents.

Patrick appeared with Chloe's and Holden's breakfast then, setting down platters with eggs, hash browns, toast, and fruit, all of which looked delicious.

"Eat while it's hot," Seth told them.

"We've got a meeting at nine, so we will," Holden said as he picked up his fork.

"Any idea how this happened?" Chloe asked quietly as she scooped up a bite of eggs. "I looked everywhere online but didn't see any photos."

I'd told Chloe and Hayden about the camera flash after it happened last night, and we'd managed to stay nonchalant, though we'd become more vigilant and turned our lights off, and I'd backed up my middle chair a little for added protection. We hadn't seen anyone else nearby, in the water or on land, so we'd continued to watch the boat parade and then the fireworks.

When the guys had finally arrived—Zane had ridden with Holden on the Rusty Anchor boat, and incidentally, neither they nor Seth had won the best boat award—I couldn't deny how relieved I was, even though that wasn't rational. If someone had snapped a photo of me and planned to share it with the world, there wasn't a thing Seth could do to protect me anymore.

Shaking his head, Seth said, "I've scoured my phone. It doesn't make sense."

Before anyone else could comment, two teenage girls sidled up to me and asked for autographs, and before long, there was a group gathered.

Moments like this never got less overwhelming, and in this little diner in this small town, the group was surely inhibiting business. I smiled a lot, made warm but brief conversation—a skill set I'd honed over the years—and tried to get to each person as quickly as possible, but the crowd didn't seem to shrink.

Holden and Seth and Chloe greeted everyone by name and made conversation while they were waiting for me to sign napkins and shirts and whatever else they could find, which I appreciated. The atmosphere was friendly and respectful. I felt bad for Holden and Chloe, though, and the way their peaceful breakfast had been invaded.

About fifteen minutes in, Patrick made his way through the crowd, his arms stacked with our plates.

"Okay, folks. Time to let these people eat," he said with authority. "Back to your tables, please. Hot plates coming through."

I was more than a little stunned when everyone followed

the server's orders and went back to their places, whether I'd had a chance to talk to them yet or not. My brows crawled up my forehead as I looked at my three table mates. "Wow."

"Patrick doesn't take any static," Holden said. He and Chloe were close to finished with their meal.

"Sorry about your breakfast, you two," I said quietly, ever conscious that, while everyone had given us physical space, they could still hear whatever we discussed if they tried.

"Back at you," Chloe said, grinning.

"Great chance to catch up with folks," Holden said, unbothered as usual.

Seth was only a couple bites into his pancakes when he said, "Excuse me. I'll be back in a few."

He made his way to the back corner of the diner, toward the restrooms, but instead of going in, he approached a woman who was sitting at the counter. After Seth said something to her, she stood and went over to the side with him, and they became engrossed in a private conversation that didn't appear from here to be casual or *hi, how are you.*

Holden followed my gaze. "That's Sage Jensen. Her dad owns the newspaper, sister runs the editorial."

"Oh," I said. "So she's the press?"

"Sage is actually the brains behind the town app," Chloe said. "She developed it herself and runs it. She seems to be really intelligent."

"She's a tech head with a journalism background," Holden said. "Nice girl, knows everyone."

"Like someone else I know," Chloe said with a smile at her husband.

The pancakes were some of the best I'd had, or maybe it was just that I hadn't eaten any for a few years, but I had to put some concentration into not wolfing them down, remembering that even though no one was hovering over our table anymore, likely more than a few were paying close attention to my every move.

I kept one eye on my surroundings, including Seth, who'd moved on from talking to Sage and gone to the restroom. As I turned my attention back to my plate, I noticed a man in uniform making his way from one table to the next. I stuffed another bite of glorious pancake in my mouth and watched him surreptitiously. He spent a couple of minutes addressing the people at one table, joking with them too, it seemed, and then he'd move to the next. Every once in a while, he glanced our way.

Seth returned to the table and must have noticed where my attention was directed, because he said, "That's Sheriff Lopez."

"What's he doing?" I asked.

"I'm not sure."

"What'd you talk to Sage about?" Holden asked.

Seth forked a large bite of pancake, but before he shoved it in his mouth, he said, "Mystery is solved." He stuck the bite in and chewed, and the rest of us were stuck waiting for him to explain.

"We need to leave in five minutes, man. Spill it," Holden said as he tossed some bills on the table that would likely cover all four of our meals.

After Seth swallowed his food, he said, "As I understand it, that was Finn McNamara in the kayak last night. Third oldest," he said for my benefit. "The guy has a photography hobby, and he was out shooting up the holiday yesterday. Late last night, he posted a dozen or so of his photos to the town app, including the one of you three."

My heart picked up speed and I wondered if Seth had missed the posting. Obviously, it didn't matter now, because word was out.

"Sage herself happened to be browsing the app when he posted it, and she recognized you immediately and saw it for what it was—a potential problem for your privacy."

"Normally media outlets thrive on candid shots like that,"

I said suspiciously. I'd picked up a slice of bacon and had torn a bite off, but I was too engrossed in Seth's story to put it in my mouth.

"I wouldn't say Dragonfly Lake journalists are normal," Holden said. "They're community based, not bloodthirsty."

"Sage of course had heard your recent story, knew you'd disappeared after a wedding that didn't happen, and when she saw Finn's photo, she guessed that you'd chosen Dragonfly Lake to hide away."

Like Chloe had said, the woman must be smart. I narrowed my eyes, still waiting for the bad news. Were they going to blackmail me? Insist on an exclusive interview?

"She pulled the photo within a minute of it being posted," Seth continued. "Considering it was after two a.m., hardly anyone saw it."

"But obviously someone did," Chloe said.

"She was able to go into the back end and see that there were nine impressions served before she could yank it down, she being one of the nine. She knew she couldn't do anything about them except hope they didn't recognize you or respected your privacy."

"Apparently that didn't pan out," Chloe said, "otherwise there wouldn't be pandemonium here this morning."

"Hold on," I said, my eyes narrowed. "Back up. I'm confused. Why did she pull the photo down if she knew who I was and if she could tell others had already seen it too?"

"According to Sage, she didn't want any possibility of an out-of-town media outlet to get hold of it."

"That..." I'd never heard of such a thing. Usually they were throwing their "exclusives" in competitors' faces. "Why?"

"To quote Sage directly, 'If she wants to hide away in Dragonfly Lake, then we should let her hideaway in Dragonfly Lake'," Seth said, his voice going up to mimic a feminine tone.

"Except..." I skimmed the diner with my eyes, saying without words, *Everyone knows I'm here.*

"These are all locals," Seth said.

Holden was peering around at each table. "He's right. Every last one. Which makes sense. Normally the tourists come out between nine and ten. The early wave of diners each day is almost all residents."

"Okay..." I was still confused.

"Basically, this town loves a juicy story for itself, but it will also protect its own," Chloe explained.

"That's it exactly," Seth said. "They love that you're here, but they'll do whatever they can to keep you off the larger media's radar if that's what you want. Sage is smart enough to figure out that's what you'd want. So between her staff at the app and her sister's at the paper, they'll see to it that there are no mentions in print or online of you being here in town."

"They're protecting me?"

"Like one of our own," Holden said with a boyish grin.

"Howdy." The sheriff, who was anything but a stereotypical fifty-something old guy, sauntered up to our table. "Hello there, Ms. Ash. Welcome to Dragonfly Lake."

"Thank you," I said. It was impossible not to notice that Sheriff Lopez was, well, hot as hell. "It's a great little town—at least the bits I've seen of it. I'd love to explore more."

"We'd love to have you explore it. I just wanted to let you know that we intend to keep your whereabouts out of the media. I'm afraid privacy in this town isn't a possibility, but there won't be anyone going to the Nashville media outlets or selling out at your expense."

"You're going to enforce that?" I asked with a disbelieving laugh.

"I don't have to. This town loves its gossip, but there's one thing it loves more—keeping our secrets to ourselves. You're our secret now. You've been staying here all along?"

I glanced at Seth, and he gave a barely perceptible nod.

"I have. At a rental property." Seth and Holden and maybe even Chloe might trust this guy, but I wasn't going to be accused of being completely naive and giving him more info than he needed.

"We've got your back, Ms. Ash. Anyone who doesn't will deal with me personally. I hope you enjoy the rest of your stay. Y'all have a good day." With a nod, the sheriff strutted away, and I sat there with my mouth likely gaping open and my eyes wide.

"Is he for real?" I asked.

"He is," Holden said earnestly.

"It's a small-town thing," Chloe agreed.

Seth nodded. "He meant every word."

"There's no way he could enforce that," I said.

"He doesn't have to. It's just how the town is," Seth said. "They've decided to protect you like one of their own. That's not to say someone from the outside couldn't spot you and spread the word, so we'll need to be cautious for the rest of your time here, but the residents of Dragonfly Lake have your back."

I looked from Seth to Holden, seeing nothing but sincerity in their eyes. I shifted my gaze to Chloe, next to me, and she shrugged in a way that said, *What they said*, as if she didn't quite get it either, having been away from town for more than a decade until just a few months ago.

"It's okay," Seth reassured. "They might butt into your breakfast, they might ask for an autograph at the ice cream shop, but they won't be snapping a photo and selling it to the highest bidder."

Knowing Seth's distrust of the media in general, particularly because of his own past, I was certain he understood my situation as well as any non-famous person could. I trusted him with just about everything. My God, I'd trusted him with my privacy since day two. I studied him for several more seconds and saw in his eyes that he believed what he was saying, believed the sheriff's words too.

This wasn't normal. But then, I'd already gotten the sense that Dragonfly Lake was not a run-of-the-mill place. Maybe it would be okay. Maybe I could enjoy the last few days of my escape from real life without worrying about the entertainment sites or the paparazzi.

I could either run back to the apartment, pack up, preemptively return to my Nashville life, and miss out on time with Seth or I could trust what people were telling me, explore this town until Saturday, and then go back to Nashville.

"What are you thinking?" Seth asked.

I held up the bite of bacon and said, "I'm going to savor this bacon and these pancakes, and then I want to explore all the shops, including a stop at Sugar, and did you say there's an ice cream shop?"

Laughing, he said, "Yes, ma'am. I'll call in and let Riley know I won't be in today. We'll make a full day of it."

"I'm thinking a few days," I said. If I had to leave Seth in four days, I intended to stuff as many amazing memories into them as humanly possible so I could take them all back with me when it came time to leave.

CHAPTER 25

The moment I'd been dreading for days—weeks—came sooner than expected.

Saturday morning, my last morning with Everly, I awoke to an empty space on her side of my bed, which jolted the drowsiness away with the speed of a bucket of cold water. I shot up to a sitting position and scanned my bedroom, looking for Everly or signs of trouble or… anything to tell me why she was no longer curled up along my side.

Her clothes from yesterday, which had been carelessly tossed onto the armchair in the corner, were gone, as was her phone from the nightstand. The sun was shining in around the blinds, and I didn't get any sense of danger. My concern receded as disappointment rushed in to replace it. Checking my phone, I saw it wasn't yet seven a.m.

I rose from bed, confused, with a heaviness in my chest I refused to acknowledge, just as I'd been doing all week. I'd face it down later, when Everly was gone.

She must've gone to pack. I would've liked—hell, I'd been counting on—one last morning between the sheets with her, waking together, sating each other's needs, laughing, planning the day.

Of course, the only thing to plan today was her departure.

We'd avoided discussing it all week. Instead, we'd been grasping on to every moment together, stocking up our memory banks so they'd be overflowing after she left. Or at least I had, and it'd seemed like we were of a similar mind, but my empty bed told me maybe I was wrong.

For the past four days, since breakfast at the diner, we'd gone out and about, though cautiously. The volume of tourists and outsiders was down after the Fourth but still July high. While the residents of Dragonfly Lake felt strongly about not outing Everly, everyone else was a wildcard, so Everly had done what she called low-key disguising, changing her looks enough that it wasn't immediately obvious who she was if you weren't looking for her but not so much that it looked like she was trying to hide.

We'd gone through the shops of downtown, visited the public and the private beaches, taken the boat out, and I'd taught her to stand-up paddle. With her state of physical fitness, and particularly a better-than-average sense of balance, she'd mastered it quickly.

She, Chloe, and a couple of Chloe's girlfriends, Anna and Olivia, had lunched at Henry's one day, and her raving about the place afterward had won her a special place in my heart—if she hadn't already had one.

I'd worked as little as possible, going in for usually just a couple hours a day, so I could take advantage of the limited time we'd been gifted together. It'd been rewarding to see our little burg through her eyes. I knew I'd remember some of her reactions, the things she'd said, the opinions she'd shared for a long time after she left. I might even see the town I'd always liked in a different light.

Shaking myself out of my reverie, I pulled on clothes without concern for which ones, put my shoes on, and headed through the house to the kitchen. No coffee. She hadn't lingered.

Bolting out the door and down to the yard, I surveyed the apartment, the lawn, the dock, and then I spotted her dark hair on the other side of the boat rack. She sat in the sandy area between the rack and the shore, her arms cradling her legs in front of her, chin on her knees. I blew out a breath of relief, feeling a little foolish for all the bad things my mind had jumped to. I had no right to a last morning in bed with Everly. I was damn lucky to have had all the mornings I'd had, and it would be wise to remember that.

As I made my way across the lush, shaded grass, I wished I had coffees for both of us, some donuts from Sugar, because I knew that was one of Everly's favorite ways to start the day. When I rounded the boat rack, she glanced up at me with a smile. That gorgeous smile that made her eyes shine.

"Hey," she said. "Good morning."

As I lowered to the sand, right alongside her, I said, "Morning. I missed you."

She leaned to me for a short good-morning kiss, then said, "I woke up hours ago. Like, stupid early. I didn't want to wake you."

"You can wake me anytime," I said lightly, suggestively, and it got the response I'd hoped for—that heated sparkle in her eyes.

When her smile dropped quickly and she gazed back out at the water, which was glass smooth today, I frowned.

"What's going through that glorious brain of yours?" I asked.

It took her several seconds to answer. "A lot." She sighed deeply. "That *first day of the rest of my life* cliché is staring me in the face."

"You're making a lot of changes." We'd talked about those changes often. Most of them had to do with the way she handled her dad, rather than letting him handle her, her music, her career. "When do you think you'll talk to your dad?"

A stressful little laugh burst from her. "Whenever I can. I doubt I'll find him sitting at home having a relaxing beverage when I get there."

"It might be a rough discussion, but I have every bit of confidence in you. You're doing what you need to do."

"I am." Her answer seemed almost distracted. "Seth…"

Something in her tone put me on alert, and I sat up a little straighter, uneasy.

"What if we didn't end this?"

"This?"

"Us."

My heart skidded to a stop and then took off, going from zero to one twenty faster than a Bugatti as I tried to imagine the awesomeness of that. Having this gorgeous woman by my side every morning, gazing from my window at the lake with her, identifying the birds on the water. Spending weekends on the boat, sometimes having my family join us, sometimes just the two of us. Sitting around a campfire under the stars, Everly plucking away at a guitar, me with the absolute pleasure of watching her, listening to her.

I reined in my foolish self, reminding myself that wasn't reality. Reality would be… more challenging.

"How would that work?" I asked, then bit down on the inside of my lip, as if that could reel in all the fantastical, blissful imaginings my mind had gone to initially.

"Well…" Everly tilted her head and gazed over at me, a shy smile forming on those kissable lips. "I don't know. There's an awards show coming up where I'd love to have you as my plus-one, for starters."

I swallowed and tried to temper my reaction, at least on the outside. Inside, my mind went to a disappointed but realistic hell no. As much as I liked having Everly in my life, our lives were two entirely different worlds.

"This past month has been" —I let out an overwhelmed, emotional, nervous laugh—"incredible," I finally settled on. "Some of the best weeks of my life."

Her smile was gone in a flash and she narrowed her eyes. "I hear a but."

"It's been like a fantasy, a damn perfect fantasy, in part because it's temporary. We've always known it was temporary. I don't fit into your world, Ev."

I'd put half my life on hold for the past four weeks so I could cherish every moment with Everly while she was on her sabbatical, as she'd been calling it. Had that pause in my life been worth it? Every damn bit. But I knew I had to make this decision with more than my emotions or my dick. This had to be a rational decision, and my brain had a laundry list of reasons it would be a bad idea.

I didn't want to be seen in the media as her small-town chump with a sordid past. Didn't want to be the kept man that Everly Ash was in the position to have. It wouldn't do her image any favors, and what the hell would I do in that world anyway? I was a small-town guy who ran a small-potatoes restaurant, a family restaurant.

Besides, my judgment when it came to romance and feelings wasn't reliable.

When I thought she would debate with me, she said, "You could fit, but you're right. We did say it was temporary. It's just been so good. Good like I didn't know it could be, but it's true that some of that is because it was temporary. I know you weren't officially on a sabbatical like I was, but we've existed in a bubble, huh?"

I let out a breath, relieved and so fucking sad at the same time. "One hell of a bubble, Ev." I wove our fingers together. "I wouldn't change a minute of it... except the turmoil that brought you here originally."

"But it brought me to the good stuff," she said wistfully, "so I can't even regret any of the wedding mistake."

We sat like that for several seconds, gazing at each other with goofy-ass smiles on our faces, then Everly took her phone from her back pocket and checked the time.

She dropped my hand, straightened, then stood. I did as well.

"Can I drive you home?" I asked, wanting to steal another hour with her even knowing it was a bad idea. We had to cut these ties at some point, and prolonging it was doing neither of us any favors.

"I actually called my driver. She's picking me up in a few minutes."

And that, folks, was exactly why we didn't belong together. Why we were ending it. She was Everly Ash. The Sweetheart of Country Music. She had a fucking driver and a full wing in her parents' mansion and a high-dollar contract with a national record label.

"It's not Drea and her husband, is it?" I asked, trying to keep it light.

It worked. Everly laughed. "No. I'd give anything to see Drea, but this is Jules. The driver my dad employs to take me anywhere—except to my secret hideaway when I pull a runaway bride stunt."

"I can see why you wouldn't want to rely on someone employed by your dad in that case."

Light banter. This was what we needed. I didn't want to dwell on the dread of saying goodbye. Didn't want to ruin our last few minutes together with sadness.

"Did you already pack?" I asked.

"I finished just before the sun peeked over the horizon," she said, glancing toward the east. "You didn't miss anything. Today's sunrise show was mediocre compared to some of the ones we've seen in the past couple of weeks."

I wasn't bothered by missing the sunrise so much as by missing her waking up one more time, but I shoved that out of my mind.

"Can I help you bring your bags down then?" Maybe if I kept talking, swallowed a couple dozen times, this lump in my throat would go the hell away.

"Absolutely. I hope you don't mind that I gave your address to Jules."

With a laugh, I said, "I'll just double my rent and start advertising it as the apartment where Everly Ash stayed. I'll be able to retire in a year."

We walked around the boat rack, toward the stairs to the apartment, my eyes locked on the ground, my focus on where to put my foot for every step. At the stairs, Everly sprinted up them, and I followed, sensing she was as full of dread as I was.

"Here we go," she said. Both her suitcases—the one she'd shown up with a month ago and the second one she'd bought online to get all her new stuff home with her—stood just inside the doorway.

I glanced around the place, looking for anything she'd left behind, but there was nothing. It looked neat enough to turn around to another renter at check-in time this afternoon. I didn't have another renter yet, because I'd taken the listing down until Everly was gone. Maybe holding out hope that she'd decide to stay longer?

"You didn't have to clean," I told her. "You paid a cleaning fee when you moved in."

"I was antsy at five a.m. It kept me busy," she confessed as she picked up one of the suitcases and a big bag. I couldn't help but wonder where she'd stuffed that wedding dress she'd had in the Walmart bag.

"I suppose I should be impressed that the Sweetheart of Country Music knows how to clean," I teased as I hefted the other suitcase up.

She shoved at my arm. "You know me better than that."

I did. She might've shown up as the Sweetheart, but she'd

morphed into a self-sufficient, sexy-as-fuck badass who I had no doubt was going to rock her new life.

"Ready?" I asked, forcing nonchalance into my tone.

Everly sucked in a big breath, her chest rising, and said, "Ready. Wait."

I stopped on my way to the door.

"Kiss me here."

So her driver—and the world—didn't see us. Of course. I was glad one of us had the presence of mind to remember that.

I set the luggage down. "Come here." I pulled her to me, eliciting a sexy little gasp from her as my lips settled insistently on hers. My final kiss with Everly Ash had to last me a long-ass time.

Shutting out all the thoughts, I turned my attention to the softness of her lips, the heat of her mouth, the taste of her tongue. I hoped I put all of my feelings for her into that kiss, all the joy and connection and discovery and lust that had made up our time together. With both of my hands around her middle, I grasped her to me, forcing myself to revel in the physical perfection instead of the loss that was imminent.

A couple minutes, or maybe more, had slid by when Everly laughed into our kiss. "Seth. My driver's probably here. I need to go."

With my entire being yanked back to reality, I straightened, loosened my hold on her, pressed a single quick kiss to her lips, and stepped back. "Of course." I smiled, trying for it to look genuine, then grabbed both of her suitcases.

"I can get one," she said.

I nodded at the door. "You're back to being the Sweetheart of Country Music." I strived to insert a light, teasing tone into my voice. "Allow me to get them for you."

Everly rolled her eyes and laughed, and though I was certain she was trying for nonchalance too, there was a thread of nervousness in the sound. "You're a nut," she said, then led me out the door.

At the car—a smooth, luxurious Lincoln SUV that undoubtedly cost more than I would earn in a year—Everly greeted her driver, who'd hopped out and opened the back door when we'd appeared. I continued to the back of the vehicle, where Jules opened the door and loaded Everly's luggage, then nodded at me, like one member of the help to another. I nodded back and told her thank you.

"Goodbye, Seth," Everly said from the interior as I walked back by. I could be the luggage boy for all the warmth in her voice, but I knew that's how it needed to be.

With just a hint of a smile, I nodded at her too and said, "Safe trip back."

I kept walking to the corner of the house, then continued around it, toward the deck steps. Not looking back once. Because I was pretty damn sure I couldn't keep my emotions off my face.

CHAPTER 26

By Thursday evening, I was exhausted and miserable.

I'd been working ridiculous hours at Henry's for a couple of reasons. One, to catch up on all the crap I'd let slide last week to spend time with Everly. Two, to avoid going home to a deafeningly quiet house.

It was just after ten o'clock. Although the bar was still open, the restaurant had been closed for an hour. Most of the staff had gone home, and the few customers left were not the noisy, drunkenly type. People went to the Barn or the Fly by Night for that.

Whitney Neal was the closing bartender tonight. When I'd walked through a few minutes ago, I'd checked in with her to make sure she could handle everything. She could, of course. There were only a handful of patrons left, so I'd not hesitated to head out to the docks. I wasn't even supposed to be at work, so my absence now made no difference to Whitney.

I sat on one of the benches in shadow by the shore. The area was quiet, not another soul around that I could see, though I'd learned after the canoe outing with Everly not to trust that illusion. There could be eyes anywhere.

I'd been fighting off thoughts of her for the five days since she'd left, reminding myself there was no point in thinking about her. The sooner I got her out of my mind, the sooner I'd feel better.

I apparently had a long fucking time to go, because she was always there in my head, even when I was occupied with something else.

"Whitney said you were out here."

My shoulders jerked at the sound of Cash's voice nearby.

Asshole.

"I would've thought you'd go somewhere else then," I snarled.

"Guess I'm just a glutton for punishment."

My older brother came over to my bench and sat right next to me, as if he was going out of his way to piss me off. Not that it took much.

For several minutes, he didn't say anything, just breathed in my fucking air and grated on my nerves. The whole world had been grating on my nerves, but Cash was abrasive on a good day.

"What the hell do you want?" I finally growled at him, thinking that, if I just got him to say whatever it was he'd come out here to say, I could get rid of him faster.

"For you to stop being a miserable asshole. You've been toxic all week and everyone's tired of it."

"Everyone who?" I could admit I wasn't in the best of moods, but I hadn't exchanged heated words with anyone that I could recall.

"Whole staff. I've had half a dozen people come to me to say that you've been awful to work with. I'm not the HR department, and I sure as hell am not the peacemaker."

"Then why are you here?"

"Because someone needs to tell you to get over yourself and do something about Everly."

Just hearing her name out loud was like a jab to my chest. I tried to ignore that and humor him so I could eventually get my peace back. "What do you think I should do about Everly, Mr. Love Expert?"

"Whatever you need to do to get her back in your life."

As irritated as I was by his intrusion, the thought of having Everly in my life tugged at me like a bottle of vodka must to an alcoholic. I didn't like anything having control over my life or my brain. My heart?

Fuck.

Tempering myself, I informed him, "Our lives aren't compatible."

"Bullshit."

Our parents had raised us to understand that violence didn't solve anything, but I'd never wanted to punch Cash's lights out more than at that moment.

"She's Everly fucking Ash. I know you pretty much exist with your head up your ass, but she's world-famous and a little busy."

"Uh-huh," he said in a patronizing tone that had me cracking my knuckles. "I know who she is and I also know you're in love with her."

I winced inwardly. "You don't know shit."

"Keep telling yourself that. While you're at it, tell yourself if you'd just face up to the shit you're afraid of, you might be able to have her in your life."

I closed my eyes, thinking maybe if I acted like I was bored or falling asleep, he'd walk away. Thinking he had some balls to try to lecture me on relationships. Thinking anything I could to keep my mind off what he'd said. Because there was a part of me that suspected he was right.

"What are you more scared of, Seth? Trusting the wrong

person again or having the whole world find out you made a mistake in the past?"

I clenched my jaw hard enough to break a tooth. "You have a fucked-up way of putting me in a better mood."

"Look, I can tell you're miserable, and I can understand where you're coming from," he said, his tone less combative. He leaned his elbows on his thighs, still wearing his chef whites.

"Wouldn't you rather go home?" I asked, my ire fizzling out a little from sheer fatigue. I didn't have the energy to keep arguing with my hardheaded brother.

"Sure as hell would, but then you'll show up to work tomorrow and be an asshole again."

He was right. I didn't see any relief in sight. I was so sick of feeling like this, but I didn't seem to have a lot of options.

"Does she know how you feel?" Cash asked.

He'd worn down my shields, so I answered honestly. "No. I don't want to distract her from her career. We hit it off under artificial conditions."

"Based on the way you looked at each other, I'd say you did more than hit it off."

I shrugged. It didn't matter, did it? I chewed on a thought, debated whether to give it life by saying it out loud. "I don't fit in her real life. She asked me to go to an awards show, for fuck's sake. Can you see me at an awards show?"

He let out a chuckle. "That's rough. But you could if you wanted to. Just think of all those pretty-boy bastards who'd be jealous of you."

I looked over at him. "The strangest things motivate you."

It was his turn to shrug. "You two come from different worlds. So what? You could make it work if you wanted to. If you tried. That's not the true issue and you know it."

A few minutes ticked by. Crickets chirped. Cicadas and frogs serenaded. A fish or two splashed at the water's surface. These sounds of nature were normally my meditation, my calming force, but tonight their racket made my brain hurt more. My heart hurt more.

"Seth, how many serious relationships have I had?"

I scowled. "How should I know? You don't tell us much."

"You know how many," he said.

"There was Karla," I said of his ex-wife, then racked my brain. "There was Ava back in the day. I don't know of anyone else." I'd been away at college for several years, and he'd been in the navy, so I wouldn't necessarily know.

"That's all," Cash said. "So how many of those did I fuck up?"

"I'm guessing a hundred percent."

"You're guessing right."

"What's your point?"

"Everyone messes up relationships, chooses the wrong person, whatever. You chose wrong once. Years ago. In my book, that makes you normal."

"Most bad relationship choices don't result in people dying."

"Your decision did not cause anyone's death."

I'd been over this countless times with my therapist back then, and I'd finally gotten it through my head that what Cash said was true. "You're right," I acknowledged quietly. "I know that."

"Good," he said with emphasis. "That situation was fucked up, but that wasn't on you, Seth."

Cash wasn't one to offer encouragement about anything, so to have his support on that made a deep impression, stirred up gratitude, and had me reminding myself once again that what he'd said was true. Who knew an older brother's understanding could burrow so deep inside of a person?

"Thanks," was all I muttered.

"So if that's not what's holding you back, I can only think of one other possibility."

My body tensed and I knew I didn't want to hear this. I

thought about getting up and walking away, but that would be cowardly, and the bastard would probably just follow me home.

I sat there and braced myself.

"You don't want the whole town to know you screwed up all those years ago. You're still embarrassed."

"Wouldn't you be?"

He shrugged. "Whole town knows about my relationship failures. Is what it is. You, though…"

"What about me?" I prompted, ready to lash out again because he might've gotten too close to the truth.

Or he might've nailed it on the fucking head.

"You've always hated being wrong or making a mistake with every fiber of your being."

"You like to screw up?"

He scoffed. "No. No one likes it. But you take it to an extreme. I remember when you were in middle school, maybe eighth grade. You got an B plus on a test in your English class—"

"It was a paper," I corrected, knowing immediately what he referred to because it was one of the only times in my life I didn't get an A.

"The worst part of it," he continued, "was that your teacher made a joke about it in front of the whole class. 'Seth Henry had an off day' or some shit, so everyone knew. That's what pissed you off the most. I heard you tell Mom."

I couldn't deny any of that, but I could still argue. "That was more than twenty years ago."

"The deal in college was nearly fifteen. And yet here we sit."

The insect symphony was the only sound for a couple of minutes while my brother kept blessedly quiet, but it didn't really matter, because his words had me thinking, wondering, examining whether his point could be valid.

"What if you're letting this decades-old fuckup hold you

back from the woman you love?" he suggested eventually. "What if, by not letting your past have any power over you anymore, you could have Everly in your life?"

My gut clenched with uneasiness. I wanted to tell him he was full of shit. Wanted to deny every word he said. But I wasn't sure I could without lying to myself. So I said nothing.

Eventually, Cash stood, shrugged, and walked back toward the restaurant, leaving me in the quiet. There wasn't, however, any peace.

I hated that he might be right.

Almost as much as I hated ever being wrong.

And didn't that give me a shit ton to think through?

CHAPTER 27

'm not going to lie—my emotions were all over the flipping map once I got "home."

First off, it didn't really feel like home anymore. My parents' home, yes. The place I'd grown up in, the house I'd lived in for years. But it no longer felt like where I needed or wanted to be.

I'd debated for days between buying and renting my own place, and Drea had suggested that if I wasn't sure I wanted to buy, I should rent to give myself time. That resonated, so I'd gone through a half-dozen apartments but had committed to none of them. I wasn't in the right mindset to commit yet. I was committed to moving out, but I needed time to decide what area I wanted to live in, what features were important to me, how much I wanted to pay.

More urgently, I needed to confront my dad about a list of things, and he'd been on the West Coast for business since I'd arrived last weekend.

My mom was ecstatic to have me back. I'd shared some of my thoughts with her about Trey, even gotten her to understand, finally, I think, but she still couldn't comprehend why I'd want to move out. They'd given me everything I could ever want, even long after I'd started earning big money, and she couldn't understand why would I want to deal with the "hassle" of real-world details if I didn't have to.

It would be an ideal situation for a teenager, but I was years overdue. Finally, I was ready for it all, good and bad, easy and challenging.

It sucked that while I was pushing toward all of this, my heart hurt nonstop.

I couldn't decide if I was more angry or heartbroken that Seth had turned me down. I missed him every minute of the day. We'd spent so much time together during my month in Dragonfly Lake, nearly every moment of spare time he'd had, and I'd gotten spoiled, so spoiled, but not like the spoiling by my parents for the twenty-nine years before I'd met him.

My parents had made my life easy, as long as I went along with their ideas. Seth didn't make things easy on me necessarily. He'd helped me get through one of the toughest times in my life, acted as a sounding board, which helped me get to know myself and grow more in a month than I had in the ten years prior. On top of that, he'd shared his life with me, trusted me with his secrets before anyone else, which made me believe it hadn't been a one-sided relationship. But honestly, I was questioning all of it now, especially in light of how it had ended.

Maybe I was naive. I was undoubtedly less experienced in love and sex than most women my age. But I didn't think I was stupid. I could have sworn Seth had been growing some real feelings for me, maybe even as real as I felt for him.

I couldn't deny it, at least not to myself. I loved him. And I was in love with him. I wanted more than anything to have him in my life, for him to be a part of my future. I'd given him the chance to move forward with me, but he apparently didn't feel the same way. That or he couldn't stomach being a part of the admittedly crazy life I lived in the spotlight. I could understand that, but if he felt as strongly about me as I did about him, it seemed worthwhile to at least try to find a way forward together, to create a life that would make both of us happy. I'd made no secret that I didn't love the spotlight part of my world either. Maybe there were compromises we could make? But he'd shut me down without giving us a chance.

I slammed my brain shut on those thoughts for now, because it was Friday evening, and my dad was finally home, waiting for me in his home office. This confrontation was not going to be fun, and I needed all my attention on it instead of uselessly bemoaning what could have been.

Eddy Ash's home office was in my parents' wing of the house, at the far end of a long hall on the first floor. As I headed that way, I couldn't help but remember some of the other times I'd made the long, quiet walk. Many of those times, it was with anticipation, excitement, positive expectations, usually about a song we'd just released or award nominations or other milestones. I didn't remember ever approaching that extra-tall door with so much trepidation. But of course, before today, I'd been playing the game his way.

I reached the closed door and stopped, gave myself a pep talk, reminded myself how justified my thoughts, my feelings, my decisions were. They were my decisions, at long last, and my dad didn't have the right to run over them or dissuade me from them. Especially not the decision to break up with Trey.

With a deep, lung-expanding breath that steadied my heartbeat some, I lifted my hand and knocked.

When my dad invited me in with a curt, "Enter," I let his gruffness feed my anger and determination to get through to him.

"Hi, Dad," I said as I went through the door with my head up, hoping I was pulling off an attitude of confidence.

"Everly."

His eyes searched me head to toe as I made my way to his masculine, minimalistic desk, which was a slab of stone on chunky iron legs. I'd always thought it didn't seem conducive to a lot of paperwork so much as high-powered deal making, though the number of deals executed in this private office was, in fact, low. Those were made elsewhere, and this office served as my dad's ego headquarters, with built-in book-shelves displaying his countless awards, from Grammys to CMAs to other prestigious accolades. On the walls were photos of my dad with some of the biggest names in the industry over the past three decades.

The room was a testament to his career success, which no one could debate. I wasn't here to do any such thing, only to defend my personal decisions and set some new boundaries and directions moving forward. There was a chance my dad would no longer want to produce my music, and I was prepared for that, maybe even at peace with it if it came to that. Bottom line, I needed changes.

But first, the issue of my broken engagement.

I lowered myself to one of the two leather armchairs, my back straight, my hands clasped in my lap. "Mom said you're upset about what I did," I said, then bit down determinedly on my tongue and narrowed my eyes at him, daring him to admit it.

My dad leaned both his elbows on his desk and took his glasses off, always the sign that he wasn't happy. "Everly," he began, and his tone immediately had me ready to lash out. I bit down harder and waited. "Everything you do in your career reflects on mine—"

"No," I let out with more than a little venom. "I'm not listening to that lecture again for a couple of reasons. First, I know it by heart, frontwards, backwards, and upside down.

I've heard it a thousand times, and I've done everything in my career so far to make sure it reflected positively on yours and made you proud. Second, and you need to hear this, Dad—really hear it—this is *not about my career or yours*. This is about my life, my future, my happiness. And guess what?"

His brows shot up near his salt-and-pepper hairline as he stared at me.

"I'm done putting anyone's career over me and what I want," I continued.

He put his glasses back on and studied me, tilting his head. "What happened to you while you were gone, Everly?"

I let out a laugh-like scoff. Was this really the man I'd looked up to for so long? Was he really that clueless or self-absorbed or dense?

"What happened was that, for the first time ever, I took the time to think about *what I want.*" I enunciated the last words as if speaking to a preschooler. "Breaking up with a guy can do that to a person, especially when your personal decision is so public. When I left right before the wedding, I was acting on instinct. Following my gut. There was something, thank God, that told me marrying Trey wasn't the right thing to do. It wasn't until I got away, by myself, that I had time to think, to rationally consider why my gut had been screaming at me. It turns out that Trey Gilbert is not the right guy for me."

"Trey's a great guy—"

"Yes! He is. But that doesn't mean he's the person who will make me happy for the rest of my life, Dad. Can't you understand that?"

He crossed his arms over his chest and looked to the right, toward one of the tall, arched windows. "I thought he was, Everly," he said quietly. His brow furrowed. "I honestly thought he was." There was regret in his tone. Sadness. Because my relationship had failed? Because he felt like I'd let him down? Before I could get good and pissed off, he said, "I didn't realize you weren't happy, Evsy."

The childhood nickname that only he had ever used for me put the brakes on my anger, nearly gave me whiplash, and tugged hard at something inside me. It'd been years since he'd called me that. When I'd turned twenty-one and we'd officially started working together, the nickname had been left behind. Our relationship, I realized now, had shifted into a more professional one, even when we were at home, because this career wasn't one you easily set aside when you got home from the "office" at night.

I didn't want to be swayed by one endearment. He seemed genuine but…

"Why did you think I left him?" I asked, because what other reason could there be besides not being happy?

My dad turned to look at me then, really look at me. He blew out a gust of air and his shoulders sagged as he perched his elbows on the desk, folded his hands together, tapped his knuckles to his chin. Several seconds ticked by as he averted his eyes. "I figured it was another ploy for publicity."

"How could you think that, Dad?" I asked in utmost disbelief. "Do you know what they're saying about me?"

His jaw went taut and his eyes flashed dark. "I can't read a fucking word of that bullshit." He clenched one of his fists and sat back. "I'm sorry, Everly. I was so happy for you, so proud of you. I woke up that day the beaming father of the beautiful bride. When we got word that you'd disappeared…" He shook his head. "We didn't believe it. Your mother and I thought maybe you and Trey had run off together. You two've been all about the publicity from the start and damn good at it. That's just where our minds went. It didn't occur to me that you could be going through a rough time."

"I didn't plan it," I told him. "I woke up thinking I'd marry Trey Gilbert."

He studied me, the sadness in his eyes making him look older. Tired. In that moment, he looked more like my loving dad than world-famous overachiever Eddy Ash. "Then what happened, Evsy?"

I bit my lip, debating. When I'd stormed in here, I'd been so mad I hadn't had any intention of sharing my reasons with him, but the tenderness in his eyes, his love, they were there, radiating out to me, and it softened me. Made me want to get him to understand.

"What did Mom tell you?"

"She tried to tell me you'd really broken up, but I wasn't in the right frame of mind to hear her."

"But you are now?"

"I'm asking, honey. I want to understand."

I believed he did want to understand now, so I told him. I explained how I'd gotten caught up in the excitement and the momentum and, yes, the publicity. The fan love. My team's enthusiasm. "Everyone was so happy about our relationship. I think we all wanted it to be this perfect match so badly that I bought into it without listening to my heart."

When I finished, my dad was quiet for a long while as he gazed pensively out the window. "I'm sorry, Everly. I was upset you didn't come to us. Sometimes I forget you're a grown woman and I want to fix everything for you."

"You can't, Dad."

He nodded. "I know that here," he said, pointing to his head.

"I'm sorry I didn't explain sooner. And I'm sorry for any problems my bad publicity caused you."

He waved that off as if it wasn't important. "If Trey isn't the right man for you, I'm glad you figured that out."

"He's not. Also…" I drew in a deep breath, peering at the ceiling, working up my nerve to continue. This would've been easier if I was still mad. "I did a lot of thinking while I was away, and a lot of things aren't right for me." Before he could say anything, I blustered forward. "I don't love where my career is, Dad, or maybe I mean where it's going. I've loved working with you," I rushed to add. "I appreciate everything you and Mom have done. So much."

Frowning, he said, "We couldn't have done any of it if you didn't have the talent, honey."

"My talent has been in the mix but my heart hasn't."

The frown turned a little scowly. "What do you mean?"

I weighed my words, trying to get them just right, not wanting to hurt him more than necessary. "You and Mom and the team have steered me to more success than I ever could've dreamed possible," I said. "I've learned"—I shook my head, unable to find an adequate word—"so much," was all I could come up with.

My dad tilted his head, a questioning look on his face, like he sensed I was going somewhere with this.

"The Sweetheart of Country Music… I don't feel like that's me anymore." If it ever was.

"You'll always be the Sweetheart of Country Music," he said lightly, and I knew he believed that. In the best possible way. But it just showed how much I hadn't let him know me in recent years.

Something on my face must have clued him in, because he went serious and said, "This is something that's really bothering you, isn't it?"

I nodded and sat forward in the chair. "I love writing music, Dad. I spent a lot of the past month playing around with an old guitar"—I fought not to think about the night I'd gotten that guitar from Seth—"writing songs."

"Oh? Let me hear them, Everly. Maybe we can put one or two on the album."

Shaking my head, I told him, "They aren't Sweetheart songs."

My dad's fuzzy brows wrinkled in confusion. "What are they?"

I hesitated, trying to think how to answer. "Everly Ash songs. Like, what comes out when I listen to myself and do what feels right to me."

He studied me for another long stretch. "So you're saying the songs we've been doing, the entire brand, is bad?"

"Not bad. Just… not me. Not what I want. Not who I am. I know I'm under contract to do the other stuff." I hadn't planned this part, but the words were on the tip of my tongue, and I was compelled to air them out. "I'm thinking about buying my way out."

I was watching his face carefully, otherwise I probably would've missed it—a flicker of anger flashed across it before he blanked it. It took him several seconds to say anything, during which I failed to breathe.

"What happened, Everly?" he finally asked. "When did everything change?"

"I've always wanted to write my own songs."

"You never told us that."

"I'm sure I did. A long time ago."

"And you don't like the music we've been selecting?"

"It's okay music. Obviously it speaks to a lot of people," I said honestly. "But it hasn't felt 'right' for a long time."

"You've never said so," he challenged.

"I've mentioned it. A few times over the years."

My dad rose, paced toward the window, peered outside for a few seconds, then whirled around. "Is this something you feel strongly about, Everly? Getting out of a contract isn't a little thing."

"I know that. I've given it a lot of thought." Even though I hadn't planned to go that far during this conversation, I'd weighed it over for days on end. Maybe longer. "I met a woman who recently finished classes to become a producer. She's a friend of a friend. We played around with some of my songs, for fun."

Another something flashed in his eyes, but this time it looked more like disappointment.

"She's not Eddy Ash," I said lightly, because let's face it, no one was Eddy Ash, "but we gelled. She's gifted, and she gets me."

"And I don't," he said, sounding more than a little defeated. "I didn't see any of this dissatisfaction, Everly. If you mentioned it, it came across as just a thought in passing."

"I know. Maybe I should've been more adamant."

"Absolutely. I just..." He looked totally, completely baffled. As if he'd been blindsided. "You never fought for what you wanted, Everly. If you don't fight for what you want, how's anyone going to know how important it is to you?"

His words hit me with the force of a concrete block.

You never fought for what you wanted.

Oh, God.

I wasn't a fighter.

I tried to get along with people, not rock the boat.

With this one conversation, that single sentence from my dad, it hit me. That tendency wouldn't get me the life I wanted.

It was true about my career, and it was true about my feelings for Seth.

What had I done? Or rather, what had I *not* done?

My dad was saying something, but there was so much noise in my head that I didn't hear anything else.

I felt like my heart was going to jump out of my chest.

I fought to get my head back in the present moment, to finish this vital conversation with my dad/producer. I couldn't be sure which one I was talking to right now. Maybe it would help if I would tune back in to what he was saying.

"What's this newbie producer's name?"

"Gin Verdinelli Steele. She's married to Tucker Steele—"

"Of Steele Hearts?"

I nodded and couldn't miss the attitude change in my dad at hearing of her ties to a band that had three songs on the charts right now.

"She's an honest-to-God musical genius in her own right. A virtuoso cellist who dropped out of an elite music program and moved to Nashville a few years ago. She was burnt out and had no plans to get back into music, but then she met Tucker, fell in love, and was sparked to go to school for production. I had really low expectations after working with the best of the best"—hey, I knew how to play to my dad's ego… besides, it was true—"but we totally clicked."

"So what are you going to do? Go indie and use this brand-new producer?"

There was some doubt in his voice, but that was to be expected. When you came from our world, which was ruled by record labels and publicity agents and managers and what have you, it sounded ridiculous.

I was okay with "ridiculous," as long as it was new and sparked me. Gin Verdinelli Steele sparked me. The things she'd done with my raw new songs were already blowing my mind.

"I'm not sure yet," I told him, because Gin and I hadn't talked business, only music. "All I know is that I need to do something that's more me. I hope you can respect that as a producer, even if you can't understand it as my dad."

After perusing me thoroughly, his shoulders relaxed slightly and he said, "Did you record anything with Gin Steele? Maybe something I could listen to as your dad?"

"It's rough. Just something on my phone. I can send it to you, but I just remembered something I need to take care of. Is later okay?"

"Yeah. Evsy, come here." He approached from the window, holding out his arms, offering a hug.

I'd never imagined this conversation would end in a hug. I was itching to get out of there and figure out what to do about Seth, but I stood and walked into my dad's arms, grateful he'd come around this much already.

"Promise me one thing?" he said as he hugged me.

"What's that?"

"Don't sign anything without having someone look it over."

"Of course not," I told him. "I might be new at calling the shots, but I've had two of the best teachers anywhere, Dad. Thank you. And now I need to go."

I had a future to figure out and a man I needed to fight for.

CHAPTER 28

Nothing said *I'll do anything for you* quite like me getting in a wobbly canoe and paddling my fool butt halfway across Dragonfly Lake.

That was the situation I was faced with, and that's what I was going to do.

After my conversation with my dad, I'd packed a bag and grabbed the keys to my Jaguar SUV, one of the six cars in my parents' garage. Before this past week, I'd rarely driven the car that had, of course, been a gift from my mom and dad. This past week, I'd put a few hundred miles on it. I felt like a teenager with her first dose of freedom. It might've been long overdue, but it was no less wonderful than if I were sixteen.

I just hoped that freedom didn't lead to heartbreak tonight.

Maybe packing a bag was optimistic, but worst-case scenario, I could get a room at the Marks Resort or the Dragonfly Inn.

I'd driven straight to Seth's house since it was after eight on Friday night and he would likely be home. Without worrying much about parking in his driveway since no one here had ever seen my vehicle, I'd gotten out and headed to his front door in the waning daylight. My knock, however, had gone unanswered. I'd gone around to the deck in back to see if he was there, but there was no sign of him, not even a dim light on anywhere. His SUV was in the driveway, so he couldn't have gone far.

With a glance at the garage apartment, I'd been hit by an onslaught of memories, most of them involving the man I couldn't find. I briefly wondered if he'd re-rented the place, but it was currently dark, so I doubted it.

I'd wandered toward the shore, checking that his boat was there, and it was, but eventually I'd noticed that one of the kayaks from the rack was gone. It was obvious, because the rack held six boats—three stand-up paddleboards, two kayaks, and that godforsaken canoe—and one of the kayak spots was empty.

After standing there, staring at the empty rack, then scanning the lake for a small-craft light that could be Seth's and not finding any, I'd texted Chloe for suggestions. She and Holden lived a couple blocks away, and she'd met me here.

Apparently, Holden, Seth, and Cash had a deal where they shared their phone locations, particularly for times when one of them went on the water alone. At Chloe's request, Holden had checked and found Seth's signal just off the shore to the west, past the private beach, about halfway to the resort. It was less than a mile away, Chloe reassured me. She'd also told me we could probably reach him faster if we drove that way, parked, and walked to the shore, calling for him. Maybe I was crazy, but I'd refused.

"You're sure about this?" Chloe asked now. We'd just set the canoe in the water at the shoreline, and I was slipping my flip-flops off. She swore it was easier to get in this way, rather than stepping down from the dock.

"I'm sure. It's kind of an inside joke between us. I'm

hoping it cracks the ice," I said. To say nothing of making an impression on him, letting him know I was serious.

"Is this because of what he did earlier today?" Chloe asked as she bent down to hold the end of the boat for me to get in.

I stopped, my feet in the refreshing water just past my ankles. "What he did earlier today?"

A strange look crossed her face, then disappeared just as quickly. "Never mind. Let's get you going. You remember everything I told you about paddling, right?"

Taking a shaky breath in, I nodded. I mean, did I? I didn't really know. I'd watched Seth, so I had some idea, but I wasn't going to win any style awards. Hopefully I'd eventually get there though.

Since it was dark, the little canoe light was on. I lowered my life-jacketed self to the seat and instantly agreed, it was easier to get in this way than from the dock, particularly without a strong, sexy man hand to steady you.

With some final tips, and after pointing out the lights on shore to aim for again, Chloe shoved the canoe out, and I followed her instructions to turn myself around. My heart pounded for multiple reasons.

The canoe felt less wobbly than I remembered, but trying to move it in a straight line was a challenge. I settled for generally straight direction overall, keeping the lights in my sight as I passed a couple houses, then the private beach I'd seen from my balcony so many times.

About twenty minutes after leaving Chloe, I approached the area where Seth's signal had come from, scanning the surface for a light on a kayak. The resort was closer now, visible, but still too far away to hear the people I could see on the docks and the sprawling porch.

What if I didn't find him?

What if he'd moved since Holden had checked, maybe gone toward the resort or out to the middle of the lake?

Though I'd done a couple of workouts with James this week, my arms ached. The thought of having to turn around and paddle back made me want to weep. Even trying to get to the resort would be a challenge for my out-of-shape arms that had to paddle twice as much as a competent canoe paddler— canoer? canoeist?—due to my severely inefficient stroke.

Maybe I should've taken Chloe up on the offer to drive over here and tromp through the trees?

Maybe I was the biggest fool alive, trying to prove myself this way. What would it even mean to Seth that I'd paddled his damn awkward canoe to reach him?

When I'd worked myself into near hysteria, I spotted a dim light near the shore about forty feet ahead of me. Staring at the boat for a few more seconds, I could make out that it was a kayak.

"Seth?" I called out. I didn't want to paddle right up to the wrong person and scare the crap out of them or creep them out. Or, God forbid, be recognized.

I could make out the kayaker's form just enough to see that the person straightened. It was a man.

"Hello?" I tried again, even less sure of myself.

"Who's there?"

I nearly wilted with relief when I recognized Seth's voice.

"Seth, it's me. Everly. Please don't paddle away."

He said nothing as I did my inept, this-way-then-that-way paddle routine toward him as fast as I could.

"Everly?" he said as I came within feet of him. "What's wrong?"

I was breathing hard and so relieved I'd reached him that I could cry. So it took several seconds before his question sank in.

"Wrong?" I repeated, easing the canoe sort of alongside him. "Nothing. I wanted to talk to you."

"You're in my canoe."

"Yes. I needed a boat," I said flippantly.

"You know a kayak is easier, right?"

"I've never been in a kayak. I don't know how to paddle one."

With a grin, he said, "No offense, but you can't really paddle a canoe either."

"I made it here, didn't I?" I said sitting up taller as I rested the paddle across the top of the boat.

"Somehow." His tone was still light, until he said, "What are you doing here?"

"Like I said, I need to talk to you."

"Out here?"

"Well..." I glanced around. We were about twenty feet from the nearest rocky shore. Maybe a hundred yards from the closest dock. And seventy-some miles from Seth's house, or so it seemed. I hadn't thought through the logistics of having this important conversation boat to boat. "I guess so. Unless there's somewhere close, out of the water, where we could go."

Seth glanced around. "Follow me."

Easier said than done, but I eventually steered the canoe to the shore right next to him.

"Let me get the kayak out and then I'll help you," he said.

I couldn't get a read on whether he was happy to see me, upset, or indifferent. My heart continued to thunder, and my mouth was bone-dry with nerves.

Five minutes later, our boats were out of the water, and Seth and I had found two big rocks next to each other along a dirt path to sit on. We sat and I tried to gather my wits after what had turned out to be a lot more exercise than I'd expected. I didn't dare think about the way back, particularly if it was made in uncomfortable silence because he'd turned me down again.

"Ev? What's going on?" he finally asked. "Were you on the town app?"

"Was I... What? No. Why?"

He shook his head, looking baffled in the moonlight. Baffled and so freaking handsome.

"I was talking to my dad tonight," I began. "Finally. He was out of town all week, so it was a long time coming."

"Confrontation?" he asked. We'd talked in detail, when I still lived in his apartment, about the talk I intended to have with my dad. Back when we'd still been together. It seemed like ages ago.

"It started out that way," I said.

"And how did it end?"

"Relatively well. Peacefully. But that's not what I want to talk about. Something he said tonight helped me figure out a really important thing."

My hands were sweating and I suddenly felt as if I was sitting in front of a full-blown campfire. Roasting alive.

Seth said nothing, just watched me expectantly, and my confidence faltered.

"When I told him how unhappy I was with my branding, he pointed out that I never fought for what I wanted in my career. He had no idea how I really felt, how strongly I felt it, how important any of it was to me. And I realized I did the same thing with you," I said in a rush.

"You told me exactly how you felt about your career and the songs you've recorded and how they seemed to fit you less and less with every album."

"Not my career."

His brow furrowed and he tilted his head.

Master communicator I was not, apparently.

Just say it. Say it all.

"Last Saturday, I suggested that you and I could see each other again after I moved. Go to the awards show. See where things went. That's not what I want."

"Oh. Okay."

Was that disappointment in his tone? Or just wishful thinking on my part?

Clenching my hands together, I barreled on. "I want you in my life full-time, Seth. I want a future with you. I want to find a way for us to be together more than we're apart." I breathed, swallowed, closed my eyes for a heartbeat or two, then peered directly at him in the moonlight. "I love you, Seth. I came here five weeks ago a total mess, convinced I was a failure in every way but especially in romance, but then you taught me what romance and love are. I'm in love with you. Crazy in love. I hated being away from you all week. So this is me fighting for what I want. It's you. I want you more than anything else in this world." I blew out air and watched his face for a signal, a change in expression, anything.

After several seconds, he let out a short laugh, and my heart sank.

In the next instant, he grabbed my hand and pulled me over to him and sought out my mouth, his hands going around me as he pulled me onto his lap and kissed me.

The second his lips were on me, I melted into him, and it felt like coming home after a long trip, like finding the place I belonged, the place I never wanted to leave. Except it wasn't a place, it was a man.

A man who hadn't said a word in reply to my big, emotional pouring out of my soul.

I pulled back and pressed a finger to his lips when he came back at me for another kiss. I was trying to be a hard-ass, but I couldn't help grinning, because did I mention how incredibly hot this man was? And he was trying to devour me.

"Seth."

"Mmm?"

I laughed. "Stop for a second."

He nibbled at my mouth, and honestly, I wasn't very good at being a hard-ass at all. I was pulled in by his kisses and nibbles and every ounce of attention he was showering me with.

A couple of minutes later, with a hand to his chest, I pushed him back, lightly, lovingly, grinning again, because it seemed like he was happy with my confession. But I needed to hear that from those delectable lips.

"I just bared all for you," I said. There was more to share, but it was feeling really lopsided so far, and I needed to be sure we were hoping for the same things before I said more.

"You don't seem bare enough to me," he said, "but we could change that easily enough."

The sad thing was I looked at that dirt path under the stars, and for a few seconds, I considered getting naked out here.

Apparently the only way I would get him to talk was to stand up and separate our bodies that seemed like a magnet and steel—him being the steel, of course—that couldn't pry themselves away from each other.

I did that, laughing, catching my balance, because Seth Henry knocked me off-kilter even when I was sitting down.

"Seth! This isn't fair. I laid my heart out for you, told you everything. I fought for what I wanted, and it seems like maybe you want something similar, but help me out here—"

He surprised me by darting up from the rock and digging his phone out of his pocket.

"Are you sure you haven't been on the town app chat?" he asked, confusing the crap out of me.

"I'm sure," I answered. "I thought you had to have a permanent address here to get an account."

"You do." He unlocked his phone, swiped a couple of times, then handed it to me. "Anyone can access the tourist parts, but the chat is only residents."

I looked at him, even more confused. "What are you doing?"

"Read that," he said, pointing at the screen.

I looked down at it, shining brightly at me, nearly hurting my eyes in the darkness. It was the town app, the chat pages, which I'd seen a couple of times when Seth had pointed something out to me.

Every small town has its secrets, right? I'd hazard a guess that most small-town residents have their secrets as well, a post began, and I noted that the poster was Seth. My interest piqued, and I went back to my original rock and sat down.

I'm no exception. I've had secrets for years that will shock you.

My eyes grew wider as I read on.

I've been careful to keep them private, but recently I figured something out. Trying to keep my past hidden has held a distinct power over me and set limits on me, or rather, I've set limits on myself in order to keep those secrets. So this is me, laying out my secrets to everyone so they no longer have me in their grip.

Buckle your seat belt. Prepare to be shocked. And once you're done reading this, do what you want with it. Talk about it until you're blue in the face, laugh at me, point your finger at me, think the worst of me… I don't care. It won't change who I am.

When I went to college, I left town thinking I was the smart guy. A bunch of you thought I was the smart guy as well.

Spoiler alert: I wasn't as smart as I thought.

Seth stood in front of me, his hands in the pockets of his cargo shorts, fidgeting with something. I took one of his wrists, grasped his hand, and tugged him toward his rock, urging him to sit down. I kept ahold of him as I went back to the post.

It started when I was in grad school, studying business. In my second-to-last semester, I met a woman. She was my professor. Our attraction was instant, and though I ignored it for a few weeks, she was my contact for an independent study, and I had to meet with her weekly. I'll skip the details. Suffice it to say, we fell in love. Or I thought we did.

I read on, through the story he'd told me and his family, about the husband, the pregnancy, the suicide. Halfway through, my eyes were watering, my heart aching for him all over again. Three quarters of the way through, I felt almost as if I'd lived through it with him, and I think I even sniffled.

I got to the end of the part about his past and sucked in a shaky breath, then read the last couple of paragraphs.

Who I am, incidentally, is a man who made a big mistake last week with a woman who means the world to me. Because of these secrets.

Pretty sure I gasped.

So though I don't know how it's going to end with this woman I've fallen in love with, I do know for a fact… it will no longer be my past that prevents me from having a future with her.

I pressed my lips together, stunned. Gobsmacked. And so damn in love with Seth Henry and all his secrets and his fears and his flaws and his awesomeness.

"You love me?" I finally managed to ask.

"You need to ask after that?" he said with a nervous laugh.

"Say it to my face," I dared, standing to face him.

He stood too and took both of my hands. "I love you, Everly Ash. I'm crazy in love with you. I don't know how we're going to do this thing, but I'll go to your awards show. I'll try the long-distance thing. I'll commute to work a few times a week if it means I can be with you."

"Actually," I said, my heart overflowing at all the concessions he'd just made. Concessions that wouldn't be necessary, for the most part. "We can discuss the awards show. I can't decide if I want to go. But more importantly, the long-distance thing might not be necessary. You see, I fell in love with this little town and this little lake, and I'm thinking I might move here. You know, if I had a good place to live. Like, an adorable studio apartment would be okay. If you know of one."

Seth's brows shot up. "You think you could do your job with that kind of commute?"

"I bet I could," I said, grinning so wide it felt like my face might break, "but I don't know if I'll need to. I'm changing direction in my career. I told my dad tonight I want out of my contract—"

"Won't that cost a hefty bit of money?"

"Most likely. Luckily, I've got a hefty bit of savings. I met with Gin Verdinelli Steele. We totally meshed. She gets me. I get her. And she's incredibly talented. She's not Eddy Ash, and I don't want her to be. I told my dad all of this tonight."

"How'd he take it?"

"He was stunned. Disappointed. But he handled it. We'll work it out. Because this is what I want—control of my career, a cute place in Dragonfly Lake, and you."

Smiling, gazing down at me with his killer brown eyes, he said, "I like most of that."

"Most of it?"

He nodded. "All but the studio apartment. I think it would get cramped for both of us, and I happen to have this nearly gutted twenty-nine-hundred-square-foot house on the shore. It's pretty big for a single guy, so I'd love to share it. If that's not moving too fast..."

"That's not moving too fast," I said, laughing, throwing my arms around him, feeling lighter than air with joy and hope and gratitude for this man who was so exactly perfect for me and so the center of the life I wanted. "In fact, I brought a bag for tonight if you'd like to get started on this cohabiting thing."

He kissed me, urgently, passionately, thoroughly, then managed to break away enough to say, "I'd love to get started tonight. Let's go home."

"One little thing," I said with a scowl at the boats. "I still don't love that canoe. Are you sure we can't just walk home?"

Seth laughed, kissed me some more, then said, "We'll leave the kayak here and come get it tomorrow. We'll take the canoe and get home as fast as we possibly can. The good news? Like just about everything else in life, canoes, my gorgeous Everly, are much better with two."

EPILOGUE

SETH

ONE MONTH LATER

Everly Ash, former Sweetheart of Country Music, was thriving in her new small-town life here in Dragonfly Lake. I thanked God for that—for *her*—every single day.

Because of her, I'd never felt so alive. So fucking happy. I'd never imagined life could be this sweet.

Today was Everly's thirtieth birthday. She'd wanted to celebrate in a way she'd never been able to before—with a big outdoor party with everyone we knew. Nothing fancy. In fact, she'd insisted on the opposite of fancy, requesting swimsuits and volleyball, a cookout and a campfire. I'd done everything possible to make that wish a reality for the woman I loved to pieces.

It was nearing six p.m. this sunny Saturday in August. Our yard was filled with people and laughter and the smell of food sizzling on the grill. My dad and Faye were here, plus three out of five of Faye's sons and their wives—Zane and

Hayden, with Harrison in tow, Cole and Sierra, and Drake and McKenzie. Chloe had introduced Everly to several of the Dragonfly Lake women, and Everly had told me she now had more people she could call friends than ever before. She and Gin Steele had been working together at the Hale Street Studio in Nashville a couple days a week, exploring directions for Everly's music, and Gin and her husband, Tucker, who even I had heard of, were here to celebrate.

Everly's parents had shown up too, looking only slightly out of place at our humble backyard party. I'd met them shortly after Everly had agreed to move in with me and liked them more than I'd expected. After spending time with them, including dinner at their giant home, I didn't question that they'd had the best intentions toward Everly all these years and had acted out of love, even if I didn't agree with how they'd handled her and her career. No one was perfect, and Everly had made the professional break fully, with no hard feelings between them.

Cash had left work midafternoon, taking the night off just for this—proof he had a brotherly soft spot for Everly. He was in charge of cooking the protein—burgers, bratwursts, veggie patties, and chicken breasts. I stood next to him at the grill, more interested in the scenery across the way.

Everly was involved in a volleyball match at the net we'd set up this morning. It was guys versus girls, and I was secretly thrilled the ladies, Everly, Chloe, Anna Delfico, and Gin Steele, were up by two in spite of a significant height disadvantage. Zane, his twin brother, Drake, Finn McNamara, and Nick made up the losing team. They were taking it pretty well so far, but if they didn't quit trying to showboat with big play attempts, they'd be drowning their sorrows in a Rusty Anchor beer before they knew what hit them.

When Drake messed up a spike and Zane accused him of trying to show off, I grinned but let my attention divert right back to the sexiest woman alive. Like a lot of the women here,

Everly wore a bikini along with cutoffs, giving me a tantalizing view of her slender, suntanned abdomen and perfect, triangle-covered breasts, whetting my appetite for later. *If* all went as well as I hoped.

As Finn chased an out-of-bounds ball, Everly met my gaze and blew me a kiss, giving me a rush as if I'd jumped off a cliff into the ocean, then she got in position to receive the serve.

Cash made a knowing snort-like noise.

"What?" I said as he shook his head with a half grin and flipped a burger. "Got something to say?"

He tapped the tongs on the edge of the grill, glanced across the yard at Everly then back at me, and said, "I can't decide between *you two are disgusting* and *I told you so.*"

"You told me nothing."

He laughed. "Lie to yourself all you want. You were on the verge of fucking it all up."

With a growl, I admitted, "Make no mistake. I fucked it up six ways to Sunday. I'm just lucky she's forgiving… and crazy about me." I shot a cocky grin his way.

"So no nerves about later then, huh?" my asshole brother asked, knowing full well I was nervous.

"Only thing I'm worried about," I lied, "is Holden showing up with the s'mores ingredients by the time we get the fire going."

"Where the hell is he? He's not normally late for food."

As if we'd summoned him, our younger brother appeared around the corner of the house at that moment, toting a bag from Country Market and looking frazzled.

"Hey," I said as he headed toward us. "You okay?"

"Please tell me there's chocolate in there," Hayden said as she came down the deck stairs carrying three Rusty Anchor Beach Babes and a Lunker Stout.

"Sorry I'm late," Holden said. He'd been working at the brewery today, along with Kemp, now that it was open and already doing a heck of a business. "Phyllis Sharp collapsed in front of the meat counter at the market."

"Oh, no," Hayden said. "Is she okay?"

Holden swallowed, and I knew in that millisecond before he spoke that the woman in her sixties wasn't okay. "Paramedics did everything," he said. "She didn't make it. They suspect a massive heart attack."

"That's awful." Hayden said what we were all thinking.

"You saw it happen?" I asked.

Shaking his head, Holden said, "I was in the graham cracker aisle, but I heard the commotion. I hung around in case there was something I could do but..."

"Damn," I said.

Cash, as usual, was quiet but frowned, then went to rotate the brats.

The volleyball game had apparently ended, and Everly came up to me, grinning as if the women had indeed prevailed. When she gauged our somberness, she sobered up and said, "What's going on?"

Holden told her about nearly witnessing Mrs. Sharp's death at the Country Market.

"That's terrible," Everly said. "I'm so sorry to hear it." I could tell by the look on her face she was puzzling out whether she should know who Phyllis Sharp was.

"She owns the Honeysuckle Inn," I told her. "Sweet lady, but from what I've heard, she had more than she could handle with the inn anymore."

"She's Ava's aunt," Hayden said, studying Cash, who seemed as if he hadn't heard her.

"Ava..." Everly said, as if trying to place the name.

"Ava Dean. Cash's ex from a long time ago," Holden said, his gaze also on our oldest brother.

Cash continued to act as if he was hearing impaired.

"She was a sweet girl back then from what I remember," Hayden said. "I wonder if she'll come back to run the inn."

Cash dropped the chicken breast he was turning and swore. The chicken bounced off the grill and landed on the ground. Keeping his face away from us, he bent down, picked it up with the tongs, stepped to the garbage can we'd rolled out for the party, and threw it in with the force of a starting baseball pitcher.

Hayden and I exchanged a look, telling me I wasn't the only one thinking Ava might be a sore spot for Cash, even after all these years.

Holden had set the bag of s'mores ingredients on the edge of the deck and was heading for his pregnant wife, missing Cash's display. Nick, Finn, and Cade were walking to the deck for another drink, calling out to Anna that she and her teammates had gotten lucky and they'd be up for a rematch as soon as they rehydrated.

Cash went back to the grill, and Hayden headed toward the group gathered on lawn chairs out by the shore.

My focus zeroed in on the beauty at my side as she stood on tiptoes and kissed me. "You've got yourself a volleyball champ, you know," she said, grinning.

"So I heard." I glanced toward the garage apartment, my anticipation building, hope soaring, and nerves surging all at once as I wondered how much I truly *had* her. Not wanting to give anything away, I busied myself kissing her thoroughly, trying to convey a promise for later without saying a word.

The sexy little moan from her throat told me I'd succeeded.

"You two need someone to take a firehose to you," Nick muttered as he walked by.

"Jealous much?" I cracked back, smiling widely, because how could a guy kiss this girl and not be happy as a clam at high tide?

"Damn straight. I'm stuck hanging out with these ugly dudes." Nick gestured to the two McNamara brothers next to him.

"You try putting your tongue anywhere close to me and I'll knock you into next week," Cade said to Nick.

"You McNamara boys have such gentle hearts," Everly said with a laugh. "I need to get drinks for Gin and me," she said to me, then pressed another quick kiss to my hungry lips and went up the stairs to the coolers.

"Ready for the platters," Cash barked to me.

"Yes, Chef," I snapped back sarcastically. I went up to the table on the deck, picked up the platters, and went back down to him, not wasting any time, because I didn't want my food overcooked.

"What are you going to do if Ava does come back?" I asked when I was next to his sullen, over-serious ass at the grill.

"What the hell do you mean, what am I going to do?" he snapped.

"Just curious whether there's anything lingering there."

"It's been almost twenty years. There's nothing there."

"Okay." I held the top platter while he loaded it with bratwursts. "Any idea whether Ava was supposed to inherit the inn?" As far as I knew, Phyllis didn't have any other family.

"No fucking reason for me to know any of that."

I had to stifle a grin because his defensiveness, his hostility told me everything I needed to know. There might, in fact, be more than "nothing" there. I opened my mouth to say something along those lines, but he cut me off before I could utter a word.

"Leave it. Take the brats and give me the other three plates."

I handed him the empty plates and blew out a whistle to let him know I saw through his act, knowing he couldn't take a swing at me because he had his hands full. "I'll let you know if I hear anything about her coming to town."

"Asshole," he said as I walked off, mostly hiding a half

grin. I was sorry as hell about Phyllis, though I didn't know her well, but I couldn't deny it was fun to get under Cash's skin.

For being such a hard-ass, he could be an easy target. I didn't know much about what had gone down between him and Ava, but apparently there'd been a whole lot of *something* back in the day.

I took the full bratwurst platter up the deck steps and set it on the table, which we were using for the buffet spread. Everly and Anna joined me in adding the refrigerated dishes to the others already set out. Everly had requested a potluck for side dishes, with us providing the main ones, since she'd never experienced the small-town mainstay before. There was everything from baked beans with brisket to homemade cornbread to pesto pasta salad. The desserts were at one end, and between several boxes of gourmet cookies from Sugar, a few pans of brownies, and a home-made peach cobbler Emerson Estes had brought, we had enough sweets to last a week. The highlight at the dessert end, though, was a stunning three-tiered birthday cake Olivia London had baked, with a different flavor for each tier.

We'd set up folding tables all over the yard, and once the dinner call was sounded, the multitudes descended—or rather ascended—on the food table, filled their plates, and found a place to sit. All in all, we put an astonishing dent in the chow, and the drinks were flowing steadily as the sun sank.

After the meal, a few people took off, and the rest gravi-tated to the fire pit, where my dad and Zane were building a healthy fire. The girls had saved a lounge chair for Everly, and then Everly spoiled the girls-only vibe by insisting I sit with her. I didn't even pretend to argue. Now she was on one of my favorite places, my lap, as the couple dozen who were still here chatted, bullshitted each other, and sang along—poorly

—when Carter and Alex Costello broke out their guitar and harmonica respectively.

The sun was all the way down, the fire was still going strong, and faces were rosy from a combination of heat and alcohol when Everly snuggled closer, then lifted her mouth near my ear.

"Thank you," she whispered.

"For?"

"The best birthday ever." She pressed a kiss to my jaw.

"I haven't even given you your present yet," I said as my stomach went tight with nerves.

"I thought this party was my present."

Laughing quietly, I said, "This party was your party. Your present is up there." I indicated the garage apartment with a nod.

Everly looked from me to the apartment where we'd met. "Really?"

"Really. In fact, why don't we sneak away and I'll give you your present."

Her eyes lit up in the glow from the fire. "Right now? With all these people here?"

I laughed again because I was pretty sure she thought I meant getting naked. That figured into her birthday, but I intended to start that after our guests were gone and make it last well into tomorrow. "Come on," was all I said, urging her to stand so I could too.

The group was absorbed in a heartfelt rendition of "Take Me Home, Country Roads," but as I stood, I caught Cash's eye and he gave a supportive nod. He was the only person I'd told about *all* of my plans, as I'd needed help with the setup.

I took Everly's hand and we walked to the stairs and went up to the apartment. I unlocked it and entered before her because I wanted to watch her expression when I flipped on the light.

The redone apartment lit up, and so did Everly's face.

"Seth! What…?"

"Happy birthday, Ev. I love you."

"What have you done?" She spun around, taking every-thing in

"We won't be renting this out anymore. I made it into a songwriting space for you—with Hayden's help."

She let out a happy breath that turned into a laugh as she moved farther into the room.

The bedroom and bathroom were still intact, as was the kitchenette, but with Hayden's help, we'd changed the living room to a musical den.

"My piano?" She rushed over to it and ran her fingers across the keys. "And guitars and amplifiers and my keyboard…oh, my God, Seth!"

"Your dad helped me with the instruments." She'd been using a single guitar here and doing a lot of her creative work at the studio with Gin since we were still finishing the rooms on the second story of the house. We'd planned to make one of the spare bedrooms an office for her, but then I'd had the idea to do this instead, to give her a bigger, better, custom-decorated creative space. "You can record demos here, but you'll still have to go to Hale Street for high-quality recording."

Everly burst out with another joyful laugh as she went to the pair of plush chairs that replaced the sleeper sofa. Hayden had redone all the décor to have a music theme and a creative vibe and piled songwriting notebooks and a multitude of colored pens and pencils in mugs around the room. There were floor pillows, throw pillows, blankets, and a heat-gener-ating electric fireplace to cozy up the place during the winter.

Everly whirled around and threw her arms around my neck and poured her joy into one hell of a kiss. I started to rethink waiting till later for naked time, but the nervous flutter in my gut reminded me the biggest part of the night was yet to come.

"You like it?" I asked. I trusted Hayden's skills, but neither one of us was a songwriter and couldn't predict what would make the space just right for Everly.

"Are you kidding? I love it, Seth. So much. My fingers are itching to play and create." She kissed me again. "One question though."

I held her to me, my fingers reveling in the feel of her skin as I burrowed them under the tee she'd thrown over her swimsuit. "What's that?"

"You told me the reason you were renting out this place was because it was good business. What happened to that? Don't you want that extra income?"

I pulled her even closer, encircling her in a tight hug, resting my chin on her head, then kissing the top of her head like the precious gift she was. "I found something much more important than business."

She let out a sigh of contentment, burying her face in my chest. "I love you, Seth."

"Love you too, Ev."

With a laugh, she said, "You know Holden's going to give you crap about the shortest business venture ever, right?"

"He already has." I laughed with her, then took a breath to try to steady my heartbeat. "You should check out the balcony."

"Oh? You changed it too?"

"Let's go see." I nudged her toward the French doors, my heart racing despite my deep breaths. I hoped Cash was ready.

I let Everly open the doors, and I saw her confusion when she spotted the same red-and-white-striped cushions on the same chairs. Then Cash caught his cue and a spotlight flipped on and shone on a point directly in front of her, highlighting the ring that dangled on a long thread from a tree branch above. The light caught the diamond just right, giving it a blinding sparkle.

Everly's hands flew to her mouth as she let out a gasp. I stepped up beside her, took one of her hands in mine, and lowered to one knee.

"Oh, my God," she said.

Not two seconds later, before I could say a word, Hayden's voice came from the vicinity of the campfire. "Oh, my God!"

I reached up and pulled at the thread to release the ring, then held it between us, my hand shaking. Tuning out the commotion of everyone behind me down on the ground, who had apparently heard Hayden's cue and were watching us, I said, "Everly, will you marry me?"

Tears streamed out of her eyes, alarming me, and then she laugh-cried on an exhale and pulled me up from me knee. I swallowed, fighting down panic, because I couldn't tell if she was happy or upset, and she hadn't said a coherent word like *yes.*

"Ev?"

"Yes, I'll marry you, Seth Henry. God yes!"

It was my turn to let out an exhilarated laugh. Fully aware of our audience—I'd planned it that way because I never again wanted to keep my feelings for this woman a secret—I called out, "She said yes!"

A chorus of cheers went up as I wrapped my arms around Everly and lifted her, letting out an exuberant howl into the night, feeling light enough to float away with her like a balloon. I'd be totally up for that, as long as Everly was in my arms.

Lowering her back to the balcony, I put my lips on hers and kissed her as if my life depended on it. The truth was, it felt like it did. Like I'd never be able to breathe right again without this gorgeous woman at my side.

"I love you," I finally managed. "I can't wait until you're my wife."

"I love you too," she said, her eyes sparkling with tears,

happy tears. I was now sure of it and suspected mine were damp as well.

"Get down here so we can hug you!" Hayden called, and several others agreed.

"And here lies the faulty part of my whole plan," I said so only Everly could hear. "I wanted the world to be a witness to me putting myself at the mercy of Everly Ash, because I'm done hiding, but I can't wait to whisk you away to our bedroom and start celebrating."

She pressed her body deeper into me, and with her lips a whisper away from mine, she said, "Best of both worlds. Celebrating with the people we love for thirty minutes. Then celebrating in private every night for the rest of our lives. I promise I'll make the wait worth your while, husband-to-be."

"There's not a single doubt in my mind, wife-to-be. Let's get started."

———

NOTE FROM THE AUTHOR

Thanks for reading Unsung! I hope you loved Seth and Everly. Cash's story is next! His high school sweetheart is coming home—unwillingly. Find out whether they get a second chance in Undone!

If you missed the North Brothers series, you can dive into book one, True North, in ebook format for free! Find out what happens when Mr. Socially Awkward spontaneously volunteers to be his beautiful boss's fake date.

Find both books and more in my author store at amyknuppbooks.com!

———

If you liked *Unsung,* I hope you'll consider leaving a review for it. Reviews help other readers find books and can be as short (or long) as you feel comfortable with. Just a couple sentences is all it takes. I appreciate all honest reviews.

———

Unsung is part of the Henry Brothers series, which includes:

- Untold (prequel)
- Unraveled
- Unsung
- Undone

The Henry Brothers series is a spin-off of the North Brothers series, which includes these stand-alone stories:

- True North
- True Colors
- True Blue
- True Harmony
- True Hero

ACKNOWLEDGMENTS

Many thanks to:

Melissa Chambers, for being not only my partner in the Books, Beaches, and Bellinis readers group and a dear friend but also for giving me insight into the music industry for this story. Some of your comments inspired Everly's backstory and the character of Eddy Ash.

Kay Lyons, for being my "coworker" day in and day out—the girl in the virtual cubicle next to mine (thank you, internet), talking caffeine, blurbs, and characters who don't do what we want. Thanks for the brainstorming and for being my first reader.

Rachel, Meshanna, Kathy, Heather, and Lisa, my beta readers and cheerleaders. You each have a unique point of view, and each of them is important to me. Thank you for the time you put into making sure my stories will fly.

My mom and my boys, for always believing in me and supporting me, even on the days when I snarl more than speak. I have the best family I could ask for.

Justin, for being my partner in everything: life, our chaotic family, brainstorming, plotting, teching, accounting, and all the other things this crazy business calls for. I literally couldn't do it without you. It's almost as if I knew all this that night so long ago when I convinced you to go to Benchwarmers.

ALSO BY AMY KNUPP

<u>Henry Brothers Series</u>

Untold (prequel)

Unraveled

Unsung

Undone

<u>North Brothers Series</u>

True North

True Colors

True Blue

True Harmony

True Hero

North Brothers Box Sets:

North Brothers Books 1-3

North Brothers Books 4-5

North Brothers: The Complete Series

<u>Hale Street Series:</u>

Sweet Spot

Sweet Dreams

Soft Spot

One and Only

Last First Kiss

Heartstrings

<u>Hale Street Box Sets:</u>

Meet Me at Clayborne's

Clayborne's After Hours

It Happened on Hale Street

<u>Island Fire Series</u>:

Playing with Fire

Heat of the Night

Fully Involved

Firestorm

Afterburn

Up in Flames

Flash Point

Fire Within

Impulse

Slow Burn

Island Fire Box Sets:

Sparked (books 1-3)

Ignited (books 4-6)

Enflamed (books 7-10)

OR

Island Fire: The Complete Series

Themed Box Sets:

Friends to Forever (Friends to Lovers Romance)

Working It (Workplace Romance)

ABOUT THE AUTHOR

Amy Knupp is a *USA Today* Best-Selling Author of contemporary romance and a freelance copy editor. She loves words and grammar and meaty, engrossing stories with complex characters.

Amy lives in Wisconsin with her husband and has two sons, four cats, and a box turtle. She graduated from the University of Kansas with degrees in French and journalism. In her spare time, she enjoys traveling, breaking up cat fights, watching college hoops, and annoying her family by correcting their grammar.

For more information:
amyknuppbooks.com

If you'd like to know when her next book is available, you can join her readers group, sign up for her newsletter, and/or follow her on social media.